WILD CARD

WILDCATS BOOK 3

RACHEL VINCENT

To fans of the original Shifters series.
This one's for you guys!

A WORD FROM RACHEL…

DEAR READER,

Finally! Kaci's story!

I hope you're enjoying the Wildcats series, a spinoff of the Shifters series, which launched my career. If you haven't already read it, don't forget to check out "Hunt," the short story that bridges the two series.

Since I started the Wildcats series, one of the most common requests I've gotten is for me to write Kaci's story, now that she's all grown up. If you've read the original Shifters series, you probably remember her as a traumatized thirteen-year-old "genetic recessive" shifter. As the little girl who bonded instantly with Ethan and fell in love with Jace. But after the events in Alpha, she was raised by Faythe on the Lazy S ranch, in the aftermath of the shifter civil war.

You *know* you're curious about how Faythe's "daughter" turned out!

Wild Card is a bit of a departure from the two previous books in the series. It's a little shorter and lighter in tone, and it functions as a kind of "time out" from the new characters in the free zone. And because Kaci is barely 18 years old, this

1

one is more of a sexual tension book than an adult content book. That said, it's also a fast, fun read, about half of which takes place on the Lazy S. So get ready to say hi to some old friends! (And a new baby!)

Please note, though, that I took some liberties with the more realistic aspects of the story, such as the layout of Caesar's Palace.

If you like *Wild Card*, I hope you'll consider reviewing it wherever you review books, because as an indie series (I'm putting it out myself, rather than selling it to a publisher), the Wildcats books depend **entirely** on my own publicity efforts and readers' word of mouth.

THANKS AGAIN FOR READING!
Rachel Vincent

RACHELVINCENT.COM

ONE

KACI

"THIS IS WHERE YOU LIVE?" DUSTIN GLANCED AROUND THE property as he drove us onto the Lazy S ranch through the arched gate, beneath the emblem—the letter S turned on its side. "I didn't know you were a farm girl."

"I'm not." Yet there *was* a lot Dustin didn't know about me. A lot he would never know.

Gravel crunched beneath his tires as we rounded a shallow curve in the long driveway, and the big red barn appeared on our right. "Damn." Dustin whistled. "That's straight out of, like, some old painting. You got horses in there? Or cows?"

"Nope. No animals." No farm animals, anyway. The local wildlife had been known to drive horses into a panic. Then into a heart attack. "This isn't a functioning ranch." It was more like a compound. The capital of a political authority Dustin would never even know existed.

"So, the barn's basically abandoned?" Dustin turned to

3

the right, and his headlights glinted on flaking red paint and slightly warped barn doors. He gave me a comically suggestive eyebrow waggle. "I bet we could get into a lot of trouble in there."

"That's a virtual certainty." Chances were good that he mistook the anticipation in my voice for lust. Human guys tend to give themselves credit for more than they deserve. I suspect the same goes for shifter guys, but the truth is that I wouldn't know.

"Let's go in." He slammed the gear shift into park and turned to me with excitement glowing in his eyes, reflected in starlight shining through the windshield.

"I don't think so. The ranch backs up to a national forest. We get a lot of predators skulking in the shadows."

"Don't worry, Kaci." He got out, then leaned down to peer in at me with a smutty smile. "I'll protect you."

I nearly choked on laughter. "Don't say I didn't warn you…"

Dustin rounded the front of the vehicle and pulled my door open. I let him tug me out of the car because if there was one aspect of human behavior I still understood, after five years of observing it from the other side of the species divide, it was that if you tell a guy he shouldn't do something, he won't even be able to *think* about anything else until he's done exactly that.

Was it unfair of me to push that button? Probably. But I learned at a young age that life isn't fair. Why should Dustin not have the benefit of that same experience?

He closed my car door and led me toward the barn in the glare of his headlights, where I straightened my skirt while I watched him struggle with the old doors.

"They're a little warped," I said as he pulled, tendons standing out in his neck from the effort.

"I got it." He grunted and pulled again, and I looked up to enjoy the warm, clear summer night. There was no moon, but the stars were all out, and they were more than enough light for me to see by. Though Dustin probably wasn't as fortunate.

"You want a hand?"

He tossed an amused look my way. "This thing's really jammed. It probably hasn't been opened—"

"Since last weekend." I pushed him aside and jerked on the right-hand barn door, one handed. It swung open with a squeal of rusty hinges, and Dustin gaped at me. I shrugged. "There's a trick to it." Showing him up was one thing. But if he knew I was actually three times stronger than he was, he would get back in his car and peel out of there before I'd had any fun.

And I was in *desperate* need of a little fun.

Mollified by my explanation, Dustin grabbed my hand and tugged me into the barn, where he stumbled over a large rock right in front of the door, which he obviously couldn't see. "Shit!

I laughed as I steadied him, and he took the opportunity to slide his hand over my ass. "Think that's funny?" He murmured against my neck as his hands moved up my back, beneath my blouse. "Maybe I tripped on purpose, so you'd grab me."

He hadn't.

"Maybe I meant to hit the ground, with you on top of me."

"The ground's filthy," I whispered as his lips trailed down my jaw toward my mouth. "But there's a bale of hay over there…" Right where I'd put it.

Dustin walked me backward toward the hay bale, steading me with both hands while his mouth fed from mine as if I were the only source of sustenance on the planet, and I had to admit, the guy knew how to kiss. Hay scratched the back of my calves and I sat.

He didn't even notice the blanket spread over the bale. But then, that was for my comfort, not his.

I leaned back and Dustin crawled over me, one knee wedged between my thighs, pushing up my skirt. His hand wandered beneath my blouse again while his lips traveled down my neck, and I threw my head back, giving myself over to the moment. To the adrenaline and to the need building low inside me.

So what if I'd only met him a few hours ago? So what if he thought I was a college junior partying her way through a degree in business management.

The less he knew about me the better. For his own good.

A growl rumbled through the dark from the rear of the barn.

Dustin froze above me, but I pretended not to hear the threat as I slid my hands over his tight stomach beneath his shirt, then over his chest. "Touch me," I whispered.

The growl rolled over us again, too loud this time for me to reasonably ignore, but I ignored it anyway.

"Kaci." My name was little more than a deep grumble of syllables from the shadows near the last stall.

Dustin backed off me and stood, squinting into the dark, eyes wide with the quiet kind of fear that makes deer freeze in oncoming headlights. "Kaci?" he whispered. "Something's in here with us." Which was when I realized his human hearing couldn't distinguish my name from the growling.

I shrugged as I sat up, straightening my blouse. "I told you. Predators."

"Seriously. Let's go."

"She's not going anywhere." Marc Ramos stepped into the

glare from Dustin's headlights, and even I had to admit that he looked kind of scary. "But *you* have ninety seconds to vacate the premises before I rip you into several pieces and toss them into the incinerator. The police will *never find your body*."

"What the hell…?" Dustin backed toward the open barn doors. "Is that your dad?"

I snorted. "He's old, but he's not *that* old."

"And *she* just graduated high school," Marc growled.

Dustin turned to me, brows arched in question. "You said you were in college."

I gave him another shrug. "I passed five AP tests, so technically I'm halfway through my freshman year. And people tell me I'm an old soul."

"Seventy-five seconds," Marc growled. "Then I start breaking bones."

Dustin turned and ran for his car, hay flying beneath his shoes. He started the engine and slammed the gear shift into neutral by mistake, and I could see sweat popping up on his forehead in the three seconds it took him to understand the problem. Then he reversed onto the driveway and took off toward the gate, gravel grinding beneath his tires.

I collapsed onto the bale of hay, laughing. "Thanks. That was awesome."

"This isn't a game, Kaci." Marc tugged me up by one hand and snatched my blanket from the bale.

"Of course it's a game. But it would have been a hookup, if you'd respect my right to a little privacy."

"The only place you're guaranteed privacy is in your room."

"But I'm not allowed to have guys in my room. So, you can kind of see my dilemma."

"No, you're not allowed to have *boys* in your room.

You're not allowed to have grown ass men anywhere on the face of this planet. So, you can kind of see *my* dilemma."

"I'm eighteen, Marc." I snatched the blanket from him and shook it out hard enough that the material snapped against itself; Faythe said she'd skin me alive if I clogged up the dryer vent with any more hay. "That means I get to make my own decisions."

"You're also a member of the South-Central Pride. Which means you have to follow the rules. There's a reason you're not allowed to bring your dates to the barn, or the woods, or anywhere else on this property except right through the front door of the house."

"Yeah, I can't quite remember why that is again." I folded the blanket in half, then in half again as I left the barn. "Can you please tell me for the millionth time?"

"I'm serious, Kaci. A formal introduction is necessary to keep from triggering territorial instincts. There are six enforcers on this ranch, at least two of them patrolling the property at all times, and if they scent a strange man out here with you, they *will* overreact."

"As opposed to this classic under-reaction I'm getting from you?" I gave him an impatient wave, trying to hurry him out of the barn, and when he finally stepped outside, I shoved the doors closed, rusty hinges squealing, and reiterated a truth that only he and Faythe seemed unwilling to believe. "The guys don't care who I bring home."

"Bullshit. If Faythe had snuck someone into the barn while I was an enforcer, I would have lost my shit. Every time I saw her with some other guy, I had to fight the urge to rip his head from his shoulders."

"I'm not sure whether that's psychotic or sweet. Either way, there is no parallel to be drawn between you and Faythe, and me and our current enforcers." I clamped the folded blanket beneath my arm and headed down the starlit driveway toward the house, where Faythe's office window was still lit up, though it was nearly ten p.m.

Up all night with the baby. Up all day with work. She hadn't had a full night's sleep in years.

Marc jogged to catch up with me. "Look, I understand that you're not interested in any of our guys, and that's fine."

I stopped walking to stare at him. Did he truly believe the problem was that *I* wasn't interested in any of *them*?

"But it isn't fair to parade a series of human dates right under their noses and rub it in," Marc continued.

I studied his gold-flecked gaze, trying to see the truth. "Is that really what you think I'm doing?"

He crossed bulging arms over a solid chest. "Why bring your dates back here, if you're not trying to rile up our enforcers?"

"Okay, first of all, most of your enforcers are old enough to be my dad—"

"That's not true."

"My point is that you think Dustin is too old for me, when he's all of twenty-one, yet you find it perfectly reasonable for enforcers in their late twenties to be jealous at the thought of me making out with a strange human." I ticked my points off on my fingers. "A: That's a double standard. B: It's factually inaccurate. The guys wouldn't care if I worked my way through an entire frat house, so there's no reason I shouldn't be able to bring my dates back to the damn barn, like any normal farm girl."

Marc scowled, his mouth already open to yell at me for cussing.

"Hell, losing one's virginity on a bale of hay is practically a rite of passage around here."

His mouth snapped shut.

9

Mission accomplished. Marc *still* hadn't figured out how to deal with his little "kitten" talking about sex. Which was why I was the only person on the ranch who could get away with cussing at an Alpha.

Not that I would *ever* try that with Faythe.

"Okay, but back to the factual inaccuracy," he said, once he'd mentally pushed past my utterance of the word 'virginity.' "If any of the guys had caught a whiff of your boyfriend—"

"Dustin's not my boyfriend. I just met him."

"I don't know whether to be relieved by that or horrified. But my point is that if any of the guys had—"

"Marc." I stopped walking again and looked him right in the eyes. "Their ears are as good as yours. They all heard Dustin's car turn into the driveway. They probably even heard me open the barn door. If any of them gave a damn who I was hanging out with, you wouldn't have been the only one who showed up to scare Dustin off. But you're *always* the only one who shows up. Because they…don't…care."

The South-Central Pride's enforcers were just as eager as any other tomcat to snag a tabby—according to shifter law, that was the only way any of them could have kids or become an Alpha—but they were *not* eager for that tabby to be me.

Somehow, in a population where the men greatly outnumbered the women, I was the only eligible female werecat in the country to have no suitors.

Ever.

Faythe saw that fact for what it was, and she understood the reasons. But Marc… Well, Marc was like the father of an ugly baby who believes his unfortunate progeny is the cutest bundle of joy on earth.

Not that I was hideous or anything. I had no problem getting dates in the human world. Unfortunately, I was no longer a member of that world, which meant that any relationship I struck up with a human was pretty much doomed from the start. So, what's a girl to do when the tomcats aren't interested and human relationships can't get serious?

Play the field, of course. On my home turf, so all those stuck-up tomcat bastards had no choice but to see that someone—*lots* of someones—wanted me. Not that I was interested in any of the South-Central men.

Not the enforcers, anyway…

"I'm sure you're reading them wrong," Marc said as we clomped up the front steps of the ranch-style house that was both capital of and home base for the South-Central Pride. "I'm sure the guys care."

They didn't. But Marc would never see that, because he was blinded by his own paternal perspective.

He opened the front door and held it for me as I stepped into the foyer. "They're probably just trying to figure out how to approach you, now that you're…more mature."

They weren't.

I shrugged. "Maybe you're right."

He wasn't.

"I'm going throw this in the wash and sulk over the premature end of my date." I gestured toward the laundry room with my folded blanket.

"Fair enough." Marc glanced at the time on his cell phone as Faythe appeared in her office doorway, one hand on her hip. "Just sulk quietly, please. Greg's asleep."

"I know." Just like I knew the little monster would be up at dawn, and Marc would be up with him, so Faythe could try to get four or five hours of sleep in a row. She looked like she was ready to fall over as it was.

The new baby slept soundly, when he *did* sleep, but he ate around the clock.

"Kaci," Faythe said before I could make a break for the laundry room. "Let's talk." She waved me into her office, then she closed the door. "Another playdate in the barn?" She glanced pointedly at the blanket still tucked beneath my arm as she sank onto the leather couch.

"Nothing happened." I flopped onto the sofa across the rug from her and tucked my feet beneath me with the blanket on my lap.

"And what if Marc stops showing up? What's your plan?"

"I'm an adult, Faythe."

"That's why I'm asking. Adults have to be prepared."

"I have condoms, if that's what you're getting at," I said, and to her credit, she didn't even flinch. Marc would've been hyperventilating. Or faking a heart attack to escape the conversation.

"That's *part* of what I'm getting at." She exhaled heavily, and my gaze settled on the thin white scar bisecting her left cheek, from the outer edge of her eye to the corner of her mouth. She'd *slaughtered* the bastard who'd cut her, and rather than a reminder of what he'd done, the scar had become a testament to how thoroughly fierce Faythe was—a tabby kicking ass in a tom's world. Even eight weeks postpartum. "I just want to make sure you understand what could happen if one of these boys decides he's entitled to more than you're willing to give him."

I sat a little straighter. "I understand that I'd break every bone in his hand and send him home to his mommy in tears." That, I'd learned from Faythe.

But she only frowned. "Unless Marc hears him screaming and comes running, in which case we'll have to fire up the industrial incinerator." The only part of a cattle ranch that was actually functioning at the Lazy S. Its intended use was to dispose of dead livestock, but we always seemed to find alter-

12

native applications. "So maybe just keep that in mind while you're exploring your sexuality."

"Acknowledged. Would you rather that I *explore* off the premises?"

"No. This is your home, and you should feel comfortable here. But Marc's right about at least one thing—no tabby has ever brought home a string of human men before. Not even me. I know you don't think the enforcers care, but I promise you they've noticed."

I rolled my eyes at her. "It's their job to notice everyone who comes onto the property."

"Yes. But eventually one of them is going to notice *you*."

I shrugged. I wouldn't mind being noticed, but it wasn't any of the enforcers I kept hoping to find in the barn, ready to terrify my latest human date. Nor was it Marc.

Her gaze narrowed on me, and my heart began to beat harder. My face had given too much away. "There's no hurry, Kaci. But if you like one of them, I could set something up…"

"No!" I could feel my cheeks flush. "I don't need you to make some poor guy go out with me!"

"That's not what I—"

"I'm not a social charity case." Except that wasn't true. I was an orphan—for all practical purposes—that the South-Central Pride had taken in as a kid. And no one had forgotten where I'd come from. What I'd *done*…

"Of course not—" Faythe's phone rang, and she glanced at the bassinet against one wall while she dug her cell from her pocket. "It's Rick Wade. Can you sit tight for a minute, Kaci? This is about Justus's trial."

Justus Alexander. My pulse rushed a little faster when his face appeared behind my closed eyelids, and if she weren't preoccupied with the baby and an incoming call from the

Chairman of the Territorial Council, she might have noticed my reaction.

Justus was a stray Faythe and Marc had accepted as a member of the Pride back in February, to make sure he'd get an actual trial—as opposed to a simple order of execution—for the murder and infection he'd allegedly committed in the free zone.

The *former* free zone, also known as the Lion's Den. Soon it would officially be recognized as the Mississippi Valley Territory, if Faythe and Marc could muster a couple more votes on the council.

For the past four months, Justus had been sleeping on the couch in the guest house, where the enforcers lived, waiting for his trial. His older brother Titus was Alpha of the new territory—the only stray Alpha in the country, other than Marc. Maybe in the world. But Titus's efforts to get his territory officially recognized had been complicated even beyond the council's hesitance to let strays play in the purebred sandbox by the fact that he'd accidentally taken Robyn Sheffield, the only known female stray, from the territory—and refused to send her back against her will.

And by the fact that his younger brother had committed several crimes that could have exposed the existence of our species to the rest of the world.

Like Titus, Justus was yummy in an I-would-eat-him-for-dessert kind of way. Unlike his brother, Justus was only a couple of years older than I was, which meant that it would totally not be creepy if I—hypothetically—had a huge crush on him.

Unfortunately, he was also TROUBLE in all caps.

If enforcers were the shifter version of cops, Justus was a felon, because unlike in the human justice system, in shifter society there was no pre-trial presumption of innocence.

Especially considering that we all knew damn well that he'd done it.

Justus Alexander was the last tom I should have been interested in. So naturally, I turned into a mumbling, sweaty puddle of drool every time he came around. Unfortunately— or fortunately?—I was stuck firmly in the friend zone. The totally platonic, "one of the guys" zone. The "watch old TV shows together without even brushing hands in the popcorn bowl" zone. It was like he couldn't even tell I was a girl.

I shook that thought off as I stood, before Faythe could see it on my face. "Don't worry about it. I'm just going to go to bed."

She glanced at her phone with a frown. "Wait just a minute, please, Kaci. There's one more thing." But as polite as it sounded, her request was actually an order.

I wandered toward the bassinet as she accepted the call from the council chairman. "Hi, Rick. What did they say?"

Baby Ethan was out cold, and he was a surprisingly deep sleeper, for a two-month-old. I'd seen Karen Sanders— Faythe's mother—push the vacuum cleaner right under his bed without disturbing him. But the minute the food gauge on his tiny belly tilted toward EMPTY, he would wake up screaming.

"Dr. Carver gave you a clean postpartum bill of health," Rick Wade said over the phone, and I heard him as if he were in the room with us, thanks to my shifter's enhanced auditory senses. "So…one week."

"From *today*?" Faythe sank onto one of the couches, seeming to deflate with the news.

"Yes. I'm sorry, but they weren't willing to put the trial off any longer."

"And I can't ask them to without validating their belief that I can't be a good mother and a good Alpha at the same time." Faythe sighed. "Sexist bastards. If you asked for a delay in order to catch up on sleep with a newborn, they'd commend you for your commitment to your family."

Wade chuckled. "If I had a newborn, we'd be having a very different conversation. Can you make it in a week?"

"Looks like I'll have to. But I'm bringing the whole family."

"Good. I'm looking forward to meeting the latest addition to the Sanders-Ramos clan."

"Thanks, Rick. We'll see you then." Faythe hung up her phone and set it on the end table to her left.

I gave baby Ethan's head a pat—his mop of thick, dark hair reminded me of his namesake—then wandered back toward the couch. "So, the trial's next week?"

"Looks like. And that's what I wanted to talk to you about." Faythe leaned forward, watching me carefully, which told me I wasn't going to like whatever she was about to say. "We'd like you to come."

"To Montana?" The hairs on the back of my neck stood up.

Justus's trial would be held in the same remote cabin complex where Faythe, Marc, and Jace stood trial a lifetime ago. Twice, in Faythe's case.

Okay, it had only been four and a half years before, but that was a lifetime ago for me, because that's where they'd found me, in the woods, stuck in cat form after my first-ever shift. Alone and terrified.

And completely feral.

If not for Faythe's trial, I might have wandered out there for the rest of my life. I might *still* be out there living like a cat, having completely forgotten that I'd ever been anything else.

Just the thought gave me chills.

"No, thanks," I told her. "You don't need me there." And I couldn't stand to see Justus on trial.

"You could help with the kids. No one's as good with little Greg as you are, and baby Ethan…" Faythe shrugged.

A low blow. She knew how much I loved those kids. But… "I can't go back there, Faythe. Too much…happened."

"I know. But maybe that's why you *should* go back. You know, exorcize those ghosts. Put the past behind you. Just tell me you'll think about it."

"I'll think about it," I told her. But that promise held about the same chance of coming true as my promises to Karen that I'd unload the dishwasher. "Can I go to bed now?"

"Yes. And try to sleep for both of us, if you don't mind," Faythe said with a glance at the bassinet, where baby Ethan was already starting to make fussy, hungry sounds.

"Night." I picked up my blanket and headed into the laundry room to throw it in the washer, but I hesitated with my hand on the doorknob when I noticed light peeking from beneath the door.

Little Greg had a bad habit of curling up in the dryer when the clothes inside are warm. He liked to make a nest for himself to sleep in, like a little kitten in a box. It was the cutest thing in the world. And the most dangerous. I was kind of terrified that someone would decide the towels needed another cycle and turn the dryer on without noticing him.

I twisted the knob and pushed the door open, expecting to find the dryer standing open with a sweet little face resting on top of a load of clothes.

Instead I found one of the guys going through the pockets of his pants.

He turned, and I found myself staring into the gorgeous gray eyes of Justus Alexander.

TWO

THEY'RE GOING TO CONVICT.

Eavesdropping probably wasn't what Victor Di Carlo had in mind when he'd told me to practice using my heightened shifter senses—just one of the challenges for any newly-infected stray. And, of course, I hadn't expected to overhear my own fate when I'd loitered at the top of the staircase that afternoon, frozen in place by the whispered mention of my own name.

We don't have the votes.

Though he'd said them hours ago, Vic's words still echoed in my mind with the impact of a judge's gavel. Not that there would be a judge at my trial. Or a jury. There would only be a tribunal made up of three Alphas chosen by the venerable short straw method to determine whether I would be found innocent or guilty.

Whether I would live or die.

With that truth weighing on me, I knelt in the tiny second-floor laundry room of the guest house and set my backpack in the bottom of an empty laundry basket, then I piled my dirty clothes on top of it.

Until tonight, I'd been naive enough to assume I'd at least get to testify before the votes were cast, but through the shifter grapevine—a backchannel of high-level conversations overheard by and recounted to enforcers across the country— I'd learned that the Alphas had already made their decision, though a date for the trial had yet to be officially set.

I was screwed. As good as dead.

Joining the South-Central Territory was supposed to guarantee me a fair trial, rather than the simple order of execution most strays would have gotten, but it did not guarantee me a favorable verdict. Or even, evidently, the chance to explain my actions before the votes were counted.

The "civilization" of the US territories had turned out to be a facade—a smiling mask worn over the snarling muzzle of a beast hell-bent on devouring me for the sin of being born human. Well, for that, and for the crimes I'd been manipulated into committing as a terrified, disoriented, newly infected stray.

But I would *not* stick around to be devoured.

I stood with my laundry basket and took several deep breaths, because if I went downstairs in a panic, the guys would know something was wrong. They'd hear my racing pulse without even consciously listening for it. They'd smell fear in the scent of my sweat.

Vic had taken me under his wing over the past four months, but all I'd really learned was how to flee the ranch, right under his nose. Guilt hovered at the edge of my mind at the thought of betraying him, but I shoved it back. I'd rather live with smudged honor than die with my integrity intact.

My pulse under control, I headed downstairs.

"Kaci's back." Brian Taylor paused his video game, freezing the car race on the sixty-four-inch screen, and stared out the front window of the guest house.

I stopped on the lower landing and listened, my laundry basket clasped under one arm. After a second of concentration, I heard what he'd detected: the soft rumble of an engine all the way at the front of the property.

"You want me to check it out?" Brian asked, and Vic looked up from his seat at the bar, where he was rapidly demolishing a twelve-inch meatball sub and an entire party-sized bag of Doritos.

"I got it." I dropped my laundry by the door. It would be my *distinct* pleasure to run off Kaci's latest boyfriend. She'd been just as good to me as the guys had, and chasing off the human loser would give me a chance to say goodbye—even if she didn't know that's what I was doing. "They're probably in the barn?"

Vic glanced at his cell as it began to vibrate on the counter. "Don't worry about it. Marc says he's on it."

"Awesome." Brian went back to his game, and his on-screen car leapt into motion again, barreling over a bridge onto a highway below, where he swerved to avoid a firetruck screeching as its red lights flashed.

"I don't get it." The only duty any of the enforcers ever seemed to shirk was making sure Kaci's dates left the property in a timely fashion. "What's so hard about scaring off one human asshole?"

"The date's not the problem." Brian leaned to the right as he turned his car, as if he were actually in the vehicle he was controlling. "Kaci creeps me out."

"Taylor," Vic warned, dropping his sandwich onto its wrapper.

I frowned at Brian. "What am I not getting?" According

to my brother, tabbies were rare and coveted. They were supposed to have their pick of any tomcat in the country, and most enforcers were desperate to catch their attention. Which was why the council had lost its collective shit when Robyn had decided she'd rather live with Titus in the untamed free zone than even consider any of the "natural-born" tomcats in the US territories.

Titus had told me to stay away from Kaci for exactly that reason—because the council would *not* be happy if another of their few eligible women fell for a stray. Especially, a stray charged with two capital offenses.

Yet most of the South-Central enforcers treated Kaci like she had the plague.

Brian shrugged. "She's a man-eater."

Vic stood, and his barstool fell onto the tile floor. "Faythe fired the last guy who said that. Should I tell her to start writing another want-ad?"

"No, man." Brian paused his game again. "I mean no disrespect. I don't hang out with her or anything, so for all I know, she turned out perfectly nice. And psychologically sound. But…it's true." He turned back to me. "She literally ate a human being. If anyone else had done that, they'd have been executed. Cannibalism is unnatural, and it's fucking creepy as hell."

"Brian…" Vic warned.

"Don't get me wrong," Taylor continued, hands held in front of him in a defensive gesture. "I *wish* I didn't know what I know about Kaci, because *someone's* gotta make a mom out of her. But it would take me a while to get past the thought of her eating human flesh in order to…rise to the occasion. Even if she is hot enough to make a man sweat."

"Fortunately, no one's asking *you* to rise to shit, so get over it, or get out." Vic wiped his mouth with a paper napkin, then wadded it up and dropped it on the counter. "She was a starving, traumatized kid who had no idea what she was doing. And she's more of a survivor than you'll ever be, so if I hear one more word from you about Kaci, I'll kick your ass myself."

"Sorry, man." Brian turned back to his game.

"And turn that shit down." Vic picked up his bar stool as I pulled a carton of laundry detergent from beneath the kitchen cabinet. "Where are you going?"

"Will's using the washer," I told him. "Faythe said I could use the one in the main house."

"Don't forget to clean out the lint filter, or she'll take your head right off." He sank onto his stool again and took another bite of his sub.

"Thanks, man." I clapped one hand on his shoulder. "I really appreciate that."

Vic gave me a strange look, and I pretended not to notice as I dropped the detergent on top of my laundry and picked up the basket. He had no way of knowing my gratitude was for more than just the lint filter advice. Or that I would be gone for much longer than the duration of a spin cycle.

"Okay. I'll be back," I said as I opened the door, half-convinced someone would see through my lie and try to stop me.

But neither Brian nor Vic looked up.

I crossed the lawn and headed into the main house through the back door, to see who was still awake and might catch me sneaking off. And *maybe* to run into Kaci one last time.

Former cannibal or not, she'd never been anything but nice to me. And she was the only girl I'd ever met who liked The Twilight Zone. As in, the original black and white episodes.

The door to the nursery was closed, but that didn't mean much. Little Greg was usually a sound sleeper, but babies were unpredictable, and either of my new Alphas could be found plodding between the nursery and the master suite at any time of the day or night.

Faythe's mom was in her sixties and suffered from occasional bouts insomnia, and Kaci hadn't gone to sleep before midnight once in the four months I'd been on the ranch.

Not that I was stalking her. The light from her bedroom was visible through the front window of the guest house, where I slept on the couch. How could I not notice when it was on?

Still focusing to control my pulse, I headed into the utility room. My plan was to hang out and pretend to do laundry until I was sure no one in the main house was awake to hear the car engine when I left.

As I listened for voices from the house around me, I removed an armful of baby…things from the dryer and set them on the counter for folding, then I transferred a load of wet towels into the dryer, hoping that helping with the laundry might somehow karmically balance out the escape I was planning. Though my real hope was that if I actually started a load of my clothes, when they discovered me missing they might think I'd just gone for a walk on the property to pass the time until the cycle finished. Maybe that would at least delay the discovery of the missing car.

Marc's distinctive footsteps crossed the hall into his bedroom as I pulled my backpack from the basket and dumped my laundry into the washer. While I set the cycle on the machine, I mentally catalogued all the other sounds from the main house.

Karen was snoring from her room.

Faythe and Kaci were talking in the office, but the door

was closed, so I couldn't tell what they were saying. With any luck, I could sneak right past. As soon as I—

Shit. Too late, I realized I'd hidden the keys in the basket —then dumped them in with my clothes.

Grumbling beneath my breath, I dug into the washer, trying to keep the keys from falling against the metal drum, which would be like ringing a gong for the rest of the house to hear.

It had taken me forever to find a set of unattended keys, and if I wasn't long gone before Chris noticed that he'd left them in his jeans pocket, I would lose my chance. And I'd never get another one, once they knew I was a flight risk.

Hell, they'd probably lock me in one of the jail cells in the basement.

Finally, my fingers grazed something hard and jagged. I pulled the keys out, and with them, the pair of pants they'd snagged on. As I was disentangling the lock fob from the belt loop of my jeans, the door behind me squeaked softly open. The key ring finally released my pants, which fell back into the washer, and I turned, keys in hand, to find Kaci Dillon staring right at me.

Her gaze settled on the keys and her eyes widened. Then she snatched them before I'd even truly processed the fact that I was no longer alone.

Busted.

KACI CLOSED HER BEDROOM DOOR AND LEANED AGAINST IT, glaring at me through beautiful hazel eyes. "What the hell are you doing?" she demanded in a fierce whisper.

Stalling for time to come up with an acceptable answer, I let my backpack slide off my arm onto the floor while I studied her room. It was messier than I'd expected, though I'm not sure *what* I'd expected, considering I'd only ever seen the outside of her window and her door.

Again, I was *not* stalking her.

Dirty clothes lay scattered over the floor, a couple of books stood open on her desk, and her unmade bed looked like she'd tried to wrestle her covers into submission.

With a fleeting and unexpected bolt of jealousy, I realized she might have had help destroying the bed. But then a quick sniff confirmed that she'd probably never had a guy in her room in her entire life.

Until now.

The thought that I might be the first guy ever admitted into her personal space triggered a satisfied rumble deep in my throat, but I swallowed it before the sound could escape.

"What are you looking at?" she demanded.

"Nothing." She'd mistaken my curiosity for a critique of her housekeeping skills. But it wasn't like I could criticize. The only reason my apartment in Jackson hadn't been condemned by the city was the bi-weekly cleaning service my brother had paid for.

My gaze landed on the iPad open on her desk, and I ran one finger across it. The screen woke up, showing a movie app paused in the middle of a black and white scene I recognized. "You're watching The Twilight Zone without me?" Not that I would be around to watch with her anymore.

Kaci snatched the tablet and flipped the cover closed. "Don't change the subject." She dropped it on the bed, then glared at me with her left hand propped on her hip, Chris's keys dangling from her right index finger. "What the hell are you doing with these?"

"Would you believe me if I said I found them?" Phrased

in the form of a question, my answer wasn't *technically* a lie...

"I'd believe that you found them after a deliberate and unauthorized search. Where are you going? Your trial is— Oh!" She slapped her spare hand over her mouth, muffling her next words. "You're running. You can't *run!*"

"I'm not running." I felt even guiltier about lying to her than about lying to Vic. "I'm taking a vacation."

"Right. Because everyone who's about to be tried for murder and infection decides to go hang out at the beach for a few days."

"Not the beach. Las Vegas." She opened her mouth to start yelling at me, and that time I covered her mouth with *my* hand. "Wait. I can prove it. Are you going to be quiet?"

She shoved my hand away from her face. "Like you could do anything about it if I say no."

"Okay, look." I slid my cell phone from my pocket and opened my email, then showed her the electronic boarding pass. "See? My flight to Vegas leaves in less than three hours. I'm just going to chill for a few days, before they decide to lock me up. Or execute me. One last hurrah, you know?"

"You're serious? This is the stupidest thing I've ever heard. What are you going to do in Las Vegas? You're not old enough to gamble. Or to drink."

"I am according to this." I pulled my wallet from my back pocket and showed her my fake ID. Everything on it was true except my date of birth, which had been adjusted by two years. "Come on. They're probably going to execute me. I just want to have a little fun before I die, Kaci," I whispered. "Are you really going to deny a dying man his last wish?"

"First of all, you're not going to die." But she didn't seem to believe her own words. She may not have heard what Vic had said, but she knew even better than I did how steeply the odds were stacked against me. "Second, your last wish is Las Vegas? Aren't you, like, a billionaire? You've probably been there a million times."

"My brother's the billionaire. I'm not going to live long enough to actually access my trust fund."

"Then how'd you buy the ticket?"

"Airline miles. I have a ton of them." I shrugged as I stuffed my wallet back into my pocket. "Titus sent me all over the world during school breaks the past few years, evidently to keep me from coming home." From figuring out that he was no longer human, and that his house was full of shifter enforcers. He'd had no way of knowing how soon—or how traumatically—I'd discover all of that for myself. "And I charged the hotel room with virtually the last available credit on my one card. So see? I'm not running. I can't *afford* to run. I'm just trying to have a little fun, one last time." I gave her my best pitiful look, well aware that my future now depended upon how much sympathy Kaci felt for a doomed murderer she had no reason to help. "Are you going to turn me in?"

"No." Her sexy pout grew into a smoldering grin, and I caught my breath, suddenly bowled over by the urge to kiss her. After all, there's no exit like a dramatic exit, and frankly, I was running out of chances. "I'm coming with you."

Yes.

Wait, what? "No. I can't—"

"Take me with you, or you're not going anywhere." She shoved Chris's keys into her pocket to punctuate her threat, and my gaze snagged there, on the front of her jeans. "I've never been to Las Vegas. I've never been *anywhere,* Justus."

I dragged my focus up her body, forcing myself to find her face. To push past the hypnotizing thought of running off *with Kaci* and focus on the madness she was actually proposing. "Kaci, this isn't a..." ...*vacation*. Except that was exactly what I'd told her it was. "I can't take you."

"Why not?"

"Because if I've learned anything from what my brother just went through with Robyn, it's that taking a tabby out of her territory without permission is considered an act of war against the Territorial Council. I'm in enough trouble already."

Kaci crossed her arms beneath her breasts, and I had to drag my gaze back up to her face. Again. "I know you're new at this, but you are *so* clueless. I'm *giving* you permission. And no one's going to start a war over me. First of all, I'm not defecting, like Abby and Robyn did—I'm just taking a vacation. Second, I'm not going into the free zone. Nevada's in the Southwest Territory, so the worst we're really going to have to worry about is Paul Blackwell getting pissed that we didn't ask permission to cross the border. But you're already up on murder charges, so how much more damage can a trespassing charge actually do?"

Fair point, especially considering that I had no intention of actually sticking around for my trial.

"And besides all that...I'm not one of the tabbies they fuss over around here, in case you haven't noticed." Her expression suddenly felt like armor, but there was something fragile in her voice.

"I have noticed," I admitted. "But I don't really understand why." The fact that her childhood trauma scared all the other guys away said more about them than it said about her, in my opinion.

"Think fast, rich boy. Are we staying or going?" She glanced at her wrist, as if she were wearing a watch. "Time's running out if you want to catch that flight."

If she turned me in, I wouldn't make it off the ranch again until my trial, which I might never come back from.

"June's a terrible time to go to Nevada," I told her. "It's hot. You're going to hate it."

Kaci blinked at me in incomprehension. Then her eyes lit up. She smiled, and for the first time since I'd met her, she looked truly happy.

And utterly gorgeous.

This isn't a date, Justus. This is a crime.

"So, can I have the keys now?"

"No way. I'm driving," she insisted. "And we're not leaving until you buy my ticket."

I rolled my eyes. Clearly she didn't trust me—with good reason. "Fine. Throw some things into a bag, and make it fast."

While she packed, I pulled up the airline website on my phone. "Hey," I whispered from the bathroom doorway while she dropped her toothpaste into the bag. "I don't know how to spell your name."

She motioned for my phone, and when I handed it over, she typed her information into the online form. Two seconds later, her phone dinged. She checked the text and found her boarding pass.

"Now can I have the keys?" I asked.

"No. I'm still driving." But she was grinning from ear to ear as she threw her backpack over one shoulder. "Let me make sure Faythe's office door is closed, then we'll go for it. Walk straight down the hall, but not too fast, because if it sounds like we're in a hurry, they'll come out. The front door doesn't squeak, and Chris parks facing away from the house, so that's already one stroke of luck."

"I assume we'll leave the headlights off until we get to the road?" Suddenly I was excited by the idea of this escape, though before, I'd just been determined.

Kaci shook her head. "Rookie mistake. They'll hear the engine and assume Chris is going out. But if there are no headlights, they'll know something's wrong."

"Good point." I was a little frightened by how good she was at this.

No, I was a little *impressed.*

"Ready?" Her eyes lit up, and seeing her so excited made me want to pull her close and steal some of her joy and hope, and pretend this really was just a vacation with a beautiful girl, rather than a last-ditch effort to save my own life.

Instead, I returned her smile and grabbed my bag. "Let's do it."

Kaci turned and opened the door, then sucked in a little gasp of surprise. Her spine stiffened. She slowly let her bag slide off her shoulder, then she set it on the floor next to the door, hidden from the hallway by the wall.

"Change of plans." She opened the door wider, and little Greg toddled inside, rubbing his eyes with both chubby fists. "First I have to do something about this."

"I'm 'posed to be sleepin'." Greg dropped his hands and looked up at me in confusion. Even the toddler knew I wasn't supposed to be in Kaci's bedroom. If his *father* caught me there…

He turned to look up at Kaci. "Sing."

Her expression melted and she bent to lift him onto her hip. "Okay, baby." She patted his back, and as he laid his head on her shoulder, she began to hum a soft tune. His eyes closed immediately.

A second later, his breathing slowed. The kid was passed out right there on her chest. And I had to admit, that looked like a great place to be.

"Holy shit," I breathed. "You're, like, the baby whisperer."

She smiled. "It's this new routine we have, since baby Ethan arrived. Little Greg's feeling kind of…displaced."

"Well, he looks like a lucky kid from where I'm standing."

Kaci's focus snapped up to my eyes and her cheeks flushed. Her heart began to beat a little harder. Something in her scent changed, and I had to shove my hands into my pockets to keep from reaching for her.

She cleared her throat and regrouped. "Okay, I'm going to take this little guy back to bed, then we're going to make a break for it. Got it?"

"Just give me my cue."

"I'm not leaving you for good, buddy," she whispered into the sleeping kid's ear as she headed down the hall. "I'll be back before you know it…"

I mentally followed her footsteps as Kaci took Greg back to the nursery. A minute later, she opened her bedroom door and grabbed her bag. But the true brilliance of her plan didn't shine through until I heard music playing from the nursery and realized that whatever device was projecting stars across Greg's room and filling it with a lullaby would also help cover our footsteps.

I followed Kaci past the closed office door, out of the house, and down the front steps, where she unlocked Chris's car with a very conspicuous-sounding thump. She dropped her backpack onto the rear seat next to mine, but instead of sliding behind the wheel, she stared at the front of the house.

For a second, I thought she was saying a mental goodbye. Or having second thoughts. Then I followed her gaze through the window of Faythe's office, which was still lit up at nearly one in the morning.

Our Alphas were making out on the desk, Faythe's legs wrapped around Marc's waist, as if they weren't married with two kids and a whole territory to run. As if there were nothing more important in the world at that moment than touching each other.

Kaci sighed, drawing my attention from over the car roof. She looked transfixed, not in a creepy peeping tom way, but in a wistful one. As if she were watching a fairytale play out in real life. Looking in from the outside at something she seemed convinced she'd never have.

Man-eater.

Suddenly I had the urge to delay my escape just long enough to go punch Brian Taylor in the face. It was his fault she thought she could never have that—his, and all the other asshole enforcers who treated her like a freak.

"You okay?" I whispered, and Kaci actually jumped. Her cheeks flushed again and she practically threw herself into the car.

"Yeah. Get in." She shifted into drive as I settled into my seat, then she pulled away from the house as if it were nothing. As if she escaped from the ranch every day.

I didn't exhale until she pulled Chris's car out of the driveway and onto the road. "You've done that before," I accused as I stared through the rearview mirror, half-expecting another car to come after us.

"A couple of times." The speedometer edged toward seventy, but she drove as if she'd been born with a steering wheel in her hands. "But never with both Faythe and Marc at home."

"How much trouble did you get into?"

"For leaving without permission? Hardcore grounding. But probably nothing compared to the trouble this will bring. Even now that I'm technically grown."

"We can still go back," I told her. We *should* go back. I should take her home and keep her out of this.

"Ha!" She dropped her phone in my lap. "It's unlocked. Disable tracking, will you? I need to be someone else for a couple of days. Anyone but the—"

Man-eater.

I heard it, even though she didn't say it.

"Anyone but me," she finished.

"I guess that means you're serious?" I navigated through her phone settings to disable her location services, and when I looked up, I found her staring at the road with an ironclad determination, her eyes shining in the glow from passing streetlights. She looked fierce and stunning. "You're really going to do this?"

"*We're* really going to do this, Justus."

The sound of my name on her tongue made me want to hear it again, under slightly more naked circumstances.

Okay, under *very* naked circumstances.

Though I would have settled for a kiss. For *one chance* to make her look at me the way Faythe looked at Marc—as if being with me would fix everything that was wrong with her life, rather than ruining it.

She liked me. I could tell that from the way her pulse sped up every time she looked at me. But I had no right to act upon her attraction, when soon she'd have to watch me run. Or see me executed.

We only had one day. Less, really. But that should be enough time for me to show her that she's worthy of everything she wants in life and in love—even if I can't be the one to give it to her.

THREE

KACI

ACCORDING TO THE MAP APP, THE DRIVE TO HOUSTON WOULD take just under an hour and a half. Faythe and Marc started calling about twenty minutes in, but they only called my phone at first, which told me they hadn't yet discovered that Justus was missing.

Justus plucked my phone from the cup holder, where it was plugged in and giving us directions to the airport. "You want me to put it on do not disturb?"

"I'm thinking I should answer it. Maybe I can delay the inevitable." I flicked on the blinker, then changed lanes a *little* too fast. "Answer on speaker phone, please, but be quiet. I don't think they know you're gone yet."

Justus tapped the speakerphone button, then angled himself in the passage seat to face me. Ready for the show.

"Hello?" I said, loud enough to be heard over the road noise.

"Kaci?" Faythe nearly shouted at me. "Where the hell are you? Did you take Chris's car?"

"Yes. I'm sorry, but…I had to get out of there for a little while. I can't stand the way the guys look at me. As if I'm going to shove up someone's sleeve and just…take a bite."

"What happened?"

"Nothing, I just… I'm tired of being the man-eater."

Faythe made a furious noise deep in her throat. "I will personally fire anyone who says—"

"Threats won't help. They'll still be thinking it." I paused for a moment. Then I pressed on, trying to pretend Justus wasn't listening to me humiliate myself, because I was *so close* to buying us enough time to get to the airport. "How many times had you been proposed to by your eighteenth birthday, Faythe?"

Silence echoed from the other end of the line. Then she exhaled. "Kaci, you're too young to get married. You're too young to *want* to get married."

"I don't want to get married. But knowing that no one's interested? That no one's ever going to be, because of something I can't go back and undo? People have wanted you your whole life. People fought over you like you were fu—" I aborted the profanity when I remembered that I was speaking to Faythe. "Like you were Helen of Troy. People won't even sit next to me at dinner unless there are no other chairs left. Normally I'm fine with it, but tonight, I need a break. Tell Chris I'm sorry about his car, but I'm taking good care of it. He'll totally get it back."

Faythe's new silence stretched into several seconds, and I was starting to worry that I'd misjudged her sympathy. Or her sleep-deprived, postpartum temper. "Where are you, Kaci?"

"I'm headed to Angelina Forest. I want to run in peace. Near the lake."

"By yourself? Let me send someone—"

"It's our territory," I reminded her. "And I'm grown. I'm sorry I took the car, but maybe this is a good time to revisit the discussion about me having my own?"

The car discussion was to Faythe what the sex discussion was to Marc—kryptonite. And a guaranteed subject change.

"We'll see," Faythe hedged. "If you're not in the driveway by three am, I'm sending out the guys. Either way, you're going to have to make it up to Chris on your own."

"Deal. And I will. I promise."

"Do *not* make me regret this." The exhaustion in her voice made me flinch with guilt.

"Thanks, Faythe," I said. "I really appreciate this."

"Love you, hon. Be careful."

"I will. Love you too." I glanced away from the road long enough to end the call, then exhaled a combination of relief and remorse.

"Damn." Justus whistled. "You knew just what buttons to push. You're mercenary."

"Yeah, and I feel bad about it," I snapped at him. "So, don't rub it in."

Justus went quiet for so long that I glanced at him, worried by his silence. He was staring at me. No, he was *studying* me.

"What?"

"You weren't playing her, were you? You really think no one will ever want you."

My face burned like it was on fire, but there was no use denying the truth. "You're too new to understand this yet, but the least lonely people in the world are tabbies. They're needed. They're wanted so badly that most of them have had several marriage proposals by the time they hit eighteen. Which is messed up, and not what I want. But there *has* to be some happy medium between child bride and the way our enforcers look at me like I'm something the dog hacked up under the back porch."

I heard my own words as they hung in the air between us, and suddenly I wished I could shove them all back into my mouth. I was driving a stolen car with the first tomcat to ever even look at me twice, and instead of acting cool and funny, I had to vomit needy bullshit all over him.

I must sound like *such* a loser.

Justus exhaled slowly. "Stop the car."

"What?" My pulse spiked painfully, leaving a bruising ache in my chest. *He's going to get out.* He'd rather hitchhike than ride with me to the airport.

I flicked on my blinker and shifted into the righthand lane, then slowed as I pulled as far onto the shoulder as I could get. "I know you can take care of yourself, but at least call a cab or something, okay?" The *thunk* of the gearshift settling into park echoed like regret in my head. "Don't walk down the side of the highway. Not even shifters can win a wrestling match with a car going eighty miles an hour."

Justus lifted my hand from the gearshift and laced his fingers through mine. "I'm not getting out of the car, Kaci. I just wanted to kiss you without causing an accident."

"You wanted to…?"

He leaned over the center console, and our mouths met in a soft press of his lips against mine. His hand slid over my jaw into my hair and he tilted my head one way and his own another, deepening the contact. Prolonging it.

"Oh my god," he murmured against the corner of my mouth, while my heart slammed against my sternum hard enough that it seemed to shake the whole car. "You taste so good."

Then we were kissing again, an almost desperate exploration of lips, and tongues, and even a little teeth. And when he finally pulled away, his hand slid down my arm and he looked right into my eyes. "I would sit next to you even if *none* of the other chairs were taken. Hell, I'd just pull you into my lap and share my chair with you."

It took me a second to realize I was grinning like a fool, just staring at him. "So…" I cleared my throat, struggling to make myself grab the wheel again. To focus on the road. "Vegas?"

"Unless you've already had enough adventure for one night."

No. No I had not. The taste of adventure—the taste of Justus—had merely awakened an appetite I hadn't even known I'd had. And suddenly I wanted nothing in the world but to satisfy this new hunger.

JUSTUS'S PHONE STARTED RINGING AS WE WERE GOING through security at the airport. The first call came from Vic. Then came one from Marc. When both their texts and their calls went unanswered, Faythe called Justus. Once. Then she called me, but I didn't answer.

Then *Titus* started calling Justus, and I knew the shit had hit the fan.

"They're going to kill us," I whispered as I buckled my seatbelt on the airplane.

"They're going to have to catch us first," Justus whispered back as he took my hand beneath the armrest.

Then the plane took off, and a spike of adrenaline hit me with such a burst of euphoria that I no longer cared what would happen when we got back. Or how mad Marc and Faythe would be. I hadn't left Texas except to go to school or

Pride functions in more than five years. I'd lost my family, and my friends, and my home, and my own name when they'd found me in the woods in Montana, and while I knew they'd done all that to save my life, to save my *sanity*, taking this trip with Justus was the first thing I'd done for myself— for the Kaci Dillion I'd once been—in my entire life.

And I'd be damned if I was going to feel guilty about that.

"SO, WAIT, WHAT NAME'S ON YOUR DIPLOMA THEN?" JUSTUS whispered as a man walked past us to get to the bathroom at the front of the plane. First class was pretty nice.

"Karli Sanders. Officially, I'm Faythe's cousin, who came to live on the ranch when her parents died a few years ago."

"Wow. Was it hard to remember to answer to one name at home and another one at school?"

I shrugged. "At first, but I got used to it. They probably thought I was living in my own world at school, for a while, because people had to call my name, like, three times before I answered." It was funny to think back on. Funny in a mortifying, bare-your-soul kind of way. Yet it didn't feel strange to be baring my soul to Justus.

"Sir, here's your whiskey and soda." The flight attendant set an unopened can, a plastic cup of ice, and a small bottle of Jack Daniels on his tray. "And your soda," she added as she set another cup of ice and a can on mine. "May I get you anything else?"

"I'm fine, thanks," I told her as I popped the top on my can.

"I'm fine too."

When she'd moved back to the galley, Justus opened his tiny bottle of whiskey and offered it to me. "She won't be able to tell which cup we poured it into," he whispered. "For all the good it'll do."

"What do you mean?"

"It's *really* hard to achieve a buzz as a shifter. Vic says it's the increase in metabolism. We process alcohol much faster than humans do, so it doesn't affect us as strongly. Have you never tried it?"

"Nope," I admitted. "I think that's one of those things natural-born cats take for granted and just kind of assume everyone else knows." And I probably wouldn't have been willing to have my first drink on an airplane, if not for that new bit of information.

"Wait, aren't you…?" Justus frowned at me, then took a subtle sniff in my direction. "You're not a stray."

"No, but I—" The flight attendant turned her back, and I dumped his bottle into my cup while she wasn't looking. Then I poured soda over it. "You haven't heard about my…circumstances?"

He took the empty bottle and set it on his own tray. "Just that they found you in the woods, and you were… Um…"

"Eating someone?" I picked up my glass and took a long drink, then coughed when the burn seemed to stretch all the way down my esophagus.

People across the aisle leaned forward to look at me.

Justus pounded on my back. "She's okay. It went down the wrong pipe."

That made me laugh, which made the coughing worse.

"You should probably sip it, at least until you're used to it," he whispered when I could talk again.

"Sorry. That line about eating people felt like something I should punctuate with a drink of something…real."

"So, it's true?"

"Yeah," I said as he poured soda into his own cup. "I had

a really rough patch at thirteen. But to truly understand that, you have to know that my parents were normal. Human. As was my sister. I'm somewhat of a rare case."

"A shifter born to human parents?" His eyes narrowed on me as he sipped from his cup. "I've never heard of that."

"I told you. Rare. It's something about recessive genes. You have them. So does Titus. You have to have a shifter in your bloodline somewhere in order to survive being scratched or bitten. People who don't have that recessive gene don't live through the infection."

"How would I possibly have a shifter in my family and not know it?" he asked.

"Oh, it could be waaay back. At some point, someone in your family hooked up with a shifter—almost certainly a tomcat—and made a baby. The most common theories involve one-night stands, which is what toms are best at, and affairs. Since most toms never get married, over time they've evidently gotten really good at getting…tail. Pun intended."

Justus laughed so loud everyone turned to look again.

I couldn't help but smile. "Okay, yeah, it sounds funny when you put it like that."

"*You* put it like that," he pointed out.

"My point is that you have to have the recessive gene to survive being infected. And *I* am what happens, very rarely, when two people with those recessive genes have kids."

"Your sister didn't…get it?"

"Nope. And I have no idea why. We did a little bit of basic genetics in biology, but nowhere near enough for me to understand why when she turned thirteen, she got insta-boobs and her period, but *I* turned into a big black cat." I took another long sip from my cup and managed not to choke that time. "Seriously, I drew the shortest straw in the entire history of puberty."

"Holy shit." Justus's smile faded into a look of concern that quickened my heartbeat. "I thought I had it rough, because I didn't know I was infected. I had no idea I was going to shift—or even that that was possible—until it happened. But I was twenty. I can't imagine going through that at thirteen. Your family must have been really freaked—"

The obvious conclusion seemed to hit him all at once.

"What happened to them?"

"My mother and sister found me behind the house. I'd just shifted for the first time, and I was *out of my mind* with terror. Obviously, they didn't know it was me. All they knew was that my clothes were on the ground, ripped to shreds, and there was a big black cat in our yard.

"They started shouting and swinging things at me, trying to protect themselves, and I…did the same thing. I…" I turned up the cup and drained it, relishing the burn in my throat like penance for a sin I could *never* be forgiven for. "I'm sorry. I've never actually told anyone."

"Faythe and Marc don't know?"

"They know. *Everyone* knows. But they found out on the internet. They looked me up once they got me to tell them my name, and the story was…there. My dad was still looking for me at the time. He was convinced for a long time that I'd somehow survived the 'wild cat' attack that killed my mother and sister, because they didn't find my blood at the scene. But eventually he stopped looking. And I let him." I shrugged. "That was the best thing I could do for him." I'd let my father mourn me and move on. "I look him up online every now and then. He remarried a few years later. He has two more kids now. Both boys."

"Holy shit," Justus breathed. "I feel like I should order you another drink."

"For all the good it would do," I said, repeating his words, and he smiled.

"So, did you eat…your…"

"My family? No. When I realized what I'd done, I was terrified. Traumatized. I ran from my backyard into the woods before my father came home, and I eventually made my way south of the border. From Canada."

"You're Canadian?"

"Yes. From British Colombia. But 'Karli Sanders' is American." I poured the rest of the soda into my empty glass. "Anyway, I didn't know how to shift back into human form, or even if I could, so I just kind of lived in the woods. For, like, two and a half months. I wandered into Montana without knowing it, and Faythe and her family found me. They were there for Faythe's trial, the same place they're holding yours. It's the northern free zone, which is considered neutral territory. That's why they hold murder trials there." Another shrug. "Not that there are many of those."

"Do you remember her trial?" A flicker of fear flashed across Justus's face—the first I'd seen from him, even though he seemed sure the court would find him guilty.

"I wasn't actually there in the room with the tribunal, and I was still pretty…traumatized. I really only remember images from that first week or so, after being stuck in cat form for months. Faces. A very confused jumble of emotions. The taste of my first meal that wasn't raw meat since the day I'd turned into a cat."

"Damn."

"Yeah. Faythe was the first person I let near me." I leaned closer to him over the padded armrest, to keep the people in front of and behind us from overhearing a *very* strange whispered conversation. "I'd been in cat form so long that I was basically feral, even in on two feet, and she thought I might

43

respond better to the scent of another girl. She had to sneak in to see me. She says I just kept hissing at her, at first." I shrugged and sipped from my soda. "But she stuck with it. She stuck with *me*. And she got results, so it was hard for the Alphas to say much about her breaking their rules. Though I suspect they were still pretty mad."

Justus shook his head, eyes wide. "It's hard for me to imagine Faythe not being in charge."

"I know. Her dad died a few months after I came to live with them, and she's been the boss ever since. I hardly remember back when she was just an enforcer, but I've heard lots of stories. She broke *all* the rules. She was a total thorn in the council's side. She still is, kind of."

"She and Marc are the only reason I'm getting a trial," Justus said. "Strays aren't considered citizens, and if they hadn't taken me in, the council could have done whatever they wanted with me."

"You feel guilty now, don't you?" I could see it in his eyes.

He nodded slowly. "The last thing I wanted to do was piss them off. Or seem ungrateful. I just... I don't know a lot about the council. I don't really know anything about natural-born cat society, except what I've learned from Vic and the guys, but what I do understand is that the council has a very long history of siding against strays. And it's hard for me to imagine them doing anything else in my case." Justus leaned closer to whisper to me, his cup held in front of his mouth, as if to foil any attempt to read his lips. "I mean, it's not like I'm innocent. I actually infected those people. I actually killed Drew Borden. And the thing is that I don't really regret it. He deserved what he got. He deserved *worse*, for what he did, and if I could do it again, the only thing I would change is how mercifully quick he died."

"You don't have to *tell* the tribunal that."

"I'm not going to lie about it, and even if I did, they wouldn't believe me. Not that any of that matters." Justus glanced at his cup as if he suddenly regretted giving me his whiskey. "They've already decided, Kaci."

"What does that mean?" But I was pretty sure I got the gist of it, even without the details.

"I overheard Vic talking. The tribunal members already know how they're going to vote, without hearing a word I have to say in my own defense. There's *no way* I'm going to leave that trial alive."

There was something in his voice. Something in the determined set of his jaw, and the way his focus seemed to be not on the seat in front of him, but on something I couldn't see. Something in his past, or in his fu—

And that's when the truth hit me like a knife straight to the chest. "You son of a bitch. You're not going back, are you? You're *running*."

And I had helped him escape.

FOUR

"KACI. CAN WE TALK ABOUT THIS?" I WHISPERED, AS CLOSE to her as I could get without looking like a psycho stalker as we got off the plane and walked down the narrow, enclosed jetway toward the airport gate.

She only swung her backpack onto her shoulder as she walked, forcing me back a step to keep from getting hit.

"Kaci!" I hissed as we stepped into the airport, where hundreds of impatient passengers were waiting to board the plane we'd just disembarked. And now that we were free of the jetway, she took off at a jog, dodging passengers waiting in line for coffee and soft pretzels, business men and women hauling suitcases and talking on their phones, and a couple of small children turning in circles in the middle of the broad aisle between gates, their eyes closed, oblivious to life going on around them.

"Wait," I called as I caught up to her, hoping the rest of the world saw a couple running late for their connecting flight, rather than a young woman fleeing a guy chasing her. "Let me explain!"

She stopped so fast I nearly crashed into her, then she turned on me, eyes flashing with fury. "A vacation," she snapped. "You said this was a *vacation*. You said you were coming back to stand trial." Her voice dropped into a whisper on the last two words, and suddenly we were having a very quietly obvious argument in a very public place. "But what you were actually doing was using me to aid your escape."

"That is *not* what happened," I whispered. "You *black-mailed* me into bringing you."

Kaci's hazel eyes widened. Then she frowned. "Okay, that is *not* the point. The point is that I thought you were coming back. That this was just a trip. But this is—"

"This is me running for my life," I said in as firm and as soft a voice as I could manage. "You're on vacation, but I'm fleeing certain death at the declaration of a bunch of men I've never even met. I didn't mean to drag you into this. I didn't *want* to drag you into it. But I *had* to go, and you gave me no choice but to bring you."

Her frown deepened as she studied my face, conflict written clearly on hers. Then she glanced around the airport, as if she were just then realizing where we were. "Why the hell would you escape to Las Vegas? This isn't even the free zone. If you think Paul Blackwell won't find you here you're crazy."

"This is only the first part of the plan." I hardly dared to breathe with the admission, for fear of pissing her off again. I wasn't sure how far into the airport I could chase her before security decided I was a threat.

"What's the rest of it?"

"Can we talk about that some place less public?" I

glanced pointedly around at all the people who shouldn't overhear anything about shifters, and murder, and escape.

Kaci exhaled slowly. "It's not like I have a choice. Where are we going?"

"To Caesar's Palace."

A flicker of her earlier excitement flashed over her face. "I'm so mad at you I almost forgot we were in Las Vegas." Her gaze wandered over a long row of slot machines stretching down the aisle between gates. "I should drag you back onto a plane to Houston without even leaving the airport. But I *really* want to go see a show…"

I opened my mouth to tell her that wasn't exactly on my list of escape plan bullet points. "Yes. We can do whatever you want."

Son of a bitch. Where the hell had that come from?

I told myself that keeping her happy was a newly necessary part of my plan—if she told anyone where I was before I had what I'd come for, Marc would show up and drag me to my trial in handcuffs.

But then she smiled at me again, and I spared a moment to thank the universe that Kaci Dillon wasn't a con artist or a gold digger, because in that moment, I would have given her everything I owned to keep that smile on her face. To keep her looking at me like that. As if I—the guy who'd snuck her out of her territory under kind-of false pretenses—were somehow the only light shining in her world.

"HOLY CRAP," KACI BREATHED AS SHE STEPPED INTO THE hotel room.

I laughed. She'd said the same thing about the fountains outside, the statues in the lobby, and the ornate main floor, as we'd passed it when I gave her a brief tour. Unfortunately, even if she'd had a fake ID, no one would have believed she was twenty-one. Which put a definite cramp in my plans, unless I was willing to leave her in our room or abandon her at a show while I hit the poker tables.

And so far, I'd hardly been able to drag myself from her side long enough to check us in.

She dropped her backpack on the long gray sofa and wandered into the bathroom. "Holy crap!" Her voice echoed out at me. "This place is huge. This *tub* is huge. This shower is huge. This sink… Well, the sink's pretty normal sized, but there are two of them!"

I leaned against the bathroom doorjamb, watching her as if I were seeing it all for the first time with her.

She turned to me, hazel eyes wide. "You don't look impressed. I assume you've been here before?"

"Not this specific room, but one like it."

"It's so expensive!" She edged past me into the main room and sank onto the couch, then twisted to look out the window. "I saw you pay in cash. If you're broke without your trust fund, where did that money come from?"

"I have a credit card. Titus pays the bill. Yesterday I took out a cash advance."

"So, I have him to thank for this little not-vacation?"

"No. He's the executor of my inheritance. He pays my bills out of that."

"It's messed up that you're fully grown, yet can't access your own money."

I'd turned twenty in April, and my new Pride had thrown me a small birthday party. Cake. Music. A bunch of shifter-specific gag gifts, like the catnip mouse Kaci had given me. It was a simple event compared to the international birthday trips Titus had taken me on nearly every year since our parents had died, but they'd made me feel like family.

Unfortunately, twenty was still five years too young for the first lump sum from my inheritance.

"Ironically, that's to keep me from blowing it all on something…well, exactly like this, while I'm still young and stupid," I explained.

Kaci's smile faded. She tugged me onto the couch next to her. "It's not too late. We could still stay the night and have some fun, then go home and face the music. This could still just be a vacation."

"If the tribunal isn't going to play by its own rules, why should I? They're going to execute me, Kaci. I can't go back."

She sighed. Then she nodded. "Okay. Tell me what we're doing here."

"I will. But first…" I leaned in and kissed her, and what I expected to be a short, soft reminder that she actually might like me, in spite of the lie I'd told, became a long, deep, hungry connection I could hardly stand to break.

When she finally pulled away, her focus was glazed with the same need building inside me. "What was that for?"

I shrugged and rubbed my thumb over her bottom lip, still damp and swollen from our kiss. "One last taste, in case you won't let me do that again after you hear my plan."

"Well let's hear it then. And please tell me it's a little more sophisticated than 'win a bunch of money downstairs and flee the country.'"

"Okay, it's pretty much exactly that, but it's much more realistic than it sounds."

"Oh good!" Her brows rose in mock excitement. "For a second, I was worried you were one of those delusional assholes who think they can step into a casino for the first time in their lives, slap down a twenty dollar bill and walk out with a million dollars. One of those delusional *underage* assholes," she amended, crossing her arms over her chest. "Seriously, Justus, tell me there's a plan B."

"This isn't my first time in a casino, and I'm prepared to slap down much more than a twenty," I assured her.

"And would that be more magical money from your credit card?"

"From the cash advance, yes. Titus pays it off every month, which means I have excellent credit. Earlier tonight, I hitched a ride into town with Vic, and while he was in a sandwich shop, I hit up an ATM for some cash."

Her gaze narrowed suspiciously. "How much cash?"

"My full limit of fifty-thousand dollars."

Kaci's hazel eyes widened dramatically. She shoved me in the chest. "You're walking around with fifty-thousand dollars in cash?"

"Forty-nine thousand, after the cab ride and the hotel, which I paid for up front, so I wouldn't have to charge it."

"Because the police can track you through your credit card?"

I laughed. I couldn't help it. "Yes, gambling underage is a crime, but I'm much more worried about evading Alphas than the cops right now. Titus is authorized on my credit card, and the first thing he would have done when he found out we were missing is check the recent charges. Which is why I took out cash in eastern Texas, rather than at the airport in Houston or here. And why I'm not charging the hotel. He may guess that we're here eventually, but he won't know that for sure unless we give him proof that I'm not already lounging on a beach in Cancun or staying in a castle in Scotland. Either of which I could do with a passport and a pocket full of cash."

"So then, why aren't you in Cancun or Scotland?"

"Because that withdrawal was the only one I'm going to get. I'm at my cash limit, and even if Titus pays it off, I can't draw again without showing him where I am."

"What makes you think he'd tell the council? Faythe said he'd do *anything* to keep you safe."

"He probably would. But I'm not the only stray he has to protect, and the council is never going to recognize his territory if they think he's aiding and abetting a criminal. I have to keep him on their side in this. By cutting him out of it."

"So, your plan is to go downstairs and win a fortune at a game of chance? Playing what, craps? I'm not even sure what that is. Blackjack?"

"Poker," I told her. "It's a game of skill, not a game of chance."

"You're not even old enough to legally gamble, so how would you have acquired that skill? Was there some kind of backroom poker game on the Millsaps campus?" She kept drilling me with questions too fast for me to answer. "Even if you're a college-level expert, what on earth makes you think you have enough experience to win serious money in Las Vegas? Isn't this where all the experts come to play? Like, professional gamblers?"

I took her hand, and she finally stopped talking. "Yes. And I'm good, but I'm not delusional. I'll be playing against tourists, not professionals."

She rolled her eyes. "And they're going to be wearing name tags that tell you they're ready lose their life savings to a guy who could buy and sell them a hundred times over? How convenient for you."

"They won't have name tags." Though the thought made me smile. "But tourists will look and act like tourists. And I didn't learn to play at school, Kaci." I intertwined my fingers with hers, because touching her seemed to make everything better. I learned to play overseas. In most of Europe, the legal gambling age is eighteen."

"Oh." She looked a little chagrined as she stood and headed for the dresser. "I didn't know that."

"Remember all those airline miles? Titus and I used to travel together a lot, but a couple of years ago, he stopped coming with me. As it turned out, he couldn't go to any place where there was a local Alpha with an anti-stray policy." I shrugged. "If he *had* come, I probably would have spent my time in museums and restaurants—which is where I told him I was going—instead of casinos. As it is, I can't tell a Monet from a Renoir, but I know when to fold and when to raise."

Kaci grabbed a bottle of water from a tray of snacks and cracked it open. "So, you're just going to go downstairs with your fake ID and turn forty-nine thousand dollars into, what? Half a million?" She took a sip from her bottle. "How much do you need, in order to live the rest of your life on the run?"

"I only have to tide myself over until I'm twenty-five and I get the first lump sum from my trust fund. It was set up in Switzerland, and Titus can't stop me from getting it. And he's not legally entitled to know anything about its release—including when or where it will happen."

"So, you want to win enough cash here to get you through the next five years—"

"Four years and ten months."

"—at which point you'll inherit enough money to let you tell the whole world to fuck off?"

"Yes. I'll retire to an island nation where there are no other shifters—turns out that's most of them—and…I don't know. Carve things out of driftwood for neighborhood children until I die a happy old man. Leaving all my money to local orphans, of course."

"Of course." She actually smiled as she screwed the lid on her water. "Funny *and* generous. How much money are we talking about?"

"Um…about two hundred million in liquid assets. And a stake in my dad's company that's worth several times that, but I won't be able to collect on the shares without contacting Titus. So, it's basically just the cash."

"Basically just the…" Kaci sank onto the tile on her knees, as if her legs would no longer hold her up. Her water bottle hit the floor and fell onto its side. "Basically just the *two hundred million in cash*?"

"Well, a third of that when I'm twenty-five. Another third when I turn thirty. And the last of it when I turn thirty-five." I reached down and tugged her up onto the couch with me.

"Okay, I know that's a lot of money. It's *so much* money," she said. "But is it worth giving up all your family and friends over?"

"They're going to lose me whether I run or I'm executed."

"Justus, you heard a rumor, not a fact. You don't *know* that they'll vote to convict," Kaci insisted.

"I know what the enforcers overheard from their alphas, and I know I'd be stupid to show up for the trial on the odd chance that they misunderstood whatever they heard. And as for giving up my family, Titus is the only family I have, and I'm doing this in part to protect him. My friends…" I shrugged. "We drifted apart after high school. Different colleges and everything."

"College friends?" she asked.

"There were a few. But none who truly questioned me dropping out in the middle of the semester. Or who even tried to come see me out in Texas. I had a girlfriend, but…"

"That's right. She died." Kaci covered her mouth with both hands. "I'm so sorry."

"Yeah. *That's* what I feel really bad about." Drew deserved what he got, but I hadn't meant to hurt Ivy. I hadn't even fully understood that I was a shifter at the time, much less that scratching her would infect her with the shifter virus. Or that women almost never survive the infection.

"I heard she was—" Kaci's mouth snapped shut.

"Cheating on me?" My snort sounded more bitter than I meant for it to. "Actually, she was cheating on this other guy with me, though I didn't know it at the time. His name was Leland Blum."

I'd followed Ivy and Leland into the woods to confront them, not to hurt them, but stress and anger got the better of me in the terrifying, vulnerable period right after I was infected, and my body had shifted into cat form without permission from the rest of me.

I'd only scratched Ivy and Leland in self defense. Because they were understandably terrified of the huge black cat I'd become. Still, her death and his infection were my fault, and they were among the things the tribunal had already decided to make me pay for with my life.

"It turns out Ivy and Leland had been together since high school. But I didn't know that until after it all went down. Until after Drew…was dead, and Titus and Robyn explained everything to me."

"Damn."

"Yeah. And as if finding out I was the other guy wasn't bad enough, the fact that Ivy was cheating on Leland with me makes it sound like I had a reason for what I did to them. A motive for murder. But that's not true. I mean, yes, I was mad, but I wasn't trying to hurt anyone, and I didn't understand what would happen."

"I get it," Kaci said, and when I looked into her eyes, I got caught there.

Since I'd been accepted into the South-Central Pride, I'd seen exactly two kinds of expressions when natural-born cats looked at me. Sympathy, from those who'd heard my story and thought to look beyond the outcome to the cause. And aversion, from those who hadn't. It wasn't revulsion, exactly, but rather a cold distance from people who found it easier to avoid thinking about strays like me—people who'd been thrown into the deep end of shifter existence without a life-jacket—rather than deal with us.

But the look in Kaci's eyes was different than both of those. In her, I found…empathy. The kind of visceral understanding I'd thought could only come from a fellow stray, infected through traumatic violence.

What we had in common wasn't how we'd become shifters, but how we'd reacted to that change.

"So, I accidentally killed my mother and my sister, and you accidentally killed your girlfriend."

"Fucked up, aren't we?" I said.

Kaci blinked at me. Then she threw her head back and laughed. "I'm sorry! It's not funny. It's just that it's somehow *so damn funny*. I know that doesn't make any sense."

"It makes perfect sense." I slid my hand behind her neck and kissed her again, slowly this time. Letting the connection linger. Because that's what I'd found. Somehow, in my attempt to flee the country—the entirety of shifter society—I'd stumbled upon the only person in the world who made me want to stay.

But if I stayed, they'd execute me. Which left only one solution.

"Come with me, Kaci." I pulled just far enough away that

I could focus on her face. So I could watch her thoughts flicker as she processed my invitation.

"With you?"

"To Cancun. Or Scotland. Or one of the island nations where there are no shifters. I know that's asking a lot, and you'd be leaving behind family and friends. But I'm mentally kicking myself for spending four months at the ranch wallowing in my own self-pity instead of talking to you. And kissing you. If you come with me, we can spend every day for the rest of our lives talking and kissing on the beach somewhere. Surfing, and eating seafood, and learning to make our own alcohol from coconuts, or sugarcane, or whatever grows locally wherever we wind up."

Kaci smiled, but it was a sad smile. A face-reality, Justus smile.

I held up one hand in the universal signal for STOP. "Don't say no—"

"I'm not saying no. I'd just like to propose an alternative." She took a deep breath and set her water bottle on the coffee table. "*You* stay here with *me*."

"Kaci, I can't—"

"We'll tell Faythe and Marc what you overheard. They'll never let you sit through a trial that's been decided before it even begins."

I rolled my eyes. "It's not like the tribunal members are going to admit they've already—"

"Justus." She seized both of my hands in an iron grip. "Titus sent you here for a fair trial, and there *has* to be a way to make sure you get one. Faythe and Marc will know what to do. Now, I know Texas isn't as glamorous as some tropical island, and you have to be twenty-one to do anything really fun, but...I can't leave Faythe and Marc without even saying goodbye. They're practically my parents."

"Yes, but you're grown," I pointed out. "Birds are supposed to leave the nest."

"Birds." She shuddered. "Sorry. Flashback. There was a thing with thunderbirds a few years ago. I got kidnapped and—"

"You got kidnapped by *thunderbirds*?"

"One plucked me right off the ground. I was a lot smaller then. Everything turned out okay. Faythe and Jace rescued me. But I'm not a big fan of heights anymore. Or things with feathers. Or talons."

"Well, there are no thunderbirds in the tropics. But Kaci, if I stay here, they'll *execute* me."

"Okay, but maybe they won't. The council is much less anti-stray now than it used to be, and even five years ago they brought charges against Faythe for killing a stray." Her eyes widened with the enthusiasm of her pitch. "That was kind of groundbreaking, if you think about it—the council being willing to punish one of its own, rare tabbies for an act against someone they didn't even consider a citizen."

"My understanding is that they found her guilty of infection—which I'm up on two counts of—and innocent of murder. Which shows how little they value stray lives."

"They found her innocent because she *was* innocent. She acted in self-defense."

"But I didn't."

"You have extenuating circumstances," Kaci insisted. "Drew ripped away your human life, then he used you to frame your brother. To get him removed as Alpha."

That was all true. But... "That's not why I killed him."

Kaci frowned. "Then why...?"

"Okay. If you get called to testify against me, I'm screwed." I meant it as a joke, because I had no intention of standing trial. But she looked more curious than amused. "I didn't know how'd I'd become a shifter or who had done that to me until that night at the zoo. Drew infected me, then abandoned me. On purpose. He let me suffer through scratch fever and figure out how to shift back on my own, without any guidance or help. He didn't teach me how to control my new instincts or fight bloodlust. Again, all on purpose, as part of his plot against my brother. He let those things rage inside me, then he sent me a picture of my girlfriend sleeping with some other guy. Less than a month after I'd been infected. Fully aware that emotional stress can trigger a new stray's shift into cat form and that without training, new strays have little impulse control and difficulty thinking like a human in cat form.

"He treated me like a loaded gun, then he aimed me at Ivy and Leland, hoping I would lose control and hurt someone. Or infect someone. Or accidentally kill someone. Because he knew that my scent is so much like Titus's that everyone would assume he'd committed my crimes. Especially since they had no idea I'd even been infected.

"It was *Drew's fault* Ivy died. Hell, he killed Leland himself. That's why I attacked him. Because of what he did to them. Because of what he made me do to them. Because of what he turned me into. I'm a killer because of that bastard."

Anger on my behalf flashed in Kaci's eyes. "Tell that to the tribunal," she said. "Exactly like you said it just now. They can't find you guilty if they understand the circumstances."

"They already know the circumstances. Titus told them all of that when they tried to make him choose between me and Robyn. Armed with all of the information, at least two of the three tribunal members have decided to vote against me before the trial even starts."

"Okay, but even if that's true, you don't know they'll vote

to execute. They didn't for Robyn. Or Manx."

"Manx and Robyn are women. The council needs them, but they don't need me. They don't even *want* me. There are more than enough strays, from the council's perspective, and they're already pissed off about being forced to give me a trial."

"You don't know—"

"Kaci." I took both of her hands and captured her gaze, trying to *make* her understand. "There is no future for me in the territories. I have to go. I have to win what I can tonight, then get on an international flight in the morning. I want you to come with me. But I'll understand if you can't. I've gotten you into enough trouble as it is."

Kaci stared at our intertwined hands. She rubbed my forefinger with her thumb. Then she took a deep breath and looked up. "I'm in."

"You're in?" For a second, I was sure I'd heard her wrong. I'd asked her for something crazy. Something that made no sense. I'd been prepared for the toughest rejection of my life. But... "Seriously?"

"Yes. I'm coming with you. So, let's go downstairs and win some money." She frowned. "How do we do that? I don't think they'll even let me on the floor."

"They won't. The bad news is that I'm going to have to gamble on my own. You can stay here and get some sleep or go grab dinner. There's a great Asian place in the casino that's open all night. Those are pretty much the options, though. The spa and the pools are closed."

"Okay." She looked disappointed, but resigned. "I'll go get some dinner. Was there good news?"

"Oh. Yeah." I leaned in and kissed her again. "After I win, we're going to party. Then we're going to book a one-way flight out of here."

FIVE

LIGHT BLED THROUGH MY EYELIDS, AND THE PAIN IN MY HEAD was like an open wound, as if someone had cut off the top of my skull. The sound of running water offered an encore of sandpaper against my exposed and vulnerable gray matter.

I groaned as I pushed myself upright on something soft, and the sound of my own voice made me want to cry.

"Kaci? I'll be out in a minute."

My eyes flew open. Direct sunlight speared my brain straight through my optical nerve, and at first, all I could do was blink tears from my eyes as I waited for them to adjust.

Then the room came into focus.

A long gray couch. Gray carpet. A coffee table littered with clear plastic cups. A wall of windows, with the drapes pushed all the way open to reveal the Las Vegas strip…

Las Vegas.

Justus Alexander.

Kissing, and talking, and…drinking?

I had vague, blurry memories of pouring something clear into my soda. Several times. There was an alcohol-scented stain on my shirt.

What the hell? I tried to stand, but my legs were tangled in the covers. My *bare* legs. Shit.

Frantic, I kicked the covers off—it took several tries—and didn't exhale in relief until I saw that I was still wearing my underwear.

The bathroom door opened and Justus stepped out wearing nothing but a pair of boxer briefs stretched across a defined V of muscle below a set of abs that would have made any enforcer proud. He snapped his toothbrush into a plastic case, then tossed it into his open backpack. "Good morning."

Justus didn't look hung over. In fact, he looked…great.

He pulled me close and kissed the corner of my mouth, and my hands went automatically to his bare, hard chest, as if they'd been there before. As if they remembered something my mind did not.

"You okay?" He frowned down at me. "I'm so sorry about last night. I had no idea the drinks would hit you that fast."

"So much for shifters having trouble getting drunk, huh?" I was afraid that anything else I said would reveal how little I actually remembered of the night before. Which was pretty much nothing but the half-empty bottle of vodka sitting on the coffee table and…walking down the strip, holding hands with Justus. And not necessarily in that order.

"Yeah. So, it turns out that if you weigh a hundred pounds and you drink quickly—"

"One-ten," I corrected him, running my hands through the crow's nest that had grown on my head overnight.

"—and you've never had a drink before, except one little mini-bottle on the plane, you can actually get drunk pretty easily." He brushed hair over my shoulder and stared down into my eyes, as if he were assessing me for a concussion. "You sure you're okay?"

"Headache," I managed, as I glanced over the room, hoping to trigger more memories of whatever we'd done.

"Oh. Yeah, just a sec."

Shoes, sticking out from under the couch. Open, presumably empty soda cans standing on the bathroom counter, visible through the doorway. Pants, hanging over the back of a chair. All of it evidence of a night I couldn't remember.

"Here." Justus pressed two tablets of Tylenol into my right hand. I set them on my tongue, then took the bottle of water he offered and swallowed them. "You should drink all of that. Then several more."

I drained the bottle of water while he stepped into his jeans, mostly for the chance to think back over last night without being expected to speak. I remembered the plane and the taxi ride to Caesar's Palace, and I remembered eating noodles alone at a restaurant in the casino. But the rest was a blur.

"Justus?" My hand shook as I set the empty bottle on the coffee table. "What happened last night?"

He looked up, alarm flickering behind his beautiful gray eyes as he buttoned his pants. "You don't remember?"

"Not everything."

He waved one arm at the empty cups and the vodka bottle. "We were celebrating."

And suddenly I *did* remember.

He was sure the tribunal was hopelessly stacked against him, so he was going to run. And I was going to go with him. After he won some money playing… "Poker!"

Relief washed over his face. "You do remember."

"I remember that you were playing, and I was eating.

63

So…" I glanced around at the evidence of our celebration. "You won? Crap, what time is it?" I patted my butt for my phone, but both my jeans and my phone were noticeably absent. "What time is our flight? Are we going to make it?"

"Kaci…" Justus took my hand and led me around the coffee table to the couch. "Sit down. Drink some more water. See if you can remember anything else." He looked really worried.

"What? Did we already miss the flight?"

"No." He cracked open another bottle and handed it to me." Kaci, we weren't celebrating…poker. I lost most of my money. You don't remember that?"

"No."

"I was up two hundred thousand dollars. Then I looked up and saw some guy hitting on you in the restaurant."

I frowned at him. "You lost your money because some guy hit on me?"

"No." He chuckled. "You shoved him, and he fell over a table, and security escorted him out. It was awesome. But then I realized I didn't want to be playing poker while you were eating alone. So I doubled down, like an idiot. That would have been enough to get us out of here and hold us over for quite a while."

"But then you lost."

"Yeah."

Damn. "Then…what were we celebrating?"

Justus took my hand again, and I expected him to inter-twine my fingers through his. That was the best memory I had of the night before. Other than the kissing.

Instead, he lifted my hand into my own line of sight. Sunlight glinted off something shining on my…

"Holy crap!" I snatched my hand from him, staring in

utter shock at the ring—no, *two* rings—on my fourth finger. My *ring* finger. "Is that…?"

"It matches mine." Justus held up his own left hand, where a platinum band encircled his ring finger.

"We're married?" The words sounded like nonsense coming from my mouth. Yet…

"You don't look happy. There wasn't much of a selection at three in the morning, but we can get you a different one soon, if you want. You can design your own. Titus knows this place that—"

"How was there *any* selection of wedding rings at three in the morning?"

Justus shrugged. "It's Las Vegas. There are actually a couple of twenty-four-hour jewelry stores."

"And we… Wait." I closed my eyes and the fingers of my right hand found the rings on my left and began twisting them. Now that I'd noticed them, I couldn't *un*notice them. "How did we go from you losing two hundred thousand dollars to us getting married? I still feel like I'm missing a big piece of the puzzle here."

"It was for the money."

"The money you lost?" How was it possible that the more I learned, the less I understood?

"No, the money I'm going to inherit. I get my first lump sum when I turn twenty-five, or when I get married. Whichever comes first."

"You…!" I opened my eyes, and the glare from the ring made me want to close them again. But I scowled at him instead. "You didn't tell me that. You said twenty-five. You never said married."

"I told you last night, Kaci." He sounded…wounded. "Last night you were *happy* about this."

"Last night I was drunk! Evidently. I can't even remember

—" My focus snapped to the bed, where the tangled mass of covers made me want to cry. "We didn't...?"

Please say we didn't.

I wanted to *remember* my first time.

Justus followed my gaze to the bed. "Oh. No, you were drunk. That wouldn't have been..." He cleared his throat. "You threw up. Then you fell asleep."

"Without my pants."

"You did *that* yourself. You were...eager. But then you passed out."

"Oh my god." I buried my face in my hands, and the ring felt cold against my scalding cheek. "Alcohol is the *devil*."

"Kaci." Justus pulled my right hand away from my face and held it, but I kept my eyes squeezed shut. I couldn't look at him. Not knowing that I'd evidently begged him to sleep with me. To free the poor, man-eating tabby from her virginity. At three in the morning. Drunk on vodka. "Kaci. Look at me."

Finally, I opened my eyes. But tears filled them almost immediately, blurring his face.

"Kaci. Oh, please don't cry. I would never have touched you while you were drunk. No matter what you said you wanted. I—"

"Aaaghhhh!" I pushed him away and stood. "You're just making it worse. No girl wants to hear that she got married while she was drunk. That she begged for sex, then didn't even get it. Not that not remembering it would have been any better."

"Wait, you're mad because I *didn't* sleep with you?"

"No!" I grabbed my pants from the back of the chair they were hanging from and leaned against the wall while I pulled them on with angry, jerking motions. "And yes. I'm mad about everything, Justus. *All* the things. This is all wrong."

I was never one of those girls who dreamed about her wedding day. By the time I realized I'd be expected to marry a tom, I already knew that none of them would be interested. I also knew, thanks to Faythe and the glass ceiling she'd shoved her way through, that I wouldn't be forced into marriage with someone who didn't love me.

But as much of a relief as that understanding was, the knowledge that I'd probably spend my entire life alone kept me from truly celebrating the feminist victory Faythe believed she'd passed down to me.

"I don't understand, Kaci." Justus stood as I buttoned my pants. "I'm sorry, but I don't know what I did wrong. I mean, other than the charges I'm facing."

"Well then, let me see if I can explain this in asshole-friendly terms." I glanced around the room in search of my socks, until I realized I hadn't worn any. My shoes were slip-ons. "Yes, as the world's only unwanted tabby, I am lonely and pathetic in a way that no one else on earth, as far as I can tell, will ever truly understand. But I was used to that. I was *dealing* with my emotional shit through a regimen of sexually unsatisfying human hookups that—at least so far—hadn't gotten anyone hurt. Then *you* came along, and you were exciting, and funny, and *so, so pretty*, and—"

"Why do your compliments feel like bullets, Kaci?" Justus looked hurt.

"—and you were interested in me. You kissed me like you wanted me, when we both know you could have any girl in the whole damn world. And I thought you meant it. I thought we were the same, except for the fucking trust fund. Then I wake up this morning and find out that we're married, even though I don't remember saying 'I do.'"

"I might have a video." He reached into his pocket for his cell phone, but came up empty. "The wedding package came with one, but I don't know if they've sent it yet. I can check my—"

"That is not the point!" Though my memory loss was at least point-adjacent. "What I'm saying is that I was falling for you. I was going to run away with you. Then you got me drunk and married me just to get your hands on your fucking money five years early."

"Four years and—"

"Do not say four years and ten months," I snapped at him. "*Do not say four years and ten months!*"

"Kaci." He reached for me, but I pushed him back again, and I hated myself for noticing how hard his abs felt. How gray his eyes were. How sad his beautiful mouth looked.

"Don't touch me."

"Okay. Look, I'm not touching you." He backed away from me, his hands in the air as if I had a gun on him. "Just listen. I didn't marry you for the money." He frowned and shook his head. "I mean…we did get married for the money, but *we* did it *together*. So *we* could both get out of here. We're going to the island, remember? I didn't get you drunk so you'd marry me. I didn't even know you *were* drunk until you got onto the coffee table and started imitating the thunderbirds who took you hostage."

"I did *not*—" But then the memory slammed into me like a slap to the face. I'd stood on the table with my arms bent like wings, flapping them and squawking, after I'd told him how terrifying it was to be ripped from the ground by a giant bird, then flown over the earth with my feet dangling over the treetops.

"Well, whether you knew it or not, I was drunk. And now I'm married." I scowled at my shoes as I stepped into them. "How the hell can I be old enough to get married, but not old enough to gamble? If they'd let me into the casino last night, *none* of this would have happened."

"Kaci, I'm *so* sorry that you can't remember. But it'll come back. I've been that drunk a couple of times, and the memories came back after a while."

"I don't want to remember making a fool of myself, Justus." I grabbed my backpack and stomped into the bathroom, where I grabbed my toothbrush and dropped it into my bag.

"That's not… You were never a fool." He followed me into the bathroom. "You were funny, and adorable, and sexy enough to make me *really* wish you weren't drunk."

"Don't think about me being sexy." I glared at him in the mirror. "I don't even know what I mean by that, but…don't think about me like that. This isn't real. We're not married."

"Yes, we are. Will you please stop packing for a minute? We need to figure out what we're—"

"No!" I pushed past him into the bedroom. "Justus, *this* is not *real*. We didn't even…" My focus landed on the bed and stayed there. "We didn't even have sex. Wait a minute." I dropped my backpack on the floor and ducked to check under the bed. "There was this movie I saw where a guy had his marriage annulled because…" There was nothing under the bed. The bed was built over a box, which must have made vacuuming the hotel room much easier.

"I saw that. He got an annulment on the grounds that his marriage was never consummated. But Kaci, I don't think that's a real… What are you doing?"

"Looking for my cell." I grabbed the edge of the comforter and ripped it from the bed in one motion. Then I shook it, snapping it like a kitchen towel. But no phone fell out.

"You had it last night. You decided you wanted to take a

one-way cruise, instead of a flight, because you've never been on a boat."

"Don't—" I exhaled slowly, trying to stop the flood of embarrassment that washed over me with every new detail about Drunken Kaci's humiliating late night performance. "Just stop telling me what I did, okay?" I already knew I was dumb enough to fall for a rich, beautiful con artist. I didn't need the recap.

"Fine. But I don't think non-consummation is actually grounds for an annulment. I think that's…fiction."

"It's not." It *can't* be. "Where the hell is my phone?"

Justus picked up one of the pillows and shook it out while I pulled the top sheet from the bed. Nothing. Then he picked up a second pillow, and my phone fell out of the case.

Oh yeah. After I'd given up finding a cruise to the Lost City of Atlantis, I'd tucked my phone beneath my pillow so I wouldn't lose it.

Damn it.

"Here." He tossed me my phone, and I caught it one-handed.

"It's dead."

"Use my charger. It's plugged in on the desk."

I plugged my phone in, then retrieved my toothbrush from my bag and brushed my teeth while I waited for my cell to accumulate enough of a charge to power on.

This is no big deal, Kaci. Lots of people did stupid things in Las Vegas. That was why what happened there stayed there.

When I emerged from the bathroom with my wet toothbrush in its case, Justus had thrown all the empty plastic cups and soda cans into the trash, and my phone screen was lit up.

I sank into the desk chair so I could research annulments while it continued to charge. And as it turned out, there were several grounds for having a marriage annulled, one of which seemed to be tailor made for our situation. "Lack of consent!" I shouted as I stood in triumph.

Justus looked up at me from the duffle bag he was digging through. "You consented, Kaci."

"Yes, but lack of consent includes the lack of mental capacity to consent, and that includes the states of either insanity or intoxication. Both of which could be considered accurate in the case of a drunk eighteen-year-old who marries a guy she hardly knows."

"Current behavior aside, you're perfectly sane. And you weren't drunk yet when we got married. They wouldn't have performed the ceremony if you had been." He pulled his phone out of his pocket. "The video came through, if you want to see for yourself. I can forward it to you. What's your email address?"

"Don't you think that's an odd question to have to ask your own wife?"

Justus frowned. "Do you want the video or not?"

"No." He wouldn't offer to send it to me if I looked drunk in the footage, and if it wouldn't get me out of this marriage, I didn't want to see myself falling for the guy who used me to get at his inheritance early.

I turned back to my phone.

"It won't work." Justus pulled a clean shirt over his head, and I tried to pretend I was relieved not to have to look at his chest anymore. "I already looked. Non-consummation isn't grounds for a legal annulment."

"Wait…" I kept reading, until a phrase popped out at me. "Yes, it is. There." I unplugged my phone and handed it to him.

"That says impotence." He shoved my phone back at me. "I am *not* impotent."

"It says we can ask for an annulment if one partner intentionally concealed impotence or an unwillingness to consummate."

"I'm perfectly willing to consummate." He grabbed the hem of his T-shirt. "Should I take this back off? We can consummate this bitch right now."

I plugged my phone back in and rolled my eyes at him. "As romantic as *that* sounds, *I'm* not willing to consummate."

"And I'm not willing to request an annulment over that. You take as much time as you need." He dropped into the nearest chair and draped his arms over the sides. "When you're ready, I'll be here."

Anger burned like hot coals beneath my skin. "I'm not *going* to be ready, Justus. We are *not* staying married!"

"Then divorce me." He crossed his arms over his chest. "Just wait until my inheritance goes through."

"Are you admitting you don't want to be married to me? That you only did this because of the money? Because that qualifies as fraud or misrepresentation—a perfectly good reason to annul, according to the internet."

"No, Kaci. That's not what I'm saying. I know you don't want to believe this, but you married me willingly. Sober and in good cheer."

"Why would I do that? I hardly know you."

His eyes closed. Then he opened them again and pinned me with a piercing gaze. "Last night, you knew me. And I knew you. Last night, you and I walked down the strip and looked at all the lights. We ate lobster and rack of lamb at Le Cirque—turns out you don't like lamb. And we talked for *hours*."

"You're saying I married you because you fed me French food?"

"Just listen. Last night, it was like we fell under some

kind of spell. I was here last year for a friend's bachelor party, but I wasn't really very impressed with the place. I thought it was smelly, and gaudy, and way over-hyped. But everything looked different when I was with you. Everything was new, and it was all magical."

I rolled my eyes. "Anything that isn't cows and oil wells—"

"—is magical to a girl from the farm." His smile actually looked nostalgic. "You said that last night too. But my point is that we had fun together. It felt like we could probably have fun together on a regular basis. Last night, spending forever on the beach seemed like not only a possibility, but a *good idea*. So we did something crazy. Something impulsive. Something that seemed like the only way to get what we both wanted. And we *both* wanted it, Kaci. That forever on the beach. So we picked out rings and got married. Then we came back here and we drank to celebrate—which turned out to be a mistake—and we kissed for an hour straight—which I will never in my life regret, no matter how this turns out.

"Then I woke up this morning, though actually, it's already afternoon, and you were looking at me like I was Hades, dragging Persephone into the underworld."

Tears blurred my vision again. "That's my favorite myth."

"I know. And you hate the Apple of Discord and the entire Helen debacle, even though they're both basically about a woman being kidnapped by a man."

"I told you that?" I knew without looking that my face was tomato-red.

Justus nodded. "You also have a very firmly held belief that books made into movies are fine, but movies made into books are not. And for no reason I can figure out, you hate the Muppets."

My tears ran over.

73

"What's wrong? Kaci, please don't cry." Justus stood and pulled me into a hug, and I let him, because it felt so good. It felt...familiar.

"I just...I want all that. I want the kissing, and the walking, and the talking, and I want to know you as well as you evidently know me, but I can't remember it. And without the memories, this is just... I don't know what this is. But it's not a real marriage." I stepped out of his embrace, as hard as that was, and wiped the tears from my face with both hands. "I have to annul this, Justus. I'll cite my own unwillingness to consummate."

His gaze burned into me. "So, you're just going to let them execute me?"

"No." *Never.* "I'll testify on your behalf. I'll...I'll tell them what you told me about Drew." That much I *did* remember. "I'll be a character witness."

"Kaci, the votes aren't there, no matter what you say. And after this—after I took a tabby to Vegas and married her—they'll probably try to kill me on the spot. Hell, Marc may swing the ax himself."

Marc wouldn't... Would he?

"So, you're just going to leave? Even without the money?"

He shrugged. "Being poor in the Caribbean is better than being dead in the States. But you could still come with me. Even if we're not married."

"I can't." *Damn*, I wanted to. But no matter how crazy-romantic the whole thing might have seemed during a drunk night I couldn't remember, in the sober daylight, it seemed just plain crazy. "But I'll help you get out of the country. We can sell this." I glanced at the ring on my finger.

But then I realized it was probably fake. If he'd lost all his money playing poker, we'd probably just snagged a cheap cubic zirconia at an all night pawn shop, or something. "I hate to ask, but how much is this worth?"

He shrugged. "Around eight thousand dollars. It was the best I could afford at the time.

I sank into the desk chair in shock, staring at my hand. At the ring. "How the hell did you afford that if you lost all your money playing poker?"

"I didn't lose *all* the money. I just lost most of it."

That explains the lobster and rack of lamb.

"Well, we can sell this to get you out of the country." I pulled the rings off as I crossed the room toward him. "How much is a ticket to the Caribbean?"

Justus folded my fingers over the rings in my palm. "Keep it. I already bought my ticket. I bought yours too."

"Okay." I slid the rings back on, because they seemed safer on my hand than in my pocket. "So, I get that today's evidently supposed to be the start of our honeymoon and all, but...any chance that ticket can be exchanged for one to Houston?" Maybe if I went straight home, safe and unharmed, I could convince everyone that I'd made Justus take me to Vegas. Which was true.

No one had to know about the marriage...

And if they were busy being relieved about my return, maybe they wouldn't have time to chase him.

Justus shrugged. "Probably. When you get to the airport, if they won't exchange it, call me and I'll buy you a ticket to Houston."

"Thanks." I picked up my backpack and slid my phone into my back pocket. When I finally met Justus's gaze, my stomach fluttered. Why was I suddenly so nervous? Why did I feel so guilty? "I'm sorry about...all this. Sorry that I'm evidently the most impulsive, reckless drunk in the world."

Another shrug. "It takes two..."

"Okay. Well. Good luck. And don't worry. I won't tell anyone where you're going."

"Thank you."

I felt like I should hug him goodbye. Or maybe indulge in one more kiss. Instead, I opened the hotel door and stepped into the hall. Then I ran for the elevator without waiting for it to close, because if I'd taken one more look at Justus…I might never have found the willpower to leave again.

SIX

JUSTUS

LETTING KACI WALK OUT THAT DOOR WAS THE HARDEST thing I'd ever done in my life. Harder than leaving behind everything I'd ever owned and every friend I'd ever had. Harder, somehow, than preparing to say goodbye to my brother forever, via text.

Yet not as hard as seeing her take off that ring. All because of a bottle of vodka.

She was right. Alcohol *was* the devil.

But there was nothing to do now except put her out of my head. So I exhaled all things Kaci Dillon, double checked the room to make sure I wasn't missing anything, and hooked my duffle over my shoulder on my way out the door.

By some miracle, the elevator was empty, which left me nothing to do during the ride down but think about her. Which was why I thought I was hallucinating when the doors slid open in the lobby and Kaci was standing right in front of them.

Her eyes widened when she saw me. She grabbed my arm and hauled me out of the elevator to the immediate right. Behind a pillar.

"I was afraid you'd be coming down in one elevator while I went back up in another," she whispered fiercely, peeking out at the lobby from behind the pillar.

"I'm right here. What's wrong?"

"Enforcers." She pointed, and I followed her finger to where Vic stood near the main entrance, talking to Chris. "They haven't caught my scent yet, but they know we're here, and I heard Vic ask someone over the phone if he'd made it to the airport yet. You're not going to make your flight. We'll be lucky if we make it out of the hotel without an enforcer escort."

"We?" I couldn't resist a smile, despite the very real sense of urgency.

Kaci rolled her eyes. "I'm still going back to the ranch. But I told you I'd help you get out of the country, and I keep my promises."

"Maybe this is a bad time to point this out, but last night you promised to love, honor, and cherish."

"One more word, and I swear I'll punch you." She glanced at the ring on her finger in sudden fascination. "I'm guessing this thing would leave one hell of a mark."

"Am I allowed to comment on the fact that you're still wearing it?"

"Rumor has it this rock is worth eight grand. Which makes it the most valuable thing I own by about six thousand dollars. Like I'm going to take that off before I figure out what to do with it."

"Now who's married for the money?" I teased her.

She gave me a low-pitched growl, still watching Vic and Chris from behind the pillar. "We are *not* married."

Then she grabbed my arm and started running. "Come on!"

Though every instinct I had said our best escape plan did not include barreling through the lobby of Caesar's Palace at full speed, dodging women in four-inch heels and families full of bored kids staring at iPad screens, I had little choice but to hang on tight and follow her.

Now that I had her back, I wasn't letting her go again.

I glanced around the lobby as we ran, hoping that Vic and Chris had left, and that was why Kaci had decided to make a run for it. Alas, they'd only wandered over to the concierge, probably to show pictures of their "missing little sister," or whoever they would tell people Kaci was.

Because even if she was a man-eater, she was *their* man-eater.

Though I felt bad about that thought as soon as I'd had it. Marc and Faythe loved her like a daughter. Vic loved her like a sister. It was mostly the younger generation of enforcers who'd turned out to be whiny, thoughtless assholes.

We were halfway to the entrance when the echo of our pounding steps caught Vic's attention, and he turned. Then he grabbed Chris by the arm and pointed straight at us.

"Come on!" Kaci breathed, too softly for any of the nearby humans to hear.

I kicked in more speed and suddenly I was pulling her.

"Jared!" Vic shouted, as footsteps pounded across the lobby toward us, and I had an instant to wonder who he was shouting at. Then a large man in a black t-shirt and jeans— enforcer clothes—stepped right into our path.

Kaci squealed, startled as she skidded to a stop in front of him, and he grabbed her arm. "Be smart, kitten," he growled, too low for anyone else to hear.

"If I scream, you go to jail," she whispered, staring up at

him as if he were nothing more substantial than a shadow in her path. Her nerve was kind of awesome.

"You won't do that. You're in the wrong here, and you scared Faythe to death."

"Let. Her. Go," I growled, and several people turned to look. Because I had not yet mastered the art of speaking beneath the human range of hearing.

"You're in enough trouble already." Vic stepped up to my right side. Chris hemmed me in on the left, and suddenly our only way out became a very public scene, after which the police would probably discover my fake ID. And arrest me.

"Miss, is everything okay?" a security guard asked as he approached.

Kaci looked right at me. I shook my head, but the determined light in her eyes refused to die. So I was surprised when she said, "Yes." Then she jerked her arm from Jared's grip and he had no choice but to let her. "My brother's being a bit of an ass. But I'm fine."

"Come on, *sis*." Jared gestured toward the front door, and Kaci and I were escorted back through Caesar's Palace toward the parking garage, passing restaurants, gambling floors, and shops, by a very conspicuous team of three identically dressed werecat enforcers.

People probably thought hotel security had caught us counting cards.

Jared led us into the garage, and the moment we were out of sight of security, he grabbed Kaci's arm again.

"Southwest Pride?" I asked, my voice echoing over an expanse of parked cars, and he nodded. "How'd you know we were here?"

"We triggered the LoJack in Chris's car," Vic said. "When we realized it was at the airport, we checked outgoing flights and alerted Alphas in all of those territories."

"We have two Pride members living in Vegas," Jared added. "The moment we heard you might be out here, we started circulating your picture. A poker dealer at Caesar's recognized you in a matter of hours. They don't get many guys your age betting six figures in a single hand."

"Huh." I shrugged, reluctantly impressed. "Good work."

Vic snorted. "You, I get," he said. "You're young and stupid, and facing trial. But you?" He tapped Kaci's shoulder. "How'd he get you to go along with this?"

She shrugged. "That was my idea. I've never been to Vegas."

"What the hell is there to do here, for a kid?"

"Oh, *fuck*." Jared stopped walking and grabbed her left hand. "Look at *this* shit."

Vic gaped at the ring. "Kaci…" Then he turned and grabbed me by the throat so fast I never even saw it coming. He slammed me into a concrete pillar between two cars, and the force was like a sledgehammer swung at my skull, even though he was using his left hand. "What the hell did you do to her?"

"Nothing!" Kaci jerked free of Jared and pulled on Vic's arm, while I focused on bringing my double vision back together. "Let him go."

Vic turned to her, his fist tight around my trachea, and it took every bit of self-control I had to remain perfectly still. Because if I'd learned anything about dealing with angry cats who outrank me, it was *do not make things worse*. "Is that thing real?" he demanded.

She frowned at the ring. "Yeah, it's, like, a full carat, I think."

"Not the diamond," Vic growled. "The wedding. Did you really marry this little prick?"

Twenty-four hours ago, he'd been giving me advice like a

friend, and now he was calling me names. Not that I could blame him.

"I know a guy who can undo this in forty-eight hours." Jared grabbed Kaci's arm again. "No one even has to know. You take him in your car, I'll take her, and we'll meet—"

"No!" Kaci shouted as he started hauling her away from me. And that was all I could take.

I grabbed Vic's left wrist and twisted as hard and as fast as I could. His bones cracked as they broke, yet his fingernails still drew blood as I ripped his hand from throat.

"Fuck," Vic muttered through clenched teeth as he clutched his broken wrist to his chest. "Chris."

Chris came at me, and I spun on one foot, then kicked him in the chest with the other. He flew backward several feet and landed on his ass on the trunk of a car across the aisle, more stunned than hurt. By some miracle, the car had no alarm.

"*Let her go,*" I growled.

Jared froze. Kaci gaped at me.

"Son of a bitch." Vic glanced from me to Kaci, then back, still holding his wrist above the level of his heart, to slow the swelling. I could read pain in the tension in his jaw, but none of that bled through into his voice. "Justus, think this through. We didn't know you could fight. That was our mistake, but we know now. There are three of us. We can take you down if we have to, but not without hurting you. And no one wants that." He glanced at Kaci, and I followed her gaze to see pure terror in her eyes.

She was afraid they would hurt me.

"Especially your new bride," Vic added. "So why don't you make this easy on everyone and just get in the car."

"Fine," I growled. "But she and I go in the same car, or I break every bone I can before you take me down."

"No," Jared barked.

Vic rolled his eyes at the Southwest enforcer. "Yes. Be smart, man. They're already married, and he's clearly not going to hurt her."

"Thank you," I said, and I wasn't sure he knew how sincerely I meant that until he gave me a solemn nod.

"Not gonna lie, kid," Vic said. "You two messed things up pretty bad."

Kaci huffed. "There's no rule against us getting married."

"But there *is* a rule against either of you coming into the Southwest Territory without permission from both your Alpha and mine," Jared insisted. "If Blackwell presses charges, that's one count for you, and one more in a long list for your new husband."

"Let her go," I growled again, but Jared only stared right at me without releasing Kaci's arm.

"Let her go, man," Vic snapped. "We've got them. There's no need to make this any worse than it is."

"Fine." Jared glared down at her. "You better not run."

"She's not going anywhere without him," Chris said with a nod at me. And the fact that even he could see that made me feel oddly optimistic about my new marriage, in spite of the fact that my bride was desperate for an annulment, and we were being taken into custody and charged with trespassing— a very serious offense in shifter circles, where territorial boundaries meant much more than the lines on a map would suggest.

"Sorry about your wrist, man," I said as Vic and Chris escorted me toward the car behind Jared and Kaci, who now walked on her own.

Vic shrugged. "Occupational hazard. Gotta say, I'm impressed. I had you pegged for a rich college boy who never got his hands dirty."

"You had me pegged right," I admitted. "If you add ten years of private MMA training to that. Which, incidentally, shifter strength has greatly enhanced."

Jared stopped next to a clean, ten-year-old Honda Civic, in a horrible, outdated shade of blue, and opened the back door. "Get in," he growled at me.

"Her first." I was half convinced that if I got in, he'd slam the door on me, then put her in another car.

Instead, he opened the front passenger door for her.

Kaci sat up front, and I slid into the seat behind her. "I don't think he likes me," I leaned forward to whisper into her hair.

She snorted. "Picked up on that, did you?"

Jared slammed my door, then Kaci's, and as he walked around the vehicle, he pulled his phone from his pocket. "I'm calling this in," he told Vic over the roof of the car. Then he opened the driver's side door, because it was one hundred and ten degrees in Vegas in the summer. Even in the parking garage, shielded from direct sunlight.

Vic was already on his phone, and with the door open, I could hear both conversations, but I tuned out Jared's to focus on what Vic was saying to Marc. "Yeah, we got 'em, but things are...complicated."

I couldn't make out Marc's reply.

"Her left hand's sporting a piece of ice big enough to sink the Titanic, and he's exhibiting telltale but disproportionately violent behavior in her defense." He paused. "Bastard broke my wrist."

The only part of that I disagreed with was "disproportionately."

I was concentrating so hard that it took me a second to notice that Kaci was subtly, slowly inching her way toward the driver's side of the car. Over the central console.

"What are you doing?" I whispered.

She glanced at me in the rearview mirror and pressed one finger to her lips. Then she lifted her other leg over the console and sank into the driver's seat.

Kaci took a deep, silent breath. Then she leaned out of the car and snatched the key ring dangling from Jared's hand, so fast my eyes couldn't follow the motion.

"What the—?" He spun around, still on his phone, as she slammed the driver's side door and poked the lock button. "Kaci!" he shouted. "Open the door!"

Instead, she shoved the key into the ignition, shifted into gear, and backed out of the tight parking space as if she'd been born driving in reverse.

"What are you doing?" I repeated.

"Kaci!" Jared dropped his phone and pounded on the door as she shifted into DRIVE. Then she took off through the garage, way too fast, following the signs marked EXIT.

I twisted in the backseat to see Chris sliding behind the steering wheel of his rental car, while Jared and Vic spoke frantically into their phones.

"Escaping."

"Well, you better escape faster, because they're coming after us."

Through the rear windshield, I watched Vic sink onto the front passenger's seat next to Chris, but Jared was still pounding on one of the rear windows, while the other two seemed to be trying to figure out how to unlock his door. My guess was that they'd engaged the child safety locks, in anticipation of having Kaci and me in the back seat.

Kaci slammed her foot on the gas again and we spun around a curve in the garage, heading downhill. Then we shot out into the parking lot and headed left, toward the road.

I sank into the center of the back bench seat, staring at her in the rearview mirror. "You just stole a car."

"It wasn't my first time." She shrugged as she took the next left, and traffic thinned out a little. "They won't report it. We don't take shifter business to the police."

"Yeah, but the council will be pissed."

Another shrug. "What are they going to do? Ground me? I never leave home anyway."

"They could declaw you. Or lock you up." My blood boiled at just the thought.

"Nah. Those are only for capital crimes. Which means I have nothing to lose by helping you get out of the country." She took the next right, a little too fast. "Can you come up here and navigate, though? I'm totally winging this, and I have no idea where I'm going."

I glanced in the rearview mirror again but saw no sign of Chris's rental car, so I climbed over the center console, careful not to elbow her in the head, and pulled my cell from my pocket. "Where are we going?" I asked as I opened the map app.

"I don't know. But we can't fly out of Vegas. They'll be watching the airport. Can you exchange your ticket for a flight out of another airport without your brother finding out?"

"Should be able to. He doesn't have access to my frequent flier account. Give me a minute…" I dragged the map around a bit, then started typing. "It's a four-and-a-half-hour drive to Los Angeles. We could fly out of LAX."

"You. Not we," Kaci said. But she didn't sound mad anymore, and where I didn't hear an outright refusal, I chose to see hope. "But if that's the closest airport, they'll be watching it too. Try Phoenix."

I typed some more. "That's five hours from here. If LA's too close, won't Phoenix be too?"

"It would be, if Arizona didn't take up half of the biggest free zone in the country."

"What?"

"Which way, Justus? Point me at Phoenix."

I tapped the directions icon on my phone and set it in the cup holder in the center console. A second later, directions appeared, pointing us toward US highway 93. "I didn't realize there was a third free zone."

"Well, there is, kind of, and it's three times the size of Titus's Mississippi Valley Territory."

Though until the council officially recognized Titus's Pride, everyone on this side of the border still called it the Mississippi free zone.

I frowned at her profile. "What do you mean by kind of?"

"Arizona and a huge swath of land surrounding the Four Corners—Utah, Colorado, and New Mexico—are considered a werecat free zone, and nothing will change that. Because a large part of that land is actually thunderbird territory."

"Holy shit. Seriously? So we'll be trading werecat enforcers for giant birds who pluck people from the ground like flying monkeys?"

Kaci laughed. "Not exactly. Unless something's changed since I was kidnapped, the thunderbirds are based just east of Alamogordo, New Mexico. About four hours south of Santa Fe. Which means that Phoenix is pretty much a best case scenario for us." She put on her blinker and merged smoothly onto the highway. "The council has no manpower or infrastructure in place in the western free zone. Thunderbirds keep the stray cat population down out there, and they do patrol the skies at night, but unless we get close to their nest or attack one of them, they should leave us alone."

"And you think we'll be safe there?"

"No." Kaci glanced in the rearview mirror, then eased her foot off the gas a little. "We won't be safe until you're out of the country. But the Council doesn't know for sure where we're going, so they'll have to split up their manpower to cover all their bases. Even if they send someone to Phoenix— and that'll probably be Vic, Jared, and Chris, since they're closest—we have a head start on them. And they still have to do something about Vic's wrist."

"Okay, but can't they just fly someone straight to the Phoenix airport to watch for us?"

Kaci scowled at the highway. "Crap. Yeah, that's a possibility. They could station a man at every terminal to watch the TSA checkpoints—the bottleneck you'd have to go through. But if they do that at Sky Harbor and LAX, they'll be using up a lot of manpower, in addition to checking bus terminals and car rental places. Also, eventually TSA will get suspicious of a guy who stands around and never gets on a plane."

"Shit." I glanced around Jared's car, noting the phone charger plugged into the cigarette lighter, a pair of running shoes on the rear floorboard, and the satellite radio receiver stuck to the dashboard with a suction cup. "This isn't a rental. This is Jared's personal car, which means he might be able to track it. We have to find another car."

She shook her head as she smoothly changed lanes again. "We can't steal from a human, Justus. That'll get us arrested. We're going to have to rent one."

"Won't work. You can't rent a car without a credit or a debit card, and Titus is authorized on both of mine."

"I have a debit card." She shrugged. 'I don't have much money, but it's probably enough."

"You have to be twenty-one to rent a car."

"Are you serious?" Kaci turned angry eyes on the road.

"So, eighteen is old enough to vote or to die for your country, but not old enough to drink, or gamble, or rent a fucking car?"

I laughed. "We Americans value our constitutional right to be completely inconsistent and hypocritical."

"I'm American enough to know that no such right exists in the constitution."

"It's in the fine print, spread out across a bunch of different amendments," I said, but she only growled in response.

"You have to tell the rental place where you'll be turning the car in, right? So, if we rent a car using your credit card and fake ID, we'll basically be telling you brother where we are, and where we're going."

"Or…we'll be sending them on a wild goose chase. We could just tell the rental place that we're driving to Nebraska, or Chicago."

"Even if your brother believes that, the council won't. They'll know that our most likely destinations from Las Vegas are Los Angeles and Phoenix. They'll expect us to try to throw them off."

"Okay, so let's do what no one expects."

She glanced pointedly at the ring still sitting on her left hand. "Because that worked out so well last time."

"I think it did. And so could this. If they expect us to head to the nearest airport so I can catch an international flight, let's do the opposite. Let's drive for a while. Let's tell them we're going to Phoenix, then take a road trip to an airport they wouldn't expect. Like Denver. That's an international hub, but it's also at least a full day's drive from Vegas."

Kaci seemed to be thinking about it as she stared at the road. And finally she nodded, then glanced at me with a smile. "A road trip. We'll be in the free zone right up until we get to Denver, which is on the western border of the Plains Territory, but north of the thickest concentration of thunderbirds. That's perfect."

I couldn't agree more. With stops for food, gas, and sleep, the drive to Denver would give me another full day to convince Kaci that the ring on her finger wasn't a con. That I wanted the money, but I wanted it for *us*.

That she shouldn't just put me on a plane—she should get on a plane with me.

SEVEN

KACI

I TOOK THE 215 LOOP AROUND THE SOUTH SIDE OF LAS Vegas and into Henderson to rent a car, because that would make it look like we were headed to Phoenix, for whatever good that would do. I wasn't convinced anyone would believe we were actually headed to the Sky Harbor airport. But I *was* convinced they would try to cover all their bases.

While Justus was inside the rental place, I sat in Jared's car with the engine running, staring at all the missed calls and unanswered messages from Faythe and Marc.

They were the only reason I'd made it out of the woods alive, when they'd found me in Montana. I owed them an explanation. Or at least the knowledge that I was okay.

I called Faythe's name to call her back, and she answered on the second ring. "*Kaci?*" The baby was crying close to the phone, but I could hear the fear in Faythe's voice, even over the noise. She sounded scared to death.

My guilt suddenly felt like an ocean I was drowning in.

"Yeah. It's me."

"Here, take baby Ethan," Faythe said over the line. "It's her."

"I got him," Karen Sanders said, and the sound of a crying infant faded into the background.

"Kaci, where the hell are you? Are you okay?"

"I'm fine. Really. I'm calling to tell you not to worry."

"You…?" A door slammed, and the crying got even softer. Leather creaked as Faythe sank into the desk chair in her office. The same one her father had sat in, before he'd died. She couldn't bring herself to replace it, even though the upholstery was starting to wear out. "Do you have any idea how scared we've been?"

"Yes, and I'm sorry. My intent wasn't to scare anyone."

"You lied to me."

"Again, I'm really sorry." I propped my elbow against the driver's side window and cradled my forehead in my hand. "But I had to get out of there."

"Where are you?"

"I can't tell you that."

"Is Justus there with you?"

"Yes, but he's…busy. He can't hear us."

"Vic said you *married* him. What the hell is going on, Kaci? You ran off to Las Vegas to *elope*?"

"No! That just kind of happened. It's complicated."

"Try me," she insisted. "I have a two-year-old, a two-*month*-old and a chronic sleep deficit. I'm knocking out crises left and right, so one more can't hurt. What's going on, Kaci?"

"It was just supposed to be a vacation. He had a bunch of airline miles, and I caught him sneaking out, so I told him that if he didn't take me with him, I'd turn him in. I've never been to Las Vegas. I've never been *anywhere*, really, and I'm an adult now, so…"

"Eighteen is not grown. It's this weird sort of in-between state, where—"

"You had a wedding when you were eighteen."

"Yes, but I left my groom at the altar."

"Are you saying that was a mistake? That you should have gotten married at eighteen?"

She groaned over the phone. "No. I was too young to know what I wanted at the time, and if I'd gotten married then, I probably always would have wondered if I'd missed out on something. On my youth. So, I seized an opportunity."

"I've heard this story. You seized that opportunity by fleeing the territory. That's exactly what I did. Only I was going to come back. It was just supposed to be a vacation."

"Was?" She sounded *so* exhausted. "What does that mean?"

"Okay, listen, Faythe, I'm going to come home, but I need your help."

There was a beat of silence. Then… "Tell me what's going on, and I'll do my best."

"You're not mad?"

"I'm furious, Kaci. I'm not gonna lie about that. But I remember what it was like to be eighteen, and I'm choosing to believe that you have a good reason for whatever the hell you're doing. So please, please, prove me right."

I sucked in a deep breath and held it for a moment. "Faythe, I like him. Justus. I mean I really, really like him."

"Oh, so *that's* why you got married!" Springs groaned as she leaned back in her chair. "You really like him!"

"The sarcasm isn't necessary," I snapped.

Faythe's chair springs groaned again. "Yet that seems to

be the only language I'm capable of speaking after three hours of sleep."

"Fine." Through the windshield, I could see Justus still standing at the rental counter. He appeared to be haggling with the clerk. "Justus knows they're going to execute him, Faythe. He overheard something in the guest house—something Vic heard through the grapevine—and he knows he doesn't have a chance. He was going to run. He's *still* going to run, and I told him I'd help him."

"You don't sound like that's what you want to do."

"The wedding was a mistake," I admitted. "Probably. Maybe. But the rest of this wasn't. Justus doesn't think of me as a kid, like you and Marc and Jace do, or as a freak, like everyone else does. He *likes* me. He looks at me like there are no other girls in the world. He kisses me like I'm the only thing he could ever want. He kissed me this morning before I'd brushed my teeth!"

"Now that's commitment," Faythe said, a hint of a smile in her voice.

And though I would never have said the rest of it to her, Justus was a total gentleman while I was passed out, not because that was the decent thing to do, or because deep down he knew it was right, but because he would *never* touch a girl who wasn't just as into touching and being touched as he was.

And I couldn't stand the thought of him touching someone else. Ever.

"Married or not, I want to give this a chance," I told her. "I want to be with him and at least see if this could work. But I want to be with him *here*. I don't want to spend the rest of my life running from the council, and that's what it would be, if I went with him."

"Oh, honey, that's what it would be *because* you went with him."

I frowned at Jared's dashboard. "What?"

"Kaci, if he flees the country, I highly doubt the council will go after him."

"Why not?"

"Because if the tribunal finds him guilty, they'll want to be rid of him, but they won't really care how that happens. Not enough to spend money and manpower chasing him across the globe, anyway. If you let him run, he'll probably be fine. But if you go with him? *You*, they'll chase to the ends of the earth."

I rolled my eyes. "No, they won't. I'm the man-eater."

She sighed. "Okay, I know that's what some of the younger, stupider enforcers are saying, but eventually one of them is going to get to know you and realize you're awesome. I know that. The council knows that. Eventually—"

"Eventually." A harsh bark of laughter exploded from my throat. "I don't need 'eventually' from a hypothetical tom who may one day decide I'm okay, probably only because some Alpha has convinced him that I'm a valuable procreation asset. Justus is offering me *forever*, right now. Just as I am." And as crazy as it sounded, I wanted that forever.

Or at least the possibility of it.

I'd rather have a crazy, sudden marriage to a guy who listens when I talk and kisses me like I'm the only thing in the world that matters than hang my entire future on the chance that *eventually* some asshole who only thinks of me as a traumatized cannibal might decide I'm good enough to carry his children. If all the other tabbies are taken.

Fuck "eventually." I'm on board with forever.

"Fair enough," Faythe said. "You have the right to make

your own choices." Though it sounded like what she actually meant was the right to make my own mistakes. "But what I'm telling you is that the council will *not* want to lose you. For the record, I don't want to lose you either, but for a totally different reason. What you need to understand is that if you run, they *will* come after you."

I shrugged, though she obviously couldn't see that over the phone. "Then I'll defect. Legally. Just like Abby did. I'll renounce all loyalty to and claims of assistance from the Pride and Justus and I can go wherever we want." As long as we weren't trespassing on someone else's territory.

"I really wish you wouldn't, but if you insist, then yes, you're free to do that. In just under three years."

"What?" I blinked, but the dashboard refused to come into focus. "No one said anything about a waiting period. Abby didn't have to wait. Neither did Robyn."

"Robyn was never a member of any of the US Prides, so technically she didn't have to defect in order to leave—she had to negotiate a way out of her plea bargain. But even if she'd been a pride member, she could have defected just like Abby did, because they're both twenty-two. You're only eighteen, and the Prides don't consider you an adult in that regard until you're twenty-one."

"That's crap! No one ever told me that!"

"It's not exactly a topic that comes up over dinner. But that's how my father had the right to bring me back, when I ran out on my wedding. He couldn't make me get married—not that he would have tried—but he *could* keep me in the Pride. And in the territory."

"You're saying eighteen is old enough to get married, but not old enough to defect?" I aimed the air vent at my face, but the cold air did nothing to temper my anger. "What kind of sense does that make?"

"None, I'm afraid," Faythe admitted. "But it's no more inconsistent than several human laws."

"I know," I huffed. "I just left a hotel where I wasn't even allowed onto the casino floor to watch."

"Exactly. So, if you really want to be with Justus, you're going to have to convince him to stay here."

"And stand trial."

"Yes," she said.

"Well, that brings me back to the help I mentioned. A favor, really. To help me come home."

"What can I do?" Faythe asked, her voice thin with a fragile thread of hope.

"It sounds like two of the three Alphas on the tribunal are going to vote against Justus. Which means he only needs to gain one more vote, right?"

"Yes, but—"

"Who's on the tribunal? You must know."

"The names are drawn at random, typically excluding family members or Alphas who might have obvious bias. Which, in this case, is Marc and me, since we're Justus's Alphas."

The door to the rental place opened and Justus came out swinging a keyring around his index finger. Grinning like a fool.

"Faythe, I have to go. I'll call you right back."

"Why—"

"I can't tell you anything else. But I'll call you back in a few." I hung up the phone just as Justus got to the car. He motioned for me to roll the window down, so I pressed the button.

"Got it." He held the keys up for me to see. "Can you follow me down the road? I thought we could grab some tacos or something and leave Jared's car in the restaurant lot, then head out. We need to go fast, though. If Titus is monitoring my card, he probably already knows where we are."

"Yeah. Lead the way."

"It's that little white one on the end." He pointed to the car on the last row of the small rental lot.

"I'll be right behind you."

While Justus got in the rental and pulled out of the parking space, I called Faythe on speaker phone.

"It's me again," I said when she answered.

"What happened?"

"Nothing." I pulled out of my parking spot and followed Justus onto the road. "You didn't think I'd call back, did you?"

"Of course I did." The tone of Faythe's voice told me she was rolling her eyes. "You still need my help. Are you driving somewhere? Is Justus with you?"

"Yes, I'm driving. And yes, he's with me, but he can't hear us. And that's all I'm telling you."

"Kaci—"

"I just... Faythe, I need you to know that I'm trying to do the right thing."

"By breaking all the rules?"

"I learned from the best."

Faythe actually chuckled. "Touché."

"We both know the right thing isn't always the legal thing, and it's not right that they're going to execute Justus for infecting people, when he didn't even know that's what he was doing. Or for killing Drew, when no one has ever deserved to die as much as that bastard did."

"I don't know," Faythe mused. "Everyone I've had to kill deserved to die."

"Then you should understand." I flicked on my blinker to

change lanes behind the white rental car. "You know what Drew did to Justus. What he manipulated Justus into doing."

"Yes." She exhaled heavily with the admission. "And sometimes I regret setting *quite* such an intrepid example for the younger generation of tabbies. Though I fully admit that's not a statement I ever anticipated saying."

"I think you did a great job." Up ahead, Justus's right blinker came on, fifty feet ahead of the taco place he was obviously leading me toward.

"Thanks. Full disclosure, though—you know I'm still trying to find you and bring you home."

"Understood. That's your job. I committed a crime." Or two. "But while you're unleashing your deductive reasoning, analyzing everything I've said, could you *please* tell me who's on the tribunal?"

"Yes. Bert Di Carlo, Ed Taylor, and Paul Blackwell."

"Shit," I breathed as Justus pulled into the drive-thru lane and motioned for me to park. And for once, Faythe made no objection to my language. Which only underlined how tired she must have been. "Obviously, Di Carlo is with us." He'd been one of the South-Central's strongest allies since long before I joined the Pride. "And Blackwell is staunchly anti-stray. So Ed Taylor's the swing vote?" I guessed as I pulled into an empty space at the back of the lot, where people were less likely to notice an abandoned vehicle. In case it took Jared longer than we expected to find his car.

"There isn't a swing vote. Taylor's been very clear with Marc that he's planning to vote to convict." Which meant that my Alphas had already known what Justus had overheard from Vic.

"But he hasn't even heard the evidence yet!"

"There is no evidence. There's only Justus's testimony, and everyone's already heard what he did and why." Faythe's chair creaked again, then I heard footsteps as she began pacing across her office floor. "Taylor insists he has sympathy for the position that Justus was in, but that we have to establish a hard no-tolerance policy on murders—including unauthorized executions. Especially where they could expose us to the public. Especially in the free zone. Especially if we're truly considering officially acknowledging the Mississippi Valley Pride. Because the new Pride would be expected to follow our laws to a T." Faythe stopped pacing, and the silence over the line was eerie. "It's kind of a brilliant position to take, politically speaking. He's indicating that he might support the acceptance of the new Pride, which keeps him in good graces with those of us supporting Titus. But at the same time, he's making it clear that he won't just let strays 'run amok.' Which keeps the old guard, like Blackwell and Mitchell, happy."

"But screws Justus over completely."

"While potentially helping his brother out," Faythe conceded.

"Then I have to convince him to change his vote." I shrugged at myself in the rearview mirror. "No big deal." As if I call Alphas out of the blue and ask them for favors every day. "Okay, thanks, Faythe. I gotta go."

"Wait!" The sound of her footsteps on hardwood told me she was pacing again, and the familiar echo made me surprisingly homesick.

"What?"

"I just…" She took a deep breath, then started over. "I know you have to do this. I understand that much. But when it's over—when you've done whatever you can for Justus— please come back home. Even if you two don't get the happy ending you're hoping for. *Especially* if you don't get that. I love you, and I can't stand the thought of you out there all alone, dealing with heartbreak, or loss, or even just a broken-down car or a dead cell phone. So when you're done, if we haven't found you yet…please come home."

I wanted to be able to tell her I would. To promise her that I would be okay. But no matter how young she considered me to be, I was old enough to understand that life doesn't come with promises. Sometimes things go wrong.

Sometimes home isn't where you always thought it would be.

So, I settled for, "I'll try. And I promise that I *will* call you again. That's the best I can do right now."

Faythe sniffled into my ear, and tears blurred the world around me. "Little Greg and the baby are my life. You know that. But *you* made me a mother, Kaci. You chose me over my mom, when you lost yours, even though I had no experience. Even though I was only a decade older than you. You and I got thrown into the deep end of this thing together, sink or swim, and we made it. I will always be here for you. No matter what happens. Please tell me you understand that."

"I do," I said, and she sniffled again. "But I have to go now. I love you."

"Love you too, Kitten."

I hung up the phone. Then I wiped tears from my eyes as Justus pulled into the parking spot next to mine.

I stuck Jared's keys between his sun visor and the roof, then locked his car on my way out of it.

"What's wrong?" Justus asked as I slid into the front passenger's seat of the rental.

"Nothing. I just…" I took the fast food bag he held out and set it in my lap. "I just spoke to Faythe, and it got a little emotional."

"She tried to convince you to come home?"

"Of course. But she wasn't unreasonable about it."

Evidently her definition of "adult" was closer to mine than to the council's.

"What'd she say?"

"She told me who's on the tribunal."

Justus shifted into reverse and backed out of the parking space.

"Don't you want to know?" I opened the paper sack on my lap and pulled out a taco. Crispy shell with grilled chicken.

"It doesn't matter," Justus insisted as he turned onto the road. "Because I'm not going. Can you get me directions?"

I set the bag on the center console and the taco on my lap, then started the GPS app on my phone. "What if I could get you the vote you need?"

He pulled us to a stop at a red light and turned to me, skepticism deepening the lines of his frown. "Can you?"

"Maybe. Hopefully." I picked up my taco. "I'm willing to try."

The light turned green and I took a bite.

"Sure. Give it a shot." We rolled through the intersection and Justus moved into the left-hand lane. "If you can get me a vote before we get to Denver, I guess I don't have to get on the plane." He shrugged. "What do I have to lose, right?"

"Yeah. Taco?"

"I can't eat that while I drive, but there's a burrito at the bottom," he said. I dug for it, then tore off the top half of the wrapper and handed it to him. "So, who's on the tribunal? What's the plan?"

"Well, it's a random draw, but you drew a pretty even hand. Which makes sense, considering that the council is pretty evenly split on the subject of strays. Paul Blackwell will never vote in your favor. He'll go to his grave shouting that strays have no place in the world. In fact, many of us

102

have been waiting for that very event for years, but that old man will never die. Marc says it's because God doesn't want him back."

He took a bite of his burrito and chewed for a minute. "I think I've heard Titus mention him."

"You probably have. He's one of the firm no-votes on accepting the Mississippi Valley Pride, which means he's kind of your family's arch nemesis. Also, he's the Alpha of the Southwest Pride, which makes him Jared's boss. And his grandfather. We're trespassing in his territory right now."

"Okay." Justus said around a bite of burrito. "That's unfortunate. Who else do we have?"

"Umberto Di Carlo. Bert."

"I know that name," Justus said as he veered left onto the highway. "Why do I know that name?"

"Bert was Robyn Sheffield's acting Alpha. She was sent to his house in Atlanta for rehabilitation/training/house arrest, after the plea bargain she made with the council. For the murders she committed."

"Damn." He took another bite of his burrito. "I'm starting to see why they think strays are savage murderers. Our track record is not awesome."

"Bullshit. Turning into a werecat when you have no idea such a thing is possible would traumatize anyone. Drew knew that. That's the only reason he was able to manipulate you. That's the reason he infected you. He was counting on the fact that you wouldn't be able to control your instincts or rein in your emotions without training. You were right—he turned you into a weapon and aimed you at his enemies."

"Sounds like the council's right: strays are the problem. They're just wrong about which strays."

"No," I insisted. "Plenty of natural-born cats have committed crimes. Manx. Jace. Faythe. A couple of Jace's brothers, and even more of his late stepfather's enforcers. Me. I mean, really, we're kind of a violent bunch. The council is trying to rein that in—I'll give them credit for that—but it doesn't do any good for them to insist that the problem lies only with the stray population. That's like taking a sledgehammer to your own glass house."

"Yeah, I guess so. But does that mean Di Carlo is another no-vote? Because Robyn chose my brother over his Pride?"

"Nope, he's on your side. *Thanks* to Robyn. He was responsible for her training. He's a good guy, and I suspect he saw how hard it was for her to master concepts that cats who grew up in Shifter society see from before they're even old enough to understand what they are. He knows the struggle is real. And he knows exactly what it will take to overcome that. He's a very good ally to have." I glanced at him with a grin as I took another bite of my taco. "He's also Vic's dad."

"Damn. Now I feel *really* bad about breaking Vic's wrist."

I shrugged. "He'll probably tag you back next time he gets a chance, but the risk comes with the job. He knows that. I can't even count how many broken bones Dr. Carver has had to come set at the ranch. Though Karen Sanders makes a pretty good field medic, in a pinch."

"She also makes a very good shepherd's pie."

"Among other things. So, the last vote comes from Ed Taylor." I turned the air conditioning down and aimed my vent at Justus. "The good news is that he's open to acknowledging your brother's Pride. At least, he says he is. Though Faythe seems to think that could just be political pandering."

"And the bad news is that he's ready to hang me up by my toenails and pluck out my eyes with a seafood fork?"

"That's a little more graphic than any sentence currently being considered, but yes. That's basically it."

"And do we know why, exactly?" Justus asked around the last of his burrito.

"I can venture a good guess, but it's kind of complicated. Ed Taylor is Brian's dad. Brian works for Faythe and Marc, and he was engaged to Abby Wade for several years. For a while, that led to a strong three-way alliance between Ed Taylor's Midwest Pride, Rick Wade's East Coast Pride, and our South-Central Pride. But then Abby dumped Brian for Jace, who—along with Faythe and Marc—helped your brother start the Mississippi Valley Pride. And that alliance kind of splintered."

"Wow. Okay. So, he wants to execute me because back before I was even a shifter, some girl I'd never met dumped his son for some guy I'd never met. That's not quite how the human justice system works."

"To be fair, we don't know that he actually wants to execute you. But that's not how our system is supposed to work either." I stuffed the last of my taco into my mouth and unwrapped a second one while I chewed. "It's possible that this is as simple as reminding Taylor of that. Of his duty to the council."

"Considering the broken alliances and grudges you just rattled off, I can't imagine that any part of this will be simple."

"Valid point. But it's worth a try." I plucked my cell from the drink holder and sent Faythe a text asking for Ed Taylor's number.

She replied half an hour later, as I was finishing my third taco. I smiled when I read her message.

"What?"

"Faythe sent me Taylor's number and told him to expect a call from me. I guess there's no backing out now."

"And there's no time like the present." Justus dropped his

empty burrito wrapper into the paper bag and challenged me with a grin. "Why don't you show me just how badass my bride is?"

Something fluttered deep in my chest. "Stealing a car wasn't enough for you?"

"Eh." Justus shrugged. "Any good wife would get her husband's murder charge dropped."

I laughed. Then I dialed Ed Taylor's number.

EIGHT

JUSTUS

KACI'S HEART RACED AS THE PHONE RANG. SHE STARED OUT her window while she waited for Ed Taylor to answer, but I could see how nervous she was in her tight grip on the fast food bag. I could hear it in the rush of her pulse.

On sudden impulse, I pulled onto the side of the road and punched the button for the hazard lights.

She turned to me with a question in her arched brows.

"He doesn't have to know we're driving," I said. Then I leaned across the center console and kissed her.

"Hello?" a man's voice said from her phone, and Kaci pulled away from me with a startled expression.

I stifled a laugh.

"Yes. Hello? Mr. Taylor? This is Kaci Dillon."

"Hello, Kaci. Faythe told me to expect your call, but I have to say, I'm not sure what it is I can do for you. I assume this is about Justus Alexander?"

"About his trial, yes." She looked nervous, but that wasn't evident in her voice.

"I was under the impression that his attempt to flee the country just days before the trial meant he wasn't going to show up."

Kaci flinched. "He didn't flee. We…eloped."

"You…?" Taylor sputtered in shock. Clearly Faythe hadn't passed that bit of news along.

"Yes. We're married. But we're still very much in the country and of course we're coming to his trial. Justus is less of a flight risk now than he's ever been," Kaci said. And she probably had no idea how right she was.

I didn't want to leave, if she wasn't coming with me.

That didn't mean I wouldn't *have* to leave. But I no longer wanted to.

"So, what is it I can do for you…Mrs. Alexander."

Kaci's face went as blank as an unmarred whiteboard, and I have to admit, it took me a second to realize what he was saying, as well. I hadn't heard her called that yet. I hadn't heard *anyone* called that since my parents had died, five years before. And we certainly hadn't discussed whether or not she'd be changing her name.

I wasn't even sure she was going to keep the ring.

Her mouth worked silently for a second, as she struggled to refocus her thoughts. I took her free hand, and she gave me a small, tense smile.

"Kaci?" Tayler said over the line.

"Yeah. Sorry. That's new. Anyway, Justus heard that you're planning to vote to convict him, but I told him that couldn't be true, because you haven't heard the evidence against him yet. You haven't even met him yet. So, you couldn't possibly have made up your mind already. Right?"

I gave her a smile, impressed. She'd backed him into a

pretty good corner, from which he really only had one option —claim to be willing to listen to the evidence.

Silence met her question. I held my breath, waiting for Taylor's response.

And finally, "Of course I haven't made up my mind yet. The trial hasn't even started. But I have to be honest with you, Kaci," Taylor said. "If his testimony corroborates what I've heard—if he really killed a stray at the Jackson Zoo, where humans could have stumbled upon evidence of our existence—I can't in good conscience vote to acquit."

"And if there were extenuating circumstances?"

"Kaci, honey—"

She made a gagging face over the unwelcome diminutive.

"I think that murder with a risk for exposure is where we have to draw a hard line. Especially if we're going to be acknowledging this new Pride full of strays. They have to know from the very beginning where we stand on the issues that affect us all. And where *they're* expected to stand on those issues."

"Okay." Kaci nodded. "I'm just a little confused by that, because I killed four people, but I was never brought up on charges at all, even though what I did made it onto the national news in Canada. That's a pretty big risk of exposure."

"That's an entirely different case," Taylor insisted. "You were a traumatized child. You had no idea what you were doing, or what was happening to you."

"That's my point. There were extenuating circumstances. Circumstances very similar to what Justus was going through when he was infected against his will—*targeted* for infection specifically to discredit his brother's authority—then unleashed in the midst of an unchaperoned, unassisted transitional period upon people who'd hurt him. I mean..." She paused, hazel eyes narrowed, and it was a shame that Taylor was missing the entire visual half of her performance. Because she was *magnificent*. "…it's almost like you're saying that what I did was okay because I'm a girl, but despite undeniably similar circumstances, what Justus did was not okay, because he's a guy. That's textbook gender bias. So, I'm pretty sure that can't be what you're actually saying. Right, Mr. Taylor?"

Holy shit, she was amazing.

I wanted to grab her phone and hang it up, then kiss her all over, right there on the highway. I'd bailed friends and girlfriends out of trouble—and out of jail—several times, but no one had ever gone to bat for me like that, other than Titus.

During the silence that followed, I pictured Ed Taylor, whom I'd never met, pulling his hair out by the roots. It must suck to be fully grown—and an Alpha, at that—and realize you've been verbally hemmed in by an eighteen-year-old.

"Of course that's not what I'm saying. And I believe I've already answered your question, Kaci. The other members of the tribunal and I will reserve judgement until after we've heard the evidence. But I would advise you not to get your hopes up, dear. I understand that you see similarities between your circumstances and Mr. Alexander's, but it's entirely likely that other people won't see those similarities."

"I'm sure you're right. People tend to see what they want to see," Kaci said. "And my advice to you, Mr. Taylor, is not to underestimate either me or Justus. We may be young, and we may not have been born into your world, but we are strong, and we are determined. And we have *nothing* left to lose."

Kaci hung up the phone and dropped it into the center console, then she leaned back in her chair, one hand over her eyes. She breathed deeply through her mouth, and the rise and fall of her chest was the sexiest, most mesmerizing thing I'd ever seen. Other than the mouth she'd just used to put a fucking Alpha in his place.

"I think I just threatened a council member." She dropped her hand and looked up at me, hazel eyes swimming in some heady combination of fear and excitement. "Why the hell did I just threaten a council member?"

"Because you're amazing. Because you're badass. Because you are the most beautiful woman I've ever seen, and you're even sexier when you talk."

She sat up, laughing, and I needed to touch her *so* badly. "I'm pretty sure you could lose your man-card for saying something like that."

"I don't need my man-card. All I need is you." I tugged some slack into my seatbelt, then leaned over the console to kiss her again.

"Why do you keep doing this?" she murmured as I kissed my way down her neck, trying to ignore the way the console dug into my side. "I can't think when you do this."

"That's part of why I do it. Change of plans." I shifted the car back into drive and flicked on my left blinker, then accelerated into traffic. "We're stopping for the night."

"But we've only been on the road for a couple of hours."

"I don't care. They don't know where we're headed, and with any luck, you've convinced them I'm no longer a flight risk. We can afford to take time out for a nice dinner and a good night's sleep." Especially considering that this was basically our honeymoon.

"Okay, but can we afford to *pay* for those?"

I nodded. "I have a little cash left."

We drove another forty minutes, until I found an exit advertising a decent hotel, then I pulled off the highway just over the Utah state line.

The hotel was nothing special, and neither was our room. But Kaci sang while she showered and though I kept my distance, like a gentleman, I couldn't help picturing her in there, dripping wet and slick with soap. I'd seen her naked at least half a dozen times, post-shift, and while I understood that nudity after a shift was not considered sexual, I remembered wondering, idly, why none of the enforcers seemed to want anything to do with her. Especially the ones near our age.

I mean, the council had been willing to start a war to get Robyn back, because women were so rare in the shifter world, and Kaci was *gorgeous*. I couldn't be the only one who'd ever noticed—"

"Your turn."

I looked up to see her standing in front of me, wrapped in a towel, her long, chestnut colored-hair dripping over one shoulder. Her face was bare, her skin fresh with the fragrance of whatever soap she used, and I wanted to touch her so badly. I wanted to taste her.

I wanted to feel her hands—

"Um…" She glanced pointedly at the bulge in my pants.

"Yeah. Sorry. Just ignore that." On my way into the bathroom, I stopped to kiss a drop of water from her bare shoulder. When she didn't object, I ran one hand down her arm and over her hip.

She made this sexy, needy sound deep in her throat, and I groaned. Then I escaped into the shower before I said something I'd regret.

By the time I emerged with wet hair and fresh breath, Kaci had applied makeup she didn't need and put on clean clothes. "I didn't pack anything fancier than a t-shirt, so I hope this dinner isn't *too* nice."

"Screw the dinner." My voice held a gravelly note—an

obvious arousal that had never been quiet so obvious before I was infected. "We could order room service, and you wouldn't have to wear anything."

"Ha, ha. I'm dressed. We're going out."

"As you wish. Our options in SmallTown, Utah include a local steakhouse, a sandwich shop, and an 'upscale casual dining' place that offers cliffside views. None of them are rated higher than four out of five stars, or more expensive than two out of four dollar signs on my review app. So, please select from the best mediocrity has to offer. And keep in mind that if you come spend forever on an island with me, I will cook for you every night."

"You cook?" She looked so impressed I hated to admit that I was joking.

"Okay, I will take a cooking class, *then* I will cook for you every night."

"I don't cook either." She unplugged her phone from the power bank on the hotel desk and slid it into her pocket. "We might actually starve, alone on an island together."

"You do realize this won't be an *uncharted* island, right? Not a *deserted* island. Just an island with no local shifter government in place to tell us we can't live there. There will be restaurants on the island. And if you still have that ring on your finger, we'll be able to afford to eat there every night. Or buy all the restaurants and make them deliver to us."

She laughed as we headed for the door. "This started out as a very romantic offer to cook for me every night of my life, but now it sounds like you'd be willing buy out every restaurant on this hypothetical island to avoid doing just that."

"Not to avoid, to give you options. And this island isn't hypothetical. It's just as yet unselected." I closed the door behind us and checked to make sure it was locked—not that we had much to steal at the moment—then I put my arm around her waist as we headed for the elevator. And she let me. "You know, I'm not opposed to letting you *choose* the island. In fact, I would go just about anywhere you want to go, if you would just get on a plane with me."

"Why?" Kaci poked the call button, then turned to me and slid her arms around my neck. She looked up at me with eyes that seemed more green than brown in the weird hotel lighting, and pressed her entire body against mine. "Why would you want to go *anywhere* with me?"

"Because I like you." Because she was beautiful, and strong, and willing to threaten an Alpha on my behalf.

"You like me now. But you might not like me next week."

"Of course I will."

"You don't know that. No matter what you think, you hardly know me."

"That is *not* true. In the past twenty-four hours, you've blackmailed me, kissed me, pushed me away, married me, stolen two cars with me, taken off your pants and then *fallen asleep next to me*, and threatened an Alpha for me. And I've loved every second of it. What on earth could you do to make me not like you, after all of that?"

"That's the easy part, Justus." She kissed me, then tugged me into the empty elevator, when the door opened.

"How the hell is any of that easy?"

"It's exciting. It's something new every other minute. It's danger, and adrenaline, and close calls. The hard part is what comes after."

"Okay, I'll bite. What comes after this?"

"Nothing."

"Huh?" I pushed the button for the lobby level.

"Forever on an island? Lying on the beach and eating seafood? What you're actually describing is a lifetime full of nothing. That might be great for a month, or maybe even a year. But eventually, you'll get bored with the tide, and the fish, and the deck chairs. And with me."

The elevator opened in the lobby, and I followed her out to the car, so I could watch her walk in front of me. "Yeah, I don't think I'll ever get tired of that," I called after her, as I watched her hips move. "But I assume you have an alternative suggestion?"

"Why would you assume that?"

I unlocked the car with the fob, then rushed forward to pull her door open before she could get to it. "Because it's rude to tear down someone's fantasy without providing an alternative fantasy."

"Then you admit the island is a fantasy?" Kaci sank into the passenger's seat and looked up at me.

I made a mental note to stop underestimating her verbal prowess. That girl could back a lawyer into a corner using nothing but his own words, against him. "I admit nothing."

"That's a solid trial strategy," she said as I slid behind the wheel. "But maybe not a very solid cornerstone for a marriage."

"So, this is a marriage now?"

"This is…insane," she finally finished, with a quiet smile. "You're insane."

"Now, *that's* a solid trial strategy."

She threw her head back and laughed, and I stopped the car with us still halfway out of the parking spot so I could lean across the console and taste the tender flesh beneath her jaw. "Seriously, we could just blow dinner off and feast on each other, Kaci," I whispered against her skin. "I'm not even hungry."

Tires squealed, and a car horn speared my thoughts. I

growled at the car stuck behind us in the aisle, and she laughed again. "Well, *I'm* hungry."

"Fine." I backed the rest of the way out, then pulled out of the parking lot onto the road. "Dinner it is. But then, I intend to taste other things."

"Sure." Kaci grinned at me. "As long as those other things include chocolate syrup, cream filling, or whipped cream."

I groaned at the dirty images her dessert cravings called to my mind. "Oh, I think we can *definitely* make that happen."

"This isn't exactly what I had in mind," I said as I tipped the room service waiter.

"I'm sorry, sir?" He glanced down at the tray he'd just set on the table, searching for the problem.

"He's talking to me." Kaci came out of the bathroom with her hair in a ponytail and her face scrubbed clean. "But this is exactly what *I* had in mind. Chocolate syrup." She pointed to the slice of cheesecake drizzled with chocolate. "Cream filling." The stuffed raspberry tart. "And whipped cream." On top of a huge slice of red velvet cake.

"You two really going to eat all that?" the waiter asked on his way out of the room.

"Oh, those are just for her," I said as I closed the door in his face. Kaci was all the dessert I needed.

"This is amazing!" She rubbed her hands together as she looked over the tray full of sweets. "I've never had room service! Maybe we *should* have just stayed here."

"You've never had room service?"

"Nope. Haven't spent much time in hotels. Shifters tend to rent cabins or houses, for privacy when they travel. And I haven't traveled much." She scooped a finger full of whipped cream from the cake and licked it off her finger. "I don't know what to eat first."

"All of them." I tucked all three sets of napkin-wrapped utensils beneath my arm, then picked up the cake and the tart. "Grab that last one and follow me." I set both plates on the middle of the still neatly made comforter, then started unwrapping silverware.

"On the bed?" She sounded scandalized, and my new goal for the night became drawing that sound out of her again— without food.

"Yes. It's like a hotel picnic. Unless you're planning to make a mess. If that's the case, I'm going to have to ask you to eat them all three…off me." I pulled my shirt over my head and dropped it on the floor. "You know, to preserve the linens."

She laughed as she carefully crawled onto the bed, holding the cheesecake plate in one hand. "Funny. Put your shirt back on."

"Take yours off, I countered."

"Not gonna happen." But she was grinning.

"Well, I think at least one of us should be topless." I started to sit, then noticed something missing. "Would you like a drink with those?"

"Just water, please. I don't care if I never see vodka again."

"That's fair, considering your first experience. But I would like to point out, in defense of alcohol everywhere, that in slightly smaller, slower quantities, it has its advantages." But I took two waters from the mini fridge and left all the little bottles of alcohol alone. If she wasn't drinking, neither was I.

"Here." I handed her an unopened water bottle, then

crawled onto the bed and sat cross-legged next to her, in front of the row of desserts.

"You know, I'm perfectly willing to share."

"Well, okay. If you insist. But you go first." I gave her a wicked smile. "And just so you know, that's my policy in all other areas, as well."

Her brows rose. "Or we could go *together*…"

"That's a lot easier with dessert than with other things, but sure, I'm game." I cut off the tip of the cheesecake slice and fed it to her.

She moaned around the bite, and the sound was…pleasant. So I fed her a bite of red velvet cake, and she moaned again. Next, I tried the tart, but some of the cream filling stuck to her lip, and she licked it off, and—

"Are you aware that you are *dirty* when you eat dessert?"

Kaci froze. "What?" she said around a mouthful of tart.

"You make erotic sounds when you eat dessert."

Her eyes went wide. She slapped both hands over her mouth and chewed furiously. "I do not!"

"Yes, you do. And that may be the hottest thing I've ever seen."

She dropped her fork onto the cake plate and pushed it toward the end of the bed. "Well I can't eat that now!"

"Why not?"

"Because you'll be sitting there thinking dirty things about me while I eat."

"Kaci, I'd be thinking dirty things about you no matter what you were doing. You're wearing a ring I gave you and sitting on a hotel bed. Also, you're gorgeous."

"You're not bad to look at, yourself." She cut another bit of cake without meeting my gaze. Then she changed the subject, as if the admission made her uncomfortable.

"Wouldn't it be great if we could eat room service every day? Neither one of us would have to cook *or* clean."

"Actually, I could probably make that happen. We could live in a hotel on our island, if you want. You could have room service for every meal, and I could feed you cake for breakfast every morning. On the balcony, or in bed…"

"You can stop trying to convince me that life is more fun when you're rich. I can't imagine anyone would argue with that premise. The problem isn't the money. It's leaving the country forever."

"*I* have to leave forever. *You* could come back and visit Faythe and Marc, and their ever-expanding litter of kidlets."

"Oh, stop it." She shoved my shoulder. "You know the boys are adorable."

"Yes. But you're more adorable." I leaned in and nibbled on the tip of her shoulder as I slid one hand beneath the hem of her tee. Slowly.

She took my hand and her gaze captured mine. "Stop."

"Why? I know you want me. I can smell arousal in your scent."

"Oh my God!" She looked scandalized. And self-conscious.

"There's no reason to be embarrassed. I think it's hot."

"It's impolite to mention romantic intel gathered from pheromone detection, Justus!"

"Well when you say it like that, it sounds much more scientific than erotic." I shrugged. "So, what? I'm just supposed to pretend I can't tell?"

"Yes! Justus, I'm not going to sleep with you."

"That's because you're afraid to admit you like me."

"No. I *do* like you. It's because I'm afraid to be married to you."

"Why?" I pushed the other plates back. "I swear on my life that I didn't marry you for the money."

"I believe you."

"Then what am I doing wrong?"

"Nothing." She leaned forward and kissed me, and she tasted like chocolate, and raspberry, and other sweet things that had nothing to do with room service. "You're not doing anything wrong. But that doesn't mean this has to end with sex."

"Sex would *not* be an ending. This doesn't have to end at all. That's the whole point of forever." I kissed her again, and my hand slid into her hair. Her tongue met mine, and then she put her hands on my chest. She explored me while we kissed, as if she'd never done that before, and with a sudden, heartbreaking epiphany, I realized that she hadn't, really, because she didn't remember touching me like this before.

And for her, that meant it hadn't happened.

For Kaci, *none* of what I remembered of the night before had happened. That must have been very scary for her. Very...confusing.

"How can this be real?" she murmured as I kissed my way down her neck. She clutched at me, as if she wanted more than she was willing to let herself have, and *damn*, I wanted to give her whatever she wanted. "How can anything that feels this good be happening to me, after—?"

"After what?" I sat up to look at her, and her eyes filled with tears.

"Justus, they're not wrong. What they say about me is true. I *am* a monster. I found that dead woman in the woods, and I was so hungry, and—"

"No. Kaci, they could *not* be more wrong about you. You did what you had to do to survive. They're the monsters, holding something like that against a little girl. You...are perfect." I leaned in to kiss her neck. "The universe owes us this," I whispered, pushing her hair back. Sliding the collar of her shirt over her shoulder, so I could taste the point where her collarbone ended. "After everything life has put us through, we deserve this, Kaci. You deserve better than I could ever give you."

She laid back on the pillow, and I lay next to her, propped on my elbow. Her hand found mine on the comforter, and she clung to it, staring up at me. "You're wrong. But I really want to believe you."

I leaned down to kiss her, and her free hand slid behind my neck. Then down my back. Her mouth opened, and she pulled me closer, lower, until I lay stretched out over her, supporting my weight on one elbow, her hand still clutching mine.

We kissed like that forever, in the closest approximation of what she clearly wanted, but would not take, and I didn't notice until much later that we'd kicked all the desserts onto the floor.

Later, she rolled toward me on the bed, still fully clothed, and laid her hand on my chest. Her head on my shoulder. Her eyes were closed, her breathing slow and even. She was nearly asleep. Or maybe she was barely awake.

"It's because you'll leave," she murmured.

"What?" I scooted closer, bunching the comforter up between us, trying to get close enough to hear sounds she was hardly even making.

"If I sleep with you, this marriage will be real. You'll get your money and you'll leave. And I can't go with you."

NINE

KACI

"SO, I'VE BEEN THINKING," I SAID AS JUSTUS OPENED THE hotel room door. "Maybe I went about things the wrong way yesterday. With Ed Taylor."

"Just a sec." He turned to the waiter standing in the hall with a full tray. "Come on in, man. You can just set it on the table."

The waiter set the tray down, and my stomach rumbled. I hadn't eaten anything since dinner the night before, except a few bites of dessert, because I drew the line at eating cake off the floor.

Justus took the padded black folder, and while he signed the breakfast bill, the waiter's gaze dropped to the carpet at the foot of the bed. Where twin chocolate and raspberry smears stained the carpet. Then he picked up last night's tray, where the misshapen remainders of our dessert had been scooped back onto their original plates. He glanced up at me with an arched brow.

I could feel my cheeks burn. "We had a little accident."

Justus laughed as he set the bill on the used tray and handed it to the waiter. "What did you mean about Taylor?" He asked as he bolted the door behind the waiter.

I sat at the table and pulled the dome from the first plate. Waffle-scented steam puffed out at me, and it took a conscious effort not to moan with pleasure. I *really* like to eat. "I mean, instead of asking him to vote for your acquittal just because that's the right thing to do, maybe we should show him that he can't afford to find you guilty."

Justus pulled out the chair across from me and sank into it. "And how would that be true?" He uncovered the other plate, and his western omelet smelled so good I almost regretted ordering in favor of carbs.

"Well, the best thing I've come up with so far is that if he votes in your favor, he could be regaining the council power alliance he lost when he got pissy because Abby choose Jace over his son."

"You're going to have to walk me through that one."

"He's said he's open to acknowledging the Mississippi Valley Pride, right?" I said as I poured syrup over my big, fluffy Belgian waffle. "If that happens, Titus will be a council member. Which means that for the first time in the history of this country, there will be eleven Alphas, rather than ten." I cut a bite with my fork and gestured with it. "That's an odd number. There will never be another tied vote. And the best way for Taylor to make sure he's on the side that wins is to make friends with the tie-breaking vote."

"Titus." Justus looks impressed. "And there's no better way to do that than by voting not to execute his little brother."

"Exactly," I said around my first bite.

He shook a bottle of Tabasco over his omelet. "Do you think he'll go for that?"

I frowned at his breakfast. "You didn't even taste that before you put hot sauce on it."

"You didn't taste your waffle before you put syrup on it."

"But syrup *goes* on waffles."

"And hot sauce goes on eggs." He looked right at me and shoveled a huge, spicy bite into his mouth. "Are you going to criticize my breakfast or answer the question?"

"I don't really see that as an either/or scenario," I said as I broke a strip of bacon in two. "But I think Taylor will go for it. That unofficial alliance will give him a *very real* advantage." I ate one half of the bacon and gestured with the other half. "Titus will clearly be allied with Faythe and Marc, who share a vote, with Rick Wade, and with Bert Di Carlo. And probably with Isaac Wade, through his connections to both Rick—his dad, who's also the council chair—and Jace—his brother-in-law. That's five out of eleven Alphas. With Taylor as the sixth, they have a majority vote, and they'll be able to push through any agenda they want. Unfortunately, the same would be true on the other side, should he ally with the other five Alphas."

"Are they split that evenly on everything?"

"No, fortunately. Blackwell tends to align with Milo Mitchell, Nick Davidson, and Wes Gardner. But Ed Taylor and Jerold Pierce are issues voters." I shrugged as I cut another bite. "Not that the others aren't. They just tend to agree with their allies on the issues. But my point is that if Taylor aligns himself with the Blackwell camp, they'll lose every time Pierce's swing vote swings the other way."

"Wow. Shifter politics makes D.C. look like playtime."

I spoke around my bite. "I know nothing about human politics."

"I started watching the news for a government class my first semester in college, and it was like digging a hole until you realize you're too deep to climb out. So, you keep digging deeper, hoping you'll find something buried in the sludge to make the effort worth it, but all you get is...filthy."

"That's depressing. But yeah, sounds about like Shifter politics. There's one big difference, though. In the justice system, at least." I dipped my last bite of bacon in syrup, then ate it.

"And that would be?" Justus watched, amused, while I chewed furiously, holding up one "wait a minute" finger.

Then I made him wait a little longer while I washed the bacon down with half my orange juice. "In the shifter justice system, you're presumed guilty until proven innocent. Which means the burden of proof is on the accused."

"What does that mean for me, in terms of the trial?"

"I'm not sure. I guess we should call Michael Sanders. Faythe's brother. He's an attorney. You don't really have the right to an attorney in front of the tribunal. At least, not the same way you would in a human courtroom. But he'll probably get to stay with you, to advise you."

Justus swallowed his last bite of omelet and set his fork on his plate. "Yeah, I was supposed to have a meeting with him, so he could prep me."

"When was that?"

"Yesterday."

I groaned. "That would have been good to know. Maybe we can reschedule. This probably counts as an emergency situation."

"You really think fleeing to Las Vegas counts as an emergency?"

I shrugged as I plucked my phone from my pocket. "I think I can spin it that way." And frankly, I was pleased that he was even willing to discuss actually standing trial. I pulled up Michael's contact information and tapped his phone number. He answered on the second ring.

"Hello? Kaci?"

"Yeah. It's me."

"I hear you're having a bit of an adventure."

For a second, I thought he was being condescending. Then I realized it was probably perfectly reasonable to characterize a trip that includes two stolen cars and being chased through the lobby of Caesar's Palace as an adventure. "Yeah, I guess. I just wanted a vacation, but you gotta roll with the punches, you know?"

He laughed. "Is Justus there with you?"

"Yeah. That's actually why I'm calling."

"Tell him he's eighteen hours late for his appointment. If I didn't already have today off, I wouldn't be free for what I assume is an emergency phone consultation?"

"How'd you guess?"

"I remember falling in love with Holly. If I'd had to choose between standing trial for my life or running off with her, I might have done the same thing."

Falling in…

I glanced across the table at Justus, and he only smiled at me. Unflinchingly. Totally not denying that he was falling in love with me. Which usually happens *before* anyone buys a ring.

"Okay. Anyway…" I put my phone on speaker mode and set it on the table between us. "Justus is kind of considering actually showing up for his trial—"

Michael snorted. "I'm going to pretend I didn't hear that."

"—and we have a few questions. So, the randomly drawn tribunal members are Blackwell, Di Carlo, and Taylor. You know more about them than I do. How do you feel about that draw? How tough will this actually be?"

"It's a decent draw. Blackwell's a lost cause, but Bert Di Carlo will be a pretty friendly face. Taylor's your real challenge."

"That's what Kaci said," Justus told him with a wink at me.

"She's a smart girl."

"Not that I don't love the flattery, but we're kind of in a time crunch here. The trial's in five days—I assume you've heard—and two sets of enforcers are looking for us. So, what we really need to know is, how can we get Taylor to find Justus innocent?"

"Well, he's not innocent, strictly speaking," Michael said. "From what I understand, he's already admitted to what he did, and there are witnesses, at least in Drew's death."

"Robyn and Titus," Justus said. "But they'll both testify on my behalf." Yet I could tell from his frown that he still didn't want to involve his brother.

"Yes, but unless they're willing to lie, that won't help. And if they *are* willing to lie, we can't use them. An Alpha lying under oath will do way more harm than good. To both of you. The goal here is to find a way to present the truth—always the truth—in a way that will exonerate Justus. Absolve him of blame for what he admits he did."

"Then what do you suggest?" I asked.

"We need to give the tribunal a reason to find Justus's actions *justified*. Then he can be found innocent by reason of…something. Traumatic stress. Temporary mental incapacity. Whatever the circumstance actually was."

"I'm *not* mentally incapacitated," Justus growled.

"That just means that in the moment you committed the crime, your understanding of right and wrong was overruled by some other factor that was beyond your control," Michael explained. "But it has to be something sympathetic. It can't just be that you were so mad your anger overtook your ability to reason. That, we just call murder."

"Drew deserved what he got," I told Michael. "If they'll just listen to Justus, they'll understand that."

"Maybe so. But that doesn't mean no crime was committed. The problem is that even if the council would undeniably have voted to execute Drew, Justus didn't have the authority to do that on his own. Not only did he commit murder, he deprived the council of the opportunity to do its job. He essentially usurped their authority, and that's probably going to stick in their collective craw."

"That wasn't my intent," Justus said. "I wasn't thinking about the council when I killed Drew. I didn't even know it existed."

"I know. Fortunately, there's another way this could work out. They could find you guilty, but have a justifiable reason to go easy on you. Which would give them a chance to save face, without ignoring the relevant extenuating circumstances."

Justus exhaled, staring at my phone. "How easy on me are we talking?"

"Probation, ideally. Or supervised training. Or even house-restriction, if it's in friendly quarters."

"And how do we make that happen?"

Michael sighed. "You two need to understand that none of this is a guarantee. In fact, it's all a long shot. Deep down, several members of the council believe that strays are inherently more violent and less prone to civilizing influences than natural-born cats, and that's what they're going to see when they look at Justus. No matter how he answers their questions. They're going to view this as further proof of the beliefs they cling to, because they can't think of themselves as the 'good' guys unless they have some other portion of society to point out as 'bad.'"

"But Taylor claims he doesn't believe that," I told Michael. "He said he thinks that accepting strays as citizens is inevitable."

"That's not exactly the same as saying that's how he thinks it *should* be. You're going to have to hold his feet to the fire. Remind him of his responsibility to vote his conscience, then give him no excuse not to."

"Okay." But I wasn't quite sure how to do that yet. "Thanks, Michael."

"You're welcome. And Kaci?"

"Yeah?"

"I'd be remiss in my duties if I didn't tell you to come home. You broke the law, and the longer you run, the worse that looks."

"Are they going to charge her with anything?" Justus's forehead furrowed with concern for me.

"They have grounds to charge her with trespassing and theft, but I haven't caught wind of any actual plans to do that. Though, I'm not on the council, so I probably wouldn't hear about that unless someone asks for legal advice."

"Okay. Thanks, again Michael."

"Wait, before you go, may I ask what your plans are?"

"Umm…" I took him off speaker and held the phone to my ear. Not that Justus couldn't hear him like that. The conversation just felt more personal that way. "We're still discussing it." I stood and began stuffing my pajamas into my backpack. "Faythe said she thinks that if he runs, they'll let him go. But if I go with him, they'll chase us. Do you agree?"

"Yes. Look, I know this isn't what you two want to hear, but the best thing you can do is go home, wait for the trial, and take whatever you have coming for trespassing. That's not a capital offense. It could just be a slap on the wrist."

"Okay. Thanks for the advice. I gotta go."

"I know. Love you, kiddo."

"I'm not a kid. But I love you too." I hung up my phone and slid it into my back pocket, and when I looked up, I found Justus staring at me. "What?"

"Did Faythe really say that?"

"Yeah." I sank onto the end of the unmade bed, careful not to step on the raspberry carpet stain. "I wouldn't blame you if you still want to go. But that's why I can't go with you."

"You're coming with me, or I'm not going. I'm never leaving you again, Kaci." He took my hand and pulled me up until I stood wrapped in his arms. My head on his shoulder. Breathing him in. My heart felt...swollen. Too big for my body. "Maybe we should take our time today. We're still eight hours from Denver. That gives us most of the day to figure out what to do before we have to make a decision."

"Well, we only have two choices," I said into his shirt. "Fly out of Denver—we'll be in the free zone until right before we cross the city limits, remember?"

He nodded, and the stubble on his chin caught in my hair.

"Or head south through the free zone and cross directly into the South-Central territory. If we're caught there, they'll take us back to the ranch. If we're caught in any other territory, they don't have to turn us over to Faythe and Marc. At least, not without some negotiating. Crossing shifter territorial boundaries isn't like crossing from one state into another. Alphas are an absolute authority, as long as they don't violate the council's rules. Tensions can run thick."

"So I hear. Okay, let's get out of here."

"Wait." I stepped out of his embrace. "I want to call Ed Taylor again, after what Michael told us."

Justus looked skeptical. "Okay. I'll finish up in here."

While I called Taylor, he checked the bathroom, to make sure we weren't leaving anything behind. This time, the phone only rang once.

"Hello?"

"Hi, Mr. Taylor, it's me again."

"Hi, Kaci. What can I do for you today?" He sounded oddly chipper for someone I'd threatened during our last phone call. He must have been pretty confident that he could find a reasonable excuse to find Justus guilty.

But I could sound chipper and confident too. "Really, it's what I can do for *you*."

"And what is that?"

"I'm going to help you vote your conscience."

"I wasn't aware that I needed help with that, but I'm listening. How do you plan to help?"

I sank back onto the edge of the bed. "To get to that answer, first let me ask you a question: What would it take for you to believe that Justus deserves to be acquitted?"

"Well, I'm not sure…"

"Please don't say you can't imagine a scenario in which he'd deserve to be acquitted, Mr. Taylor. Because that would make it sound like you've made up your mind about him before the trial even starts. And I'm *sure* that's not the case."

He chuckled. "Kaci, have you ever considered becoming an attorney?"

"You know, I just might. So. What would you need to see or hear to convince you that Drew Borden's death was justified?"

"I would need to hear that his execution had been ordered by the council—which I know for a fact did not happen—and that the circumstances were too dire to justify carrying out his execution in a more secluded place."

"Okay. Thanks. And on the lesser charges? Infection?"

"Kaci, those are not lesser charges. It's a capital offense to infect a human. Especially a woman, because infecting a human woman has always led to her death. Well, until Robyn, anyway."

"Yes, but surely you don't think he can be held responsible for infecting people, when he didn't even know that was a possibility?"

"Ideally, we'd like proof that he didn't realize that scratching or biting spreads the werecat infection. It's unfortunate for Justus—or perhaps convenient?—that the one man who could testify to that has died. At Justus's hands. Er…jaws."

"I can assure you that is *not* convenient," Justus said from the bathroom, where he'd been staring into the tub for far longer than it should have taken to make sure I hadn't forgotten my shampoo.

"However," Taylor continued, and I couldn't tell whether or not he'd heard Justus. "I, personally, would be willing to give him the benefit of the doubt on that for the first three cases of infection. The ones that happened at the cabin, where he was evidently manipulated into going."

"He wasn't just manipulated. Drew infected him on purpose, then sicced him on his girlfriend and her real boyfriend. He created a weapon, then he unleashed it, with a very specific and destructive purpose. Justus was a victim in that."

"Like I said, I think he could make an effective argument to that effect—as you just did—for the first three cases. But that fourth infection. The kid at the party? Justus would need to prove that he was still acting involuntarily, even though he was evidently sane and reasonable enough to carry on his normal human life between the two incidents."

"Okay. Thank you, Mr. Taylor."

"I'm glad I could help." Though he didn't sound entirely sure about that. "And I look forward to seeing you and Justus both at his trial."

"Uh huh," I said, in as non-committal a tone as I could muster. In case Justus still decided to run. "Bye." I hung up the phone and stared at it for a moment, processing.

"Learn anything helpful?" Justus closed the bathroom door and glanced around the rest of the hotel room.

"I assume you heard the whole conversation?"

"Yup." He grabbed my hairbrush from the top of the dresser and dropped it into my backpack. "But I suspect you and I processed that information pretty differently."

"Probably." I zipped up my backpack and tossed it over my shoulder. "So, what happened with the last guy you infected? If we've talked about that part, it's been lost to the dark, dark abyss of the other night."

Justus picked up his duffle, evidently satisfied that we hadn't left anything behind. "Exactly how every groom dreams his bride will describe their wedding night."

I laughed as I stepped into the hall and held the door open for him. And as I took his hand, I realized I hadn't laughed so much with anyone in my life, other than little Greg. And toddlers don't count. They're all adorable.

"That guy's name was Elliott Belcher." At the end of the hall, Justus pushed the elevator call button, and it opened immediately. "I didn't know him, and I only met him briefly at Titus's house, after everything went down. He's a member of the Mississippi Valley Pride now, and Titus says he's doing great."

The elevator doors slid shut, and I pressed the L button. "How'd you wind up infecting him?"

"I didn't mean to. I was at this after-hours party at a museum, trying to get drunk." I arched both brows at him, and he rolled his eyes. "I know, I know. But I had no idea what was happening to me. Every shift into cat form that I'd made had been involuntary. I'd figured out how to shift back, but not why it was happening in the first place, or how to stop it. Drinking was the only thing that still made sense. Only it was suddenly super hard to achieve a buzz."

The elevator slid slowly down from the fourth floor, and I glanced at our reflections on the mirrored wall. He had one arm around my waist, his gorgeous gray eyes totally trained on me, and we looked fucking adorable together.

"So, I was at this museum party, finally actually starting to feel the vodka, and this song started playing. I can't even remember what song it was now, but the moment I heard it, I started flashing back to the woods. To what happened at the cabin with Ivy and her...boyfriend. They must have been playing that song in the cabin, or something, because hearing it triggered a shift.

"I ran out, with my hand shoved into my pockets so no one could see that my nails were turning into claws. Everyone seemed to think I was going to puke—I'd had half a bottle on my own by then. I wound up in the alley behind the museum, hidden by the trash bin, and there was nothing I could do but let it happen."

"Right there in the middle of Jackson?"

"Yeah. It was kind of terrifying. Anyway, when it was finally over, I stood up and had to pull what was left of my clothes off with my teeth, you know?"

I *did* know. The same thing had happened to me with my very first shift. The one I hadn't known was coming.

"That's a very surreal moment, when you're shaped like a cat, but you're still wearing human clothes, and suddenly you don't seem to fit into either world."

"Exactly. I remember that."

The doors slid open, and we stepped into an empty hallway at the back of the lobby, but Justus lowered his voice, just in case. "Anyway, I was just going to hide there until I'd regained enough strength to shift back. But then this guy came around the corner of the Dumpster. It was Elliott, and he *was* puking. He didn't notice me until he was done. I didn't have anywhere to go. I was boxed in by a fence, the building, the trash bin, and him. And I was still a little drunk. Then he got scared and grabbed this long board sticking out of the Dumpster. He started swinging it at me. There were nails sticking out of the end, and he actually grazed me."

Justus pushed up his short sleeve to show me a thin white scar on his left shoulder. "So, I swiped at him. I didn't even think about it. I mean, there was no human thought process, like, 'What should I do now?' My paw just shot out, and I smacked him. I didn't even realize I'd actually scratched him until I met him in the basement of Titus's pool house."

"Then there was no malice," I summed up in a whisper, running my finger over his scar. "You were acting in self-defense, and you had no idea you could infect anyone. Do you think Elliott would testify to that?"

Justus shrugged. "I have no idea what he remembers."

"Well, we could call your brother and ask to talk to him." I glanced at the front of the lobby, then at the door leading to the lot in back, where we were parked. "Why don't you check us out, and I'll bring the car around front. It's my turn to drive."

"You're not old enough to drive a rental," he teased.

"Neither are you. Give me the keys."

He gave me the keys and a kiss. I lifted his duffle off his shoulder and hung it over my own, opposite my backpack. "See you in a minute." Then I headed out the back door, while he went toward the lobby.

In the parking lot, I popped the trunk with the button on the key fob and dropped our bags inside. Then I slammed the trunk and looked up—

Someone grabbed me around the waist. I opened my mouth to scream, and a hand clamped over my mouth. Panicked, I inhaled through my nose and instantly recognized the scent of the hands that held me.

Jared lifted me off the ground, and I kicked and thrashed, and though my shoes slammed into his shins a dozen times, he never even flinched. He just shoved me head-first into the open back seat of his car, then slammed the door.

One glance told me it was the very car we'd stolen and left for him in the parking lot of the fast food taco place, only since then, he'd screwed a rough-cut plexiglas panel into the backs of the front seats, separating me from him like a cab driver from his customers.

I pulled on the door handle, but nothing happened.

"Child safety locks," he said as he slid into his seat behind the wheel. The passenger seat next to him was filled with a large, unmarked cardboard box.

"I can pull the handles right off," I threatened.

"Yes, you probably can." He shoved his key into the ignition and started the car, then backed smoothly out of the parking spot. "And that will get you into a lot more trouble. But it won't get you out of this car. So buckle up."

"Let me out!" I yelled, as close to his ear as I could get.

"Shout all you want." He shoved something small and green into his left ear—an ear plug. "But if you do anything to wreck this car and either of us gets hurt, the Southwest

Pride is fully prepared to charge you with reckless endangerment."

"You stupid son of a bitch, you have no right—"

Jared took the curve around to the front of the parking lot too fast, and I had to grab the door handle to keep from falling over. As we pulled out onto the street, I turned to bang on the rear windshield, shouting Justus's name. I could see him through the front window of the hotel, paying for our incidental charges. I shouted as hard as I could, but there was too much distance between us. Too many doors and windows.

"Say goodbye," Jared taunted. "The next time you see your poor groom will be at his execution."

TEN

JUSTUS

I WHISTLED AS I STEPPED OUT OF THE HOTEL, SHADED FROM the morning sunlight by the covered drop-off at the front of the parking lot. The day was shaping up to be hot, even though it was hardly past nine am, but the rental car had a great air conditioner and Kaci was—

Where was Kaci?

Frowning, I rounded the side of the hotel building headed for the back of the parking lot, expecting her to pull alongside me in the car any moment. She liked to drive, and for all I knew, she'd gotten bored waiting for me and had decided to fill up the tank. And grab snacks for the road.

But the car was still in the lot, exactly where I'd parked it the night before. The trunk was closed, the doors locked, with no sign that she'd ever opened them. I tried the trunk, but it could only be opened from inside the car or with the key fob. Fear building inside me like a steady, bitter pressure, I'd just decided to break open one of the windows when the tip of my shoe landed on something that scraped against the concrete.

Keys.

Our keys. I bent to pick them up and discovered Kaci's phone lying just underneath the car. The case was scuffed, the screen cracked.

Kaci was gone.

No.

"Kaci!" I shoved the keys and phone into my pocket and raced toward the rear hotel door—the one she'd gone out— but it required a hotel key card to get in, and I'd already given ours back to the clerk. So I jerked on the door as hard as I could.

Metal groaned, but the door was solid. It held.

I pulled again with both hands, wedging one foot against the door frame. Something popped, and the door flew open. Something small and metal bounced off my shoe, but I was already pounding down the back hall before I realized it was the bolt from the busted door.

My shoes skidded on the tile floor as I raced past the elevators and rounded the corner into the lobby, then stood in front of the desk clerk, panting not from exertion, but from utter terror.

Kaci was gone.

I had let her out of my sight for *four minutes*, and she was *gone*.

"Have you seen her?" I demanded, and the clerk gave me an alarmed, but blank expression. "Kaci. The woman I checked in with. She's about five-seven. One hundred ten pounds. She has hazel eyes and long, dark hair, and she's gorgeous. You would notice her."

"I do remember her sir, but I haven't seen her since last night."

"Okay, what about...cars? Did you see any cars leave since I checked out? Is there a back way out of the parking lot?"

"The only way out is right through there." He pointed behind me, at the parking lot entrance in front of the hotel. "But I think I did see a car leave while you were checking out."

Fuck!

"What did it look like?"

"I—" He frowned, clearly trying to remember. "I'm sorry, sir, I don't remember."

"Was it a car? A truck? An SUV?"

"Definitely a car. I think. Four doors. Oh!" His brows shot up. "It was low to the ground. It nearly bottomed out on that bump in the entrance."

"Great. What color?"

"Um... Something dark. Red, or green."

A growl exploded from my throat. "Those are two *completely* different colors."

"I know, sir." He looked flustered. "But my point is that it definitely wasn't white or silver. It was a *real* color."

"As opposed to a made-up color? Honestly, I don't even know what to do with that description."

"I'm trying to help you, sir. Has she been assaulted? Kidnapped? Should I call the police?" He lifted the desk phone.

"No!" I snatched the hand piece from him and slammed it down on the receiver. "Just...are there security cameras?"

"Yes, but—"

"Let me see the footage. Please. Right now."

"I can't do that without my manager's permission, or a warrant. But it wouldn't matter anyway, because none of them face the entrance."

"None of your security cameras face the entrance to the hotel? How the hell can you call them *security* cameras, if they don't see who comes and goes?"

"They don't face the entrance of the *parking lot*, sir. So, unless whoever you're looking for came into the hotel, we probably don't have footage of him or her anyway. Now, if you'd like me to call the police for you, I'd be happy to help. But if not, I'm afraid there's nothing else I can do for you. Sir."

"Fine. Thank you." I spun, ready to storm out the front entrance, when a new possibility occurred to me. When I turned back to the clerk, he actually groaned out loud. "Just one more question. Please. Is possible that this low-riding four-door car that wasn't silver or white was actually blue?"

"Yes!" His eyes lit up in triumph, as if he'd remembered that detail on his own. "A dark blue. Like, from fifteen years ago, or so."

"Ten," I corrected. "Thank you so much."

Jared.

The Southwest Territory enforcer with the old blue Honda Civic. The car Kaci and I had stolen, then thoughtfully left safe and sound in the parking lot of a taco place two hours down the highway.

We should have left it in the bottom of a lake. With that bastard in it.

I raced around the building and back to the rental car, and I'd already shifted into reverse when I realized I had no idea where to go.

Think! Where would a Southwest Pride enforcer take his…captive?

If he stuck to I15—the only major highway in the area— the choices were north and south. North would take him farther into the free zone, according to Kaci. And within a couple of hours, south would take him back to Las Vegas. Back to the Southwest Territory.

If he was acting under the authority of the council, he would likely take the fastest route out of the free zone. But if he'd gone rogue and had taken Kaci for any purpose other than an official apprehension...

I would find him and rip his dick off and shove it down his own throat until he suffocated on it.

But if he *had* gone rogue, I had no idea where to look for him.

If I took off toward the south, I might be able to catch them before they crossed out of the free zone. But if he hadn't gone south, I'd just be wasting time while he took Kaci farther and farther away from me.

A roar erupted from my throat. My fist slammed into the dashboard, and I didn't even realize I'd swung until I was picking fragments of plastic out of my knuckles.

A little girl screamed in the parking lot, and I looked left to see an entire family staring at me. I growled at them, and the parents hustled their kids into their mini-van, then tore forward out of their space toward the road.

I brushed more shards of plastic off my lap and my focus fell to my phone, where I'd dropped it in one of the center cup holders. I could think of only one way to find out for sure whether Jared was acting on the council's orders. So I swallowed my pride and dialed.

"Hello?" Marc answered on the first ring. "Justus? Are you there?"

"Yes. I need help, and I swear I wouldn't be asking, after what I did, if it were just for me. But Jared took Kaci, and I don't know where they've gone."

"Slow down. Actually, hang on." Something brushed the phone, and his voice was muffled. "Karen, can you watch them for a minute? I have to take this. No, let Faythe sleep."

A door closed over the line, and everything got quiet. "Okay, say that again? Jared *took* Kaci? Jared who?"

"I don't know his last name. He's an enforcer for the Southwest Pride. One of Blackwell's men, right? I think Kaci said he's Blackwell's grandson."

"Jared Taylor. Big guy with a thick neck?"

"You're describing every enforcer I've ever met. He was there yesterday with Vic and Chris. At Caesar's Palace. They can tell you who I'm talking about."

"Vic's fine, by the way," Marc growled.

"Yeah, I'm sorry about his arm. I'm sorry about all of this. I never meant to drag her into anything. In fact, I'm trying to drag her back out." I sucked in a deep breath. Then I did what I should have done twenty-four hours ago. What I should have said from the very beginning. "You have to help me get her back. I swear, I'll drive her straight to the ranch, then I'll disappear. You'll never hear from me again, if you promise me you'll keep her safe."

"That's all we've ever tried to do for her. And we want the same for you. No one wants you to disappear."

"No, but several of them want me to die."

"That's not—" A frustrated growl rumbled over the line, as if Marc had stopped the lie before it could be spoken. "We'll sort the rest of this out after we've found Kaci. Okay?"

"Yes. Done." I nodded at myself in the rearview mirror, as if I were looking at Marc. "Whatever you want."

"Where are you?"

"St. George, Utah. It's two hours up I15 from Las Vegas."

"You two didn't get very far yesterday."

"We stopped to…rest."

He growled. "Do not say *anything* that even gives me the *slightest* mental image of you in bed with the girl I've raised like a *daughter*."

"I'm serious, Marc. We rested. I swear on my life I haven't touched her. I bought her dinner and we talked. That's it."

"But you're married? Faythe and Vic said you two got married."

"Not that I want to discuss the particulars of that with you right now, but yes. We're married, but not yet... Um..."

"Stop there," he snapped. "I understand."

"Thank God."

"Okay, I want you to sit tight and wait. I'm sending Vic and Chris your way from Phoenix."

"I don't need—" I bit off the objection before Marc could interrupt me. I would take whatever help he offered, if it would get Kaci back. "Okay, it's not that I don't need them. But Jared could be heading back toward Las Vegas as we speak, so maybe Vic and Chris should head that way. I need to know whether Jared's acting on the council's orders or... I need to know... Marc, why the hell would he take her, but leave me?"

"I don't know. Let me call Blackwell. I'm going to put Chris and Vic on alert, but have them stay put until I know more about what's going on. You stay put too. I'll call you right back."

"Okay. Thanks."

I plugged my phone into the car charger, then I drove across the street to fill up the gas tank and grab a cup of coffee, so I'd be ready for whatever orders came down the pipeline. Then I sat in my car and waited. And waited. After what felt like forever, I checked the time on my phone and discovered that only fifteen minutes had passed.

Somehow, Kaci had been kidnapped *and* time had slowed down.

Finally, my phone rang. Marc's name appeared on the screen, and I jabbed the talk button. "Hello?"

"Please tell me you have a full tank of gas."

My heart slammed against my sternum. "I do."

"Now tell me there's nothing illegal in your rental car, at all."

"Of course not." *Shit.* "Well, except for the fake ID I used to rent this car. And to play poker at Caesar's."

"Fine. That's nothing."

"What's going on?"

"Put me on speaker, then get on I15 and go south," Marc said. "I'll explain while you drive."

I tapped the speaker button and dropped my phone into the cup holder, then pulled out of the gas station onto the road. A quarter mile later, I merged onto I15. "I'm on the highway. What's going on, Marc?"

"It's Blackwell. He's decided to take action against Kaci for trespassing."

"That means he can just *kidnap* her?" I put on my blinker and shifted into the left-hand lane, then stomped on the gas; it was clear where I was headed. "How bad is this, Marc?"

"Bad enough that I'm going to have to wake Faythe up from her nap. And I try never to wake Faythe up from a nap. Blackwell's calling this a by-the-book apprehension, and the problem is that he's not wrong."

"What book says it's okay for an enforcer to grab a girl half his size and just take off with her? Did the council okay this? How could they have, if he didn't even tell you and Faythe?"

"The council doesn't get a say except on capital offenses —those potentially punishable by execution. Trespassing is

145

serious, but it's not a capital crime, and Blackwell has jurisdiction, because the crime occurred in his territory, against his Pride."

"And he didn't even have to tell anyone?"

"Because she's our Pride member, he has to give us the details once she's in custody, but he doesn't have to alert us beforehand."

"So why didn't he give you the details?"

"Because she's not officially in his custody until she's back in his territory. And once she *is* in his custody, in his territory, he can try her there without interference from anyone else."

Anger raged like fire in my veins, yet I saw the proverbial writing on the wall. "But if she's *not* in his custody? Or in his territory?"

"If you can get to her before Jared takes her back over the border, then get her back onto our land, we can petition the council to try her here. Blackwell would still get to sit in judgement, but he'd have to do it on our turf, and he'd have to negotiate with me and Faythe about the rules of the hearing."

"So, I'm going to take her back, right?" Adrenaline exploded in my heart and raced through my veins.

"You *have* to get her back. And to make it legal..." Marc actually groaned over the line. "I'm *temporarily* appointing you as an enforcer of the South-Central Pride. And I'm waiving the usual swearing in, due to the emergency circumstances."

"Holy shit." I swerved around some asshole going sixty in the fast lane. "I'm an enforcer? Just like that?"

"Temporarily. And without pay, or any other benefits. And please let me be clear here. I'm giving you this job not because you're the most qualified—or because you're *at all* qualified—but because you're the only one close enough to get to her. Your one job in the world is to catch up with Jared before he gets Kaci over the border, stop them *safely*, and take her *safely* into your official custody. Then bring her *safely* back here. Did I mention safely? Don't run them off the road, or do anything that could get her hurt."

"What about him?" I pressed a little harder on the gas, and the needle edged toward eighty-five. "Can I hurt him?"

"If you have to fight him, yes. Vic says you *can* fight. But nothing more than what has to be done to get her back. Do you understand? Once you have her—*if* you get her—do not strike out against him. Your authority to act against him ends when he's incapacitated. But only if he *has* to be incapacitated."

Oh, he'd have to be. I knew that from the way he'd grabbed her arm in Vegas. And from the way he'd kidnapped her when I wasn't looking, like a sneaky little *bitch*.

"There's one more thing."

"What?" I watched the needle edge toward ninety.

"If they cross over the border, *let them go*."

"No way in hell."

"Justus. Jared didn't bother with you because he knew he didn't have to. He knew that if he took Kaci, you'd follow him right into their territory. Where they can hold you on another count of trespassing and keep you in custody until your trial for murder and infection."

"I'm not going to leave her—"

"They won't hurt her," Marc insisted.

"You don't know that."

"Actually, I do. Blackwell is old fashioned. He believes women should be cherished, protected, and provided for. And that they should be mothers and homemakers. He's an asshole, but he would never let anyone hurt Kaci. However, he also believes that strays are a problem that the US prides must not accept, but confront. I'm saying this to you from one stray to another. Blackwell was part of the ruling that exiled me into the free zone several years ago. He stood by and watched Faythe removed from her position as Alpha, which nearly got her killed and got us all kicked out of our own house. Off the ranch. He won't break the rules, but he will interpret them in a manner that supports his beliefs. And that will *not* benefit you."

"I understand."

"So, you'll stop when you get to the border, if you don't have her back yet?" Marc demanded. But I wasn't sure how to answer, so I let silence speak for me. "Justus, I can't let you go after her if I know your intent is to go past the boundary, where you have no authority, even as an enforcer."

"Well then, I guess it's a good thing you don't know that. I'll call you when I have her." I hung up and turned all my attention toward the road.

Marc called me back, and I let the call go to voice mail so he couldn't *un*-appoint me as an enforcer. Then I stomped a little harder on the gas.

The needle hit ninety. I flicked my blinker on and carefully eased back into the left-hand lane. As much fun as it would've been, under other circumstances, to test the limits on a car I didn't own, if I wrecked the rental, I'd have no way to get Kaci back. Or get her to safety, once I *had* her back.

I watched the mile markers as they ticked past, counting down the miles toward Las Vegas. I passed from Utah into Arizona, then half an hour later into Nevada, where I panicked for a moment until I remembered that territorial borders don't follow US geopolitical lines. They follow natural boundaries like mountain ranges and rivers. I hadn't left the free zone yet.

As I drove, I scanned the cars ahead, trying to determine their color. Unfortunately, the morning sunlight glaring off the rear windshields kept me from seeing the colors of the cars. And for the ones in the distance, I couldn't even determine size, unless there was another vehicle nearby to compare them to.

For nearly an hour, I counted the passage of time in my own heartbeats. In the miles that raced by beneath my tires.

Please let Kaci be okay. Please let me get her back. Please, please, please…

Then, up ahead, a small car swerved into the left lane, in front of a white delivery van, and my pulse spiked. I couldn't be sure, but at a glance, it was about the right size. About the right color.

It *had* to be her.

I pushed the gas pedal all the way to the floor.

ELEVEN

KACI

"GIVE ME MY PHONE!" BUT JARED IGNORED ME, SO I LEANED back and kicked the plexiglass barricade as hard as I could. The whole thing shuddered. It was bolted to the backs of the seats and to the sides of the car itself, but not to the roof. There was an uneven, one- to two-inch gap all around the top. "Give me my phone, Jared!" I kicked again, and again the screen shuddered.

"You dropped your phone in the parking lot. You can keep kicking the panel, but that won't do any good."

But I didn't believe him. He'd clearly cut and installed it quickly, and less than professionally, to keep me from crawling into the front seat or kicking him in the head and wrecking the car. I might not be as strong as a tomcat, but I was a hell of a lot stronger than a human. If I kept kicking, eventually the screen would break.

Which meant he probably intended it as a temporary measure.

On the bright side, the very existence of the screen seemed to suggest he had nothing…personal in mind for me. If I couldn't kick him in the head, he couldn't touch me either.

"What is this?" I demanded. "You can't just kidnap people out of parking lots."

"You weren't kidnapped. You were apprehended on behalf of the Southwest Pride, on one count of trespassing. And if you don't shut the hell up, I'll add a charge for stealing my car."

"Oh, come on. I left your car in a parking lot where I knew you'd be able to track it. You did more damage to it by installing this stupid shield than I did."

"That's not the point."

"How's this for a point? *I'm* going to charge *you* with kidnapping!"

"This isn't—"

"You can't just throw me into the back of your car and call it apprehending. I'm a member of the South-Central Pride, and there is *no way* you have Faythe and Marc's permission to take me into the Southwest Territory."

"I don't need permission to remove an apprehended criminal from the free zone."

The free zone. *Shit*. He was probably right about that.

"Fine. But don't I get a phone call or something?"

Jared rolled his eyes at me in the rearview mirror. "No, you don't get a phone call. You watch too much television."

"Tele—? No one watches TV anymore. We stream—" *Damn it*. "Did you get my bag? I need my stuff. We have to go back."

He didn't even dignify that with a refusal.

"Jared, I need my stuff! I don't have any clothes."

"We'll find something for you to wear at the compound."

The compound. In California. Where Paul Blackwell was probably breeding sexism and anti-stray mentality into his great grandchildren. Which he had several of. By his age, most Alphas had long-since retired and passed on the baton to a son-in-law, but Blackwell clung to his power with a death grip that seemed stronger every year, in spite of the increasing weakness of his actual arthritic grip.

"Call Faythe. You have to call Faythe."

"My grandfather will handle that. My job is to bring you in. Nothing you say will change that."

Nothing I *say…*

I grabbed the handle of the passenger's side door and pulled until it creaked. Then I pulled a little more.

The handle broke off in my hand.

Jared glanced over his shoulder. "You're just racking up debt now, and you're going to pay for every *cent* of damage you do to my car."

"Somehow, I think whoever awards those damages might sympathize with the girl you locked into a homemade prison cell in the back of your car, like a psycho!" I scooted across the seat and ripped the other door handle off, but by then, the goal was no longer simply doing damage to piss him off. It was finding a way to make him stop the car.

If I could expose the mechanics behind the door panel, there *had* to be a way to disengage the child safety locks…

With the door handle gone, I began pulling on the "oh shit" handle over the window. The one you hold onto when you ride with Marc, and he takes all the turns too fast. I pulled and pulled, but it didn't budge, so I turned to face the door and propped both feet against it for better purchase.

The plastic casing around the handle creaked, then finally split apart beneath my hands. A jagged edge of plastic speared my palm and drew blood.

"Shit!"

Jared sniffed the air on the other side of the plexiglass. "Did you just hurt yourself?"

"Well, let's put it this way—I hope you weren't supposed to deliver me without a scratch, because that ship has sailed." I slapped my bleeding palm onto the clear divider and rubbed it around, leaving a bright red smear of blood in the approximate shape of my hand.

"You know, if you obstruct my view, I can't drive safely, and that puts us both at risk."

"Then stop the fucking car." I squeezed my palm to draw more blood, then slapped my hand against the screen again, directly in line with the rearview mirror. "As fast as you're driving, this isn't safe anyway." I frowned at the speedometer, viewed through a smear of my own blood. "Why are you going so fast? This isn't a race."

Or was it?

I spun to look through the rear windshield, leaving a bloody print on the fabric of the seat back, but if Justus were somehow following us, I couldn't see him. However, I *could* see several other cars. None were close enough to see me yet, but…

Pulse racing, I scratched at the wound on my palm to reopen it. Then I smeared my finger in the blood and began writing in reverse on the rear windshield.

I'd finished capital letters H and E when Jared noticed.

"Hey!" He twisted to look over his shoulder and the car swerved to the right. I fell over on the seat, and Jared turned back to the road. "Stop that!"

"Make me!" I shouted as I pushed myself upright. Perhaps not my most mature comeback, but whatever. I squeezed more blood onto my palm, then started on the capital L. "If you don't want every motorist who drives by to call 911 and give them your license plate number, you better stop this fucking car right now!" I finished the bottom of the L and started on the P, but my palm was scabbing over again. The cut was pretty shallow.

"Kaci! This isn't a joke. We do not bring human authorities into shifter business!"

"We also don't kidnap girls from parking lots! Stop the fucking car!"

"Kaci!" He twisted to look over his shoulder again, and I noticed that the tip of his right elbow actually dipped below the plexiglass screen. Which gave me another idea.

I glanced around at the traffic and was pleased to see that the nearest other cars were well behind us. And that there was a flat, broad shoulder leading into brown Nevada dirt. No place is a good place for a car wreck, but I couldn't imagine a better-case scenario.

"Stop the car!" I shouted again as I slid down into the floorboard of the car.

Jared glanced into the rearview mirror, and when he didn't see me, he turned again.

I stuck my unwounded hand beneath the plexiglass and grabbed his arm. The car swerved to the right, onto the shoulder of the road, and he righted the wheel with his left hand.

"Stop it!" He jabbed at my hand with his elbow, but I grabbed it again and hung on. "Kaci! Stop! You're going to wreck us!"

"Then pull over!" I let go of his right elbow, then I reached under the shield to the left of the driver's seat and grabbed his left arm. The car swerved to the left.

"Damn it!" He turned right, over-corrected, and the car began to spin. "Fuck!"

I grabbed the broken "oh shit" handle and held on while he tried to control the car. But the spin was too tight.

An inarticulate scream filled the vehicle as it tipped into a roll, and I didn't realize I was the one screaming until my impact with the roof knocked the breath—and the shriek—right out of me.

Glass crunched and metal groaned. The roof of the car dented toward me. Then we were rolling again. And again. I slammed into the roof, and the rear windshield, and the plexiglass. By the time the car finally came to a halt, I was bleeding from several gashes on my forearms and one on my head, and I could no longer read the letters I'd written on the rear windshield. Both because my vision was swimming and because I'd smeared them more with every impact.

Jared groaned from the front seat.

I pushed myself upright and realized I was sitting on the roof of the car, my head brushing the seat bottom above me.

"Kaci?" My name sounded slushy coming from Jared's mouth. I peered through a clean spot on the bloody plexiglass to see him blinking sluggishly, barely conscious, hanging upside down in his seat, pinned by his seat belt.

I really should have worn one of those.

There was a gash on his forehead and a smear of blood on the steering wheel. I felt bad for a second. Hurting him hadn't been my goal. But then I banished guilt from my mind.

The bastard kidnapped me. He deserved what he got. Which was a concussion and one hell of an explanation to make up for the police.

Not to mention his Alpha/grandfather.

I had to be gone before either of those happened. But the back doors were still locked and the plexiglass hadn't—

Wait. Our roll had dented the roof hard enough for it to hit the top of the plexiglass shield. Shoving it downward and ripping free the screws that had held it in place on the passenger's side. The panel was half loose.

Heart pounding, I grabbed the right edge in both hands, trying to ignore how much blood now covered my arms and was still oozing from various cuts and scrapes. And how badly my head throbbed.

Seated on the roof of the car, I braced my feet against the bottom—now the top—of the passenger's side door and wrapped my fingers around the top—now the bottom—of the plexiglass. Then I pulled with every bit of strength I had.

The panel creaked. Or maybe that was the remaining screws holding it in place. My vision began to swim from the strain—or maybe a concussion—but I pulled harder. Then, suddenly, the plexiglas snapped in half, about a foot from the remaining screws holding it to the driver's seat.

I fell back from the momentum, and the broken slab of shield smacked me in the face. I folded it back all the way, edging around it until I could slither beneath the headrest of the front passenger's seat and open the front door.

"Kaci!" Jared sounded more alert. His eyes were open. He fumbled with his seatbelt, struggling to press the button with hands that obviously weren't communicating very well with his brain yet.

I crawled out of the car into the dirt and stood, bracing myself against the inverted vehicle until my head stopped spinning.

"Kaci!" Jared's seatbelt clicked, then there was a thump, followed by a groan as he fell.

I stumbled back from the car, wiping a paste of my own blood mixed with dirt onto my pants, and took a look around. It was still mid-day, the sun high in the sky and already baking the top of my head. Not a good time to be stranded in the Nevada desert.

Assuming this was even Nevada. We might still be in Utah. Or maybe Arizona. I hadn't paid attention to the signs we'd passed and without my phone, I had no idea how long I'd been locked in the back of that car.

But the reason the car had flipped was suddenly obvious. We'd passed the soft, sloping shoulder I'd been aiming for and rolled off a steeper incline into the dirt at the base of a series of hills. Unfortunately, there was nowhere for me to hide in the barren, craggy landscape, and I saw no houses I could run to for help.

There was nothing but dessert brush and rocky hills.

So, I shoved hair back from my face, smearing sticky blood paste across my temples, then ran up the incline toward the highway as fast as I could make my traumatized, disoriented body go.

"Kaci!"

I looked back when I got to the road and saw Jared's head and torso sticking out of the same door I'd opened, clutching at the dirt to pull himself out of the vehicle. Damn it. I'd hoped he'd be incapacitated. Or at least unconscious.

Traffic was sparse, but there were a cluster of cars coming. I raced across the road, hoping Jared would have to stop for the traffic, if he made it up to the road in time to see me cross.

The closest half of the highway was only two lanes wide, but the line I ran across it was more slanted than straight, and I had to hold my arms out to keep from falling over. When I got to the rocky median, I had to stop and throw up. Which I recognized from health class freshman year as one of the earliest signs of a concussion.

I wiped vomit from my mouth, leaving a smear of blood in its place, then forced myself back to my feet and ran across the next two lanes. My steps felt a little steadier. On the shoulder of the road, I turned. Several cars had stopped on the other side of the highway, and their drivers stood at the edge of the road, staring down at the wreck.

"Hey! Are you okay?" one of them called out to me.

More vehicles whizzed past without stopping, and I took off running again. In the distance, to the south, I saw a line of trees—the only reasonable place to hide in such a barren landscape, utterly unlike what I'd grown up with in eastern Texas, and in southern Canada before that.

I could not *live here*.

I ran as fast as I could across the rocky dessert, stopping to catch my breath, stumbling every few steps as I tripped over pebbles I couldn't see very well with my still-blurry vision. Sweat dripped into my eyes and I wiped my face with the tail of my shirt, for all the good that did. My shirt was grimy from the wreck.

A few feet later, I tripped and went down face-first in the dirt. As I picked myself up, my gaze caught on my left forearm. Blood was still dribbling steadily from the gash, and when I looked back, I found a thin trail of dark droplets leading back to where I'd crossed the highway.

Cats can't track by scent, but Jared wouldn't need to. My trail was small, but obvious, and there was nothing I could do to hide my progress until I made it to the trees.

"Kaci!" Jared shouted, his voice hardly carrying over the distance.

I kept running, my right hand clamped over the gash on my left forearm, trying to hold it closed.

Relief washed over me when I hit the tree line and the foliage provided much-needed shade. But my relief was short-lived. The patch of trees was so thin I could see all the way through it to the narrow, shallow river that fed this lush patch in the desert.

I was alone and injured, on the run in the desert.

With no good place to hide.

TWELVE

JUSTUS

MY PULSE RACED AS I SPED DOWN THE HIGHWAY, CHASING A car that might or might not have been a blue Honda Civic with my kidnapped bride trapped inside. I must have looked like a psycho, weaving in and out of the left lane, honking my horn at assholes already doing better than the speed limit on a straight, open stretch of highway, and if I'd been driving my Z4, they might have (somewhat correctly) concluded that I was a rich asshole who felt entitled to the whole road.

Yet I'd never been farther from my Z4 or a carefree stretch of highway. I'd never in my life done anything as important as this. I'd never had anyone else depending on me, and the fact that it was Kaci—and that *I'd* gotten her into this —made me press the gas pedal harder than I should have. Harder than the poor little rental could probably take for very long.

I swerved around a delivery van and finally had a clear view of…what turned out to be an aquamarine Ford Taurus.

160

Not Jared's car. And unless Kaci's was one of the small, dark heads just peering above the rear seat, aimed at a cartoon playing on a screen strapped to the back of the front passenger's seat headrest, I'd been following the wrong car for miles and miles.

And Kaci was gone.

Fuck!

My fist flew, but I stopped it about an inch from slamming into the dash board. Hurting myself wouldn't help anything, and further damage to the car would only run up a credit card bill Titus was probably already shaking his head over.

I eased off the gas a little to keep from scaring the family in the Taurus, then I passed them like a normal asshole, rather than a psychotic street racer. And as I was pulling back into the righthand lane, using my blinker and everything, a sharp movement in the traffic up ahead caught my eye.

I looked up just in time to see a car swerve to the right and plunge over the shoulder of the road into the desert, then flip. Then flip again.

Oxygen deserted me. The sudden pressure in my chest was paralyzing. I couldn't make out the color of the car from here, but I knew without even a flicker of a doubt that it was a blue Honda Accord. And that Kaci had somehow caused that crash.

That she might not have survived it.

The cars around me began to slow. The Ford Taurus dad was already on his phone, staring at the wreck as he—presumably—called 911.

I had to get to Kaci. But when the first car stopped on the shoulder of the road to help, I realized my rescue attempt would have an audience.

Shit.

I pulled the rental to a stop on the shoulder, in the middle of a line of gawker/do-gooders, then I slammed the gearshift into park and practically vaulted out of my car, without bothering to close my door before I raced around the hood. I peered over the shoulder at the wreck, blending into the gathering crowd just long enough to verify that the car lying upside down at the base of a hill was, in fact, Jared Taylor's.

The front of the roof was crushed, the windshield shattered.

Panic seized my lungs and squeezed. *Kaci*...

I pushed my way to the front of the small crowd. "There's a man! Someone help him!" A woman shouted, and sure enough, when I got to the edge of the embankment, I saw Jared Taylor trying to crawl out the passenger's side of the inverted vehicle. Blood dripped from his temple and his hands looked scratched up, but none of that explained his trouble making it out of the car.

But my heart leapt into my throat when I saw that the rear windshield was totally covered in smears of blood. If Jared was driving, Kaci would have been in the back.

No.

"I got it," I shouted as I scrambled down the rocky embankment. "Everybody stand back. The car could blow." I highly doubted that was true, but the last thing I needed was human interference. Unless there was a doctor or nurse in the crowd who could administer first aid to Kaci.

Screw Jared.

At the bottom of the embankment, I ran twenty feet to the overturned Honda Civic, now characterized as much by dust and dents as by the dated blue paint. "Justus," Jared called, and though his voice was strong, my name came out slushy.

His slurred speech and the bloody scalp told me he had a

concussion, but I walked right past him and squatted to peer through the back window.

The rear of the car was empty, but…weird. A thick sheet of plastic had been screwed to the backs of the front seats, like the barrier between cops and criminals in a police car, and the bloody fingerprints on one end told me Kaci had snapped the damn thing in half to get out of the wrecked car.

And that she'd been bleeding when she'd done it.

She was hurt.

He would pay for that.

I squatted next to Jared, hyper aware that the crowd was still watching us, and that if I didn't at least appear to be helping him, someone else might step in. And that we were probably already being filmed on someone's cell phone.

"Where is she, you psychotic bastard?" I whispered as I peered past him to see that his legs were tangled in his seat-belt, one pinned between the steering wheel and the edge of his seat, which had been compressed during the wreck.

"She ran." Jared flinched, as if it hurt to speak, and I hoped to hell it did. "I think she's okay."

"You better hope she is, because if there's a scratch on her, I'm coming back to rip your arms off."

"Big talk from a trust fund brat," he growled, and his words sounded clearer, as if anger were giving him focus. "Your bitchy little bride caused this wreck, so any 'scratches' are her own fault."

"Is he okay?" someone shouted from behind us.

I turned to look up at the crowd, shielding my face from the sun—and any cameras—with one hand. "Yeah. His leg's caught, but I got it."

"An ambulance is on the way!" another voice yelled.

"Great, thanks!" *Damn it.* I turned back to Jared. "I'm

163

going to get you out of here, and I hope it breaks your fucking leg."

"Do it," he growled. "I can't get in a human ambulance."

But I was more motivated by his potential pain than by keeping him out of the hospital. "You know you didn't make it, right?" I said as I grabbed him beneath both arms. "You're several miles shy of the border. She's still in the free zone."

I pulled, and he shouted in pain. Then he clenched his jaw and spoke through gritted teeth. "If it were up to me, I'd tell you to take her. She's not worth this. Man-eating little bitch."

I pulled harder, and something popped. Jared screamed, and I peered into the car to see that his kneecap looked…odd. Even through his jeans.

It was dislocated. Or maybe I'd torn the damn thing off.

"She's worth *everything*, and you'll *never* get near her again."

"It's not her we want, you idiot," he growled as I hauled him onto the dirt several feet from the car. "It's you."

"Well, you're not getting either of us." Before he could argue, I turned to the crowd still gathered up the hill. "Hey, could I get some help here? I think the car's pretty stable, but this guy's heavy."

"I'm fine!" Jared called out. Then he muttered obscenities at me under his breath. But when he tried to stand, his dislocated knee folded beneath him and he crashed into the dirt with a less-than-masculine screech of pain. I might have laughed, if I weren't hyperaware that Kaci was still out there somewhere by herself. Hurt and bleeding.

As two men scrambled down from the road, I glanced around, trying to figure out where Kaci might have gone. There was nothing but desert and a few rocky hilltops on this side of the highway, but—

My gaze caught on a small trail of dark droplets in the

dirt, stretching from the car up the embankment to the road, about fifteen feet from where the crowd had gathered.

Shit. She crossed the highway.

One of the men who'd come to help saw me staring at the blood trail. "There was someone else in the car. A girl," he said. "We called out to her, but she just ran off. Must have been in shock."

"Thanks, guys," I said as he and the other newcomer helped Jared to his feet. "I'll see if I can find her." While the injured enforcer glared at me, I followed the trail of blood up the embankment toward the highway.

At the road again. I waited for a couple of cars to pass, then I confirmed that the trail led across both oncoming lanes and onto the median. I couldn't see any farther than that, but by then Kaci's destination was obvious. In the distance was a small grove of trees, an oasis likely fed by a stream or small river, and—

Movement in that direction caught my eye, and I squinted.

Kaci. My chest ached, and renewed urgency spurred me into action. It was hard to tell across the distance, but she seemed to be limping. Or stumbling.

I hurried back to the rental, relieved to see that oncoming cars hadn't yet ripped the open driver's side door off, then I started the car and swung onto the road again as fast as I could. I took the first available turnaround, then sped back toward the wreck from the opposite side of the highway. When the trees came into view, I slowed and veered carefully onto the dirt, fully aware that the rental car was a sedan, not an SUV.

I drove past the thin length of woods and parked at the end, facing the direction we'd need to head to put more distance between us and the Southwestern territory boundary. Then I got out of the car and took off through the foliage.

Kaci only had a few minutes' head start on me. I was determined to find her and make up for putting her in danger in the first place.

This was my chance to do the right thing—even if that meant risking execution to take her home.

THIRTEEN

KACI

DESPERATE, I GLANCED AROUND AS I STUMBLED THROUGH the underbrush. The woods looked thicker to the west, so I headed that way, and when I found as dense a patch of under-brush as I was likely to, I squatted in it to rest while I examined my wounds.

My head was tender, but there was a lump in my brow, rather than a dent, so I decided to call myself lucky on that front. I had to use the filthy tail of my shirt to wipe the blood from my arms. Most of my scratches were minor and shallow, but the laceration in my left forearm was long and deep, and it welled with more blood every time I tried to clean it.

The cut needed stitches, at the very least. But my only options were to try to tie the wound closed with a strip of cloth from my shirt or try to heal it by shifting into cat form. As my body reassembled itself, it would naturally begin to heal my wounds. At the very least, that would slow the bleeding in my arms and accelerate the scabbing process.

Unfortunately walking around as a big black cat would be dangerously conspicuous in the middle of the desert, especially in broad daylight, because in nature, most large cats are crepuscular; they're mostly active at dusk and dawn. I did have this handy—if shallow—patch of woods, which should shield me from human notice. However, I wouldn't be hard for Jared to find while I was leaking fragrant blood all over the place, even if he couldn't actually track me by scent.

But maybe he wouldn't bother looking for me. His car was trashed, and he'd have to explain that to both the police and to Paul Blackwell. And he was hurt. If the cops got to him before he got to me, they might make him go to the hospital, which would open a whole new can of worms for him, considering the risk of medical care exposing our species to the public.

Maybe if I hurried, I could shift to accelerate the healing of my arm, then climb one of the trees and hunker down out of sight for a while. Maybe Jared would walk right past me, if he came looking at all.

That felt like my best bet, so I knelt in the underbrush and took off my clothes, shaking from exhaustion and stress. I spread my shirt and jeans out on the ground and lay down on top of them. Then I closed my eyes and focused on breathing deeply. On blocking out the pain in my head and my arm, as well as the feline sense of urgency demanding that I *run* until I dropped dead, rather than get caught, though my human mind knew there was a better, if riskier, solution.

When my breathing was even and my hands had stopped shaking, I began to visualize what I wanted to happen. Speed was critical, but if I freaked myself out, the process would actually take longer.

My first shift had been five years ago. It was traumatic,

violent, and completely unexpected. I'd long-since learned to control the process and had never once, since the day Faythe found me in the woods, lost control of myself in cat form. But that old fear was still there. Still very real. It was still my worst nightmare.

In cat form, I still felt like a monster.

Tears filled my eyes as my jaw began to pop. That sound cascaded down my spine, then echoed through the rest of my joints, and more tears fell, not from the pain, though there was plenty of that, but from the memories.

I had never loved shifting like the others did, and I probably never would. I would never love to race through the woods and hunt and eat raw game, because where they saw sport and exercise—tapping into a primal nature that was as much a part of us as were our human selves—I saw violence and death. And this time was no different.

As my legs began to thin out and reform, shooting pain through both muscle and bone, I remembered my mother and my sister. I remembered screaming in agony in my backyard as my body tore itself apart, out of nowhere. As my fingernails grew into claws, I remembered those very claws swiping and slashing at the mother who'd given me life and raised me, because I hadn't known how to handle my own terror and confusion. Because in *her* terror, she had become a threat. Because my newly-feline self had lashed out through untempered instinct.

While my jaw elongated and my teeth moved around in my mouth, sharpening into curved points, I thought of that woman in the woods in Montana. The hiker. I remembered dragging her body into a tree through some compulsion I'd had no way of understanding.

All I'd known for sure that day, trapped in the body of a

creature I still hardly understood, was that I was hungry. And that she'd smelled like food.

Finally, fur sprouted all over my reshaped body in that tiny green patch in the middle of the desert, but my mind was still far away, trapped in past traumas. In old sins I could never forgive myself for. In violent acts I blamed on the very beast ripping its way into the world through my human flesh, because no matter how guilty I felt, I could not let myself bleed to death or get recaptured—not even to pay penance for what I'd done. The instinct to survive was stronger than anything else I'd ever experienced both now, as I lay vulnerable and exposed in the last seconds of my shift, and five years ago, when I'd killed my own mother and eaten human flesh to keep from starving.

Ultimately, my body would win out over my mind. Even if I hated myself for it for the rest of my life.

"Kaci!"

Startled, I shot upright on four legs, backing instinctively away from the voice. Heart racing, I licked my front left leg, testing out my new wound. The taste of my own blood was familiar, and in cat form, it didn't bother me. The pain was much less than before, and the gash had already started to close.

If I climbed a tree before it was fully healed, it might reopen. But if I didn't…

I looked up and judged the distance in less than a second, my feline instincts doing mental physics my human brain could never have managed. Then I leapt, without conscious thought of how far I was going or where I would land.

My claws grasped the bark of a tree about a foot in diameter, digging in with all four sets. Pain shot through my front left leg again as the laceration reopened, but I pushed that pain to the back of my mind. Then I leapt again. Straight up.

Pushing off against the bark with all four legs. I caught the tree farther up, spared a moment for balance, then leapt again.

And again.

And again.

Any higher, and the stunted desert tree would start to bow. So I took one more little leap up to a small fork in the branches thick enough to support the weight of my torso, to take some pressure off my legs. This would have to be high enough.

I hunkered down to wait. To watch.

Every bird that chirped sent alarm racing through me. Every creature that burrowed through the underbrush below made me flinch.

"Kaci! I know you're out here!" Footsteps crunched through twigs and leaves to my east. Movement in that direction caught my eye, but then it was gone.

A low, soft growl rumbled up from my throat.

"We have to go!"

What? That didn't sound like something Jared would say. In fact, that didn't sound like Jared at all. But surely that was just my unreliable ears, currently overwhelmed by the thunderous rush of my own pulse.

"Kaci! It's me! Please come out! Are you— Shit!"

The footsteps were right below me. I looked down and found someone holding the clothes I'd abandoned on the ground, almost directly beneath my tree. It was hard to tell from the angle, but he didn't look big enough to be—

The man looked around, then he walked several feet away, peering through the underbrush. Then he turned. And looked up, squinting at the trees to the east.

Justus. Where the hell had he come from? How had he found me?

A whine leaked from my throat. He looked up, still

holding my bloody, filthy clothes. "Kaci?"

The relief on his face was the most beautiful thing I'd ever seen in my life.

FOURTEEN

JUSTUS

THE SPARSE VEGETATION MADE MY SEARCH EASIER THAN IT would have been in Eastern Texas or even Mississippi, where the woods were thicker, the trees taller, the underbrush much denser. The scent of her blood was strong enough to tell me I was close, but unlike dogs, cats can't track by scent.

"Kaci!"

Focus, Justus!

Eyes closed, I mentally sorted through the myriad of sounds around me, tossing out the rodent squeaks and the frantic digging of something small burrowing into the earth. Finally, I made out a distinctly feline huffing inhalation, tinged with a soft, scared growl she probably didn't even realize she was making.

I headed toward her, and a few minutes later, I found Kaci's clothes, laid out on the ground on a bed of leaves. I bent to pick them up and shook debris from them. They were stained with blood and dirt, and the sweat that had soaked into them smelled like fear.

"Kaci!" I called again. "I know you're out here! We have to go!"

Something moved in the trees above me, and I looked up to find her staring down at me through a familiar set of hazel eyes, more green than brown in cat form.

Relief flooded me, and a little of the tension in my chest eased as she worked her way down from the tree, purring softly. "Come on. Jared's trying to fend off some do-gooders who saw the crash, and I'm sure the cops are on the way. We need to get out of here."

Her head bobbed, then she suddenly leaped gracefully onto the ground at my feet with a soft thump.

"Are you okay?" I asked, and she rubbed her cheek against my calf. That was more of an affectionate greeting in cat-speak than an actual answer, but I'd take it, for the moment.

"I missed you too." I scrubbed the fur between her ears, more like you'd pet a puppy than a one-hundred-ten-pound cat, but I wasn't sure how else to express physical comfort when I was in human form and she was not. "If this is what happens when I let you out of my sight, you can bet that'll never happen again."

She rubbed the entire length of her body against my left leg, then made her way back up my right, evidently telling me that she was fine with that plan.

"Let's go." I threw her clothes over my arm and led the way toward the rental, careful to keep an eye on her as we picked our way through the thin foliage, because in addition to a cut on her left front leg, there was a shiny patch of still-wet blood on her head, above her right eye. Though it wasn't bleeding as badly as the laceration, it could actually be the worse of the two wounds.

"I've got your stuff in the car." I kept up a dialogue as we walked, trying to think of everything she would probably be asking me, if she had the use of her human tongue. "Your phone's fine; just a little scratched up from hitting the concrete. And we'll get you some food as soon as we can. I'm sure you're starving after your shift."

She stiffened a little at that, and too late, I realized that post-shift food was probably a touchy subject for a cat whose peers called her a man-eater.

Bastards.

"I parked as far from the wreck as I could, to keep us from being seen. Jared's hurt, but still capable of causing trouble," I said, and her snort in reply sounded distinctly curious. "His leg was pinned between the steering wheel and his seat when I got to him, and I think I dislocated his knee pulling him out of the car."

Every few steps, she paused to lick her injured leg, and I remembered what Vic had told me about cat-form saliva helping to keep wounds clean. And according to Dr. Carver, it would also promote the growth of new skin cells, which helped animals' wounds heal faster than humans' wounds.

Though nothing would be as good as stitches, some antibiotic cream, and a big bandage, once we got far enough away from Jared that it would be safe to stop for first aid.

"You okay?" I asked when she stopped for the millionth time to lick her wound. She bobbed her head at me, but she looked a little woozy, so I picked up the pace, worried that her concussion would lead to her collapse before we made it to the car.

If that happened, I would damn well carry her.

We stepped out of the woods just feet from where I'd

parked the rental, and I opened the back door for her. She climbed into the bench seat and gave the upholstery a regretful look, considering the blood and dirt she was covered in. Then she noticed the fist-sized dent in the dashboard.

"Yeah, I got a little frustrated earlier," I admitted. "I really should have bought insurance when I rented the car…"

She huffed in amusement.

I slid into the driver's seat and looked back at her. "You rest, but try not to fall asleep until I've had a chance to look at your head wound. I'm going to get us out of here, and as soon as it's safe, I'll stop for food."

As I pulled onto the highway, headed deeper into the free zone and away from the Southwest territory, she sat up on the rear floorboard, holding her head just high enough for a glimpse of Jared and the wreck she'd caused as the first police car pulled to a stop along the side of the road, his lights flashing bright blue and red. As we passed, I waved to Jared, who was sitting in the back of an ambulance, his left leg splinted beneath jeans cut open to his thigh, while an EMT examined the wound on his head.

Then I took off to the east at five miles over the speed limit, before anyone could notice the big black cat riding in the back of my car.

A few minutes into the drive, I realized Kaci's breathing had grown slow and even. I tilted the rearview mirror down until I could see her, stretched across the floorboard in spite of the hump pressed against her midsection. I hadn't meant to let her go to sleep with a concussion, but as long as I could hear her breathing, I figured she was probably okay. And she was clearly exhausted.

A couple of minutes after that, I remembered to call Marc back. He answered before I even heard the phone ring. "Please tell me you have her."

"I have her. But only because she made Jared wreck the car. She's got a gash on her left front leg and another one on her forehead, but she seems okay, other than that. She's asleep in the back seat."

"And Jared?"

"When we pulled away from the scene of the crash, he was being treated by EMTs and the cops were pulling up. He's going to have to think quick to explain the plexiglass barricade he rigged up in the back of his car, and all the blood on the rear windshield."

"How much blood? Is she still bleeding?"

"I think so. I was going to stop for some first aid supplies as soon as I find a pharmacy."

"Wait until you get out Nevada, if you think you can," Marc said. "Then I want you to head back to St. George, rent a room at a different hotel, lock the door, and wait for Vic and Chris. They're still on their way from Phoenix. I don't want the two of you traveling by yourselves after this. You shouldn't have been in the first place."

"I know. I'm sorry."

"Tell that to Kaci, when she wakes up. And to Faythe, when you get back."

That, I was not looking forward to.

"Okay. I'll call you back with an address when we're settled in somewhere."

"Take care of her, Justus. Everyone else may be judging you for what you did in Mississippi, but everyone who matters will be judging you on what you do *now*."

"Understood."

"And by the way, you're fired."

No longer an enforcer. I'd known that was coming, yet the words stung more than I'd expected.

As soon as we crossed back into Arizona, I began searching

for a pharmacy, but because our route would only take us across the tip of the northwest corner of the state, I didn't find any good place to stop until we'd made it into Utah, and all the way back to St. George. And I have to admit that as I drove past the same small town I'd raced through that morning in search of Kaci, I felt like we were now farther than ever from our forever island.

Not that that would ever happen now. The safest place for Kaci was with her family. I should never have taken her off the ranch.

The GPS on my phone led me to a pharmacy a couple of minutes from the highway, and I parked at the back of the lot, hoping no one would get close enough to see the giant, sleeping cat in the back of my car. Then I rushed through the store and came out with food, a case of bottled water, a case of soda, over-the-counter pain killers, antibiotic cream, a light blanket, and every kind of bandage I could find.

Kaci was still asleep when I got to the car, and when I was sure she was actually breathing, I pulled onto the street, then into the first decent-looking motel I found. Though I'm fundamentally opposed to the very concept of a motel, I couldn't very well sneak a big cat up the elevator and down the halls of a hotel.

"Hey." In a parking space at the back of the lot, I twisted in my seat to stroke her head gently. "Wake up, Kaci."

She blinked hazel cat eyes at me, her pupils round like a lion's, rather than pointed like a house cat's. She started to sit up, but I shook my head.

"Stay down. We're back in St. George, at a hotel. I have to go get us a room, but I don't want to leave you here without telling you where I'm going." She nodded, and I pulled the new blanket from the pharmacy bag on the front seat. "I'm going to cover you with this, and I want you to just stay hidden until I get back, okay?" I shook the blanket out, and she nodded again. Then she laid down, folding her paws beneath her head on the hump in the center of the floorboard. Which was already grimy with blood and dirt.

"Okay I'll be right back." I covered her, then got out of the car and locked it.

I requested a room on the first floor, at the back, which probably made the clerk immediately suspicious. But my platinum card seemed to smooth that over, and since we were no longer on the run from both my Alphas and my brother, there was no reason not to use the card.

The clerk gave me two keys, and I parked as close as I could get to our room. Then I unlocked the door, did a cursory exam to make sure the room was acceptable, and threw the bolt over with the door open, to keep it from closing while I went back for Kaci.

When I was sure the parking lot was empty and no one was watching from any of the motel room windows, I opened the back door of the car and escorted Kaci into the room. I went back out for our luggage and the pharmacy bags, and when I returned, I found her in the tub, shifting back into human form.

While she finished her shift, I called Marc and gave him our motel information, for him to pass along to Vic and Chris. "How's she doing?" he asked.

"She's shifting back. I'll be able to ask her in a minute. I got food and first aid supplies, so we're going to get her cleaned up, then eat and rest while we wait for the guys."

"Justus? I'm going to take a shower," Kaci called from the bathroom.

"I heard that," Marc said over the phone. "Tell her to take a bath instead, until you're sure she won't faint from blood loss or the concussion. Help her if she needs it. And do *not* take advantage."

"I would *never*," I growled, beyond caring whether or not that would be considered rude to an Alpha.

Marc actually chuckled. "I believe you. But I have to say it. She's like my daughter."

"She's like my *wife*," I shot back, irritation building inside me.

"No," he said. "She's not. She's like a teenager who made a stupid mistake."

"I—"

"Shut up and listen," he snapped. "Faythe and I are not going to try to separate the two of you, because we know that will only make you cling to each other harder, and because no matter what you think, we don't believe in thwarting young love. But we *do* believe Kaci's too young to get married."

"Didn't you try to marry Faythe when she was eighteen?" I probably should have reassessed my confrontational tone, but he had *no right* to an opinion on my marriage—new though it was.

"Yes, and that was a mistake, and I paid for it for the next six years."

"It was Faythe's decision not to marry you then. Just like it was Kaci's decision to marry me two days ago," I growled.

"Agreed. But I suspect there's a reason this hasn't yet been…consummated. Don't you?"

I let silence answer for me.

"Good. Now take care of her as if she's the most important thing in the world—"

"She *is*."

"—but do *not* start thinking of her as yours, in any sense of the word."

"What the hell does that mean?"

Marc's pointed silence on the other end of the line reminded me that I wasn't supposed to use profanity when speaking to an Alpha. *Oops.* "Justus, I'm going to give you some advice," he said at last. "Because as new as you are to the biological demands and hormonal impulses of a Shifter, you're even newer to the realities of our society, and the point where those two aspects converge is particularly difficult to navigate for a man in your position."

I sank onto the side of the hotel bed, still listening with one ear for any sounds of distress from the bathroom. "What point of convergence would that be?"

"The point at which an adopted stray falls in love with a tabby. I may be the only man in the world who understands exactly what you're going through right now. Those conflicting impulses. That irrational anger when someone who outranks you gives you an order. That consuming drive to protect her from any- and everyone—even the other people who love her. Even if she doesn't need your protection."

"Titus has been in my position."

"In love with a tabby, yes. But an adopted stray? No. When your brother fell for Robyn, there was no one around who outranked him. There was no other authority to rankle his fur."

"What the—" I bit off the profanity with a roll of my eyes. That was a *stupid* rule. "What are you talking about?"

"From a hormonal, instinctive perspective, falling for a tabby makes a tom feel like he's above the rules. Like no one else has any right to tell him what to do. That's because historically, all the way back to our cave-dwelling ancestors, the tom who gets the girl rules the whole Pride. Kaci has accepted your advances, at least on some level. Your hormones are preparing you to...well, to take over. To become an Alpha. But your hormones are writing a check your body can't cash."

"All I want is to be with Kaci. I don't care about being an Alpha. That's literally never occurred to me." I didn't even know if I was going to be alive in a week.

"Yes. I'm sure that consciously, that's true. But beneath that, on a primal level, your body chemistry is pushing you to reject authority. To *become* the authority, in order to establish the strength that would have historically been necessary to protect your family. To gather a Pride around you, to help you protect that family. Times have changed. As a society, we've learned to listen to our human halves over our feline halves in matters of gender equality—though admittedly, the women learned that faster than most of the men. Hell, some of the men *still* haven't caught on. In part, that's because our hormones haven't progressed as fast as our brains."

"If you're worried that I'm going to try to get Kaci pregnant or challenge you or something—"

"No." Marc sighed over the phone, and I realized this wasn't any easier for him to say than it was for me to hear. "I think your head will prevail in those particular areas. Though in case I'm wrong, let me take this opportunity to remind you that *I will end you* if you fuck this up."

"Noted. If that's not the problem, what *are* you worried about?"

"That instinct to argue. To shrug off orders. To do things your way. You lack the experience to make those calls, no matter what your body is telling you. That could get Kaci hurt. That could get both of you killed. So, when Vic and Chris arrive, I expect you to remember that they outrank you, and they have Kaci's wellbeing in mind just as much as you do."

I found that last bit hard to believe. *No one* cared about

Kaci like I did. No one was better prepared or more deter-mined to protect her.

Wait, what?

The very strength of that thought made me wonder if Marc might actually have a point…

"Is it always like this?" I whispered into the phone, suddenly conscious of the fact that Kaci might be able to hear the whole conversation, though the bathroom door. "You're saying every tom who falls in love with a tabby goes through this?"

"No. Just the ones whose advances are accepted or encouraged. Jace went through this when he and Faythe were…a thing. But Brian didn't, back when he was engaged to Abby, which should have clued all of us in to the fact that their relationship wasn't going to work out. But all of the others—the natural-born toms—know how to deal with this. They grow up expecting it. The only exception I know of is Owen. He's shown no Alpha tendencies, even though he's been with Manx for years. But I suspect they're the exception that proves the rule."

The sound of running water came from the bathroom. "I have to go. Kaci's starting the shower."

"Okay. Don't forget to call me with updates."

The unnecessary reminder from Marc rubbed me the wrong way, and the realization that my reaction was likely hormonal in nature only further irritated me. I didn't like being manipulated by anything—even my own body. "I won't."

"Hey Justus, before you go…"

"Yeah?" I stood, already heading for the bathroom.

"There is a bright side to what's happening between you and Kaci."

Other than his unintentional confirmation that Kaci evidently felt something real for me? "What's that?"

"If your connection with her is strong enough to have triggered a hormonal reaction, then there is *truly* nothing in the world you wouldn't do to keep her safe. Even if that means putting yourself in danger."

I huffed into the phone. "I could have told you that without this entire, weird discussion, Marc."

"Yes." He chuckled. "But now I can actually believe it."

FIFTEEN

KACI

"HEY." JUSTUS KNOCKED ON THE DOOR JUST AS THE SHOWER was starting to warm up. "Marc says you should take a bath, until we're sure you won't pass out from blood loss."

I'm not going to…

Although I *did* feel a little unsteady. "Damn it. Okay." I flipped the lever in the tub, and the shower spray became a deluge from the faucet. But even when I flipped the other lever for the stopper, water seemed to be draining out of the tub. "Shit."

"Do you need help?" Justus called, and I jumped. I hadn't realized he was waiting by the door.

Did I need help? Bathing? From the gorgeous guy whose mouth was like candy and whose touch made me want to tackle him and rip his clothes off with my teeth?

Yes. I might need a *lot* of help. But if I got the kind of help I wanted, he'd be free to fly off to his island with his fortune, and leave me alone in the South-Central Pride. And as lonely as I'd been before Justus—before I'd understood how much happier I could truly be—post-Justus loneliness would no doubt be even worse.

Having something and losing it was worse than never having it in the first place.

But he said he'd never leave again.

Yes. He had. But people say a lot of things they don't mean in moments of stress or relief. And they're not even always lying. Sometimes they're just…wrong.

Justus couldn't stay unless we found him one more vote. And even if we did, who was to say that he'd stay after his acquittal? He wouldn't need me anymore, and even though he liked me now, once the novelty wore off and that inevitable boredom set in, I'd still be the man-eater, and he'd still be one of the hottest, wealthiest, most eligible tomcats in the history of ever. Even if he was a stray.

"Kaci?"

"Um…no, I'm fine," I called through the door, as I flipped the stupid drain switch again.

"You don't sound sure of that. I promise I won't try anything." The next *thunk* against the door sounded more like his head than his knuckles. "Please let me help you."

"Okay. Hang on." Against my better judgement, I wrapped myself in a towel, flinching when the motion twisted my left arm and reopened my laceration, then I opened the door. "I'm really fine. I'm just grimy, and…" I shrugged and held my left arm out. "This hurts like a bitch."

"And bath water will probably sting." He glanced at the tub. "If we're able to actually accomplish a bath." Justus sat on the edge of the tub and flipped the drain switch. But the water only drained faster. He flipped it again, then shoved up even harder with the heel of his palm.

Something clicked beneath the tub, and the water started collecting.

"Thanks." I opened a travel-sized bar of soap from the sink and set it on the edge of the tub. "Um… Could you grab my shampoo?"

"Sure."

While he was gone, I laid my towel on the floor and stepped into the tub, then tucked my knees up to my chest. Technically, this was still post-shift nudity, which should have been void of any sexual context, but the addition of a bathtub and warm water seemed to push the whole thing into a gray area. A very, very tempting gray area.

Justus came back with both the shampoo and conditioner from my backpack, and he stopped in the doorway as if he'd hit a brick wall. "Sorry. I knew you'd be naked, and I swear I'm not staring. I'm just… You're so beautiful."

"I'm covered in blood and grime." I hugged my knees to my torso.

"You could be covered in vomit and sludge and I'd still think you were the most beautiful thing I've ever seen."

I tried to cover my self-consciousness with a laugh. "I'm already wearing the ring. You don't have to say things like that anymore."

"I'm not saying them on purpose." He sank onto his knees next to the tub, on the towel I'd laid on the floor. "I don't seem to have much control over my own mouth when you're near. Especially when you're naked. But again, for the record, this is not real nudity, nor will I treat it as such. This is injured-nudity."

And I would lay my injured arm on the side of the tub to remind us both of that, if I wouldn't be exposing the side of my left breast with the motion.

"So, what can I…?"

"Um…" Normally, I'd lie down in the tub to wet my hair, but I wasn't about to stretch out naked in front of him. "Can you grab one of those?" I nodded to the cellophane-wrapped plastic cups stacked on the counter. "To help with my hair?"

He grabbed the top cup and tore off the wrapper, then sat on the edge of the tub and held it beneath the flow of water from the faucet. "Tilt your head back."

I obeyed, my eyes closed, and he poured the water over my hair slowly. "That feels so good," I whispered. "I hate being dirty."

He laughed. "Except when you eat desert."

I opened my eyes and glared up at him. "Ha, ha. Maybe you could hand me my shampoo without commentary?"

He grinned as he grabbed the bottle from the counter, but instead of giving it to me, he squirted some right onto the top of my head.

I gasped. I could tell from the weight of the glob alone that it was way too much.

"Was that wrong?" He frowned down at my head. "How do I do this? I've never washed this much hair before."

"And I had no plans to change that." I reached up, tucking my knees tighter to my chest, and showed him how to work the shampoo into a lather, while incorporating the bulk of my hair.

"Let me help."

"That's okay." I flinched when my lathering motion pulled on my laceration.

"You're in pain. Let me do it. Please."

"Fine." The shampoo *was* my favorite part of a trip to the salon. Faythe hated having her hair done, but Karen and I went every few months, so she could get her straight, gray hair trimmed back to shoulder length, and I could get mine…

well, washed and blown out. Though that was as adventurous as I'd gotten so far.

"How's that?" Justus asked. His fingers were strong, but unsure.

"It's good."

"You're lying. If you tell me something feels good when it doesn't, you're really just cheating yourself out of pleasure."

"Did you mean for that to sound dirty?" I demanded, scowling up at him.

He grinned down at me. "Will you get mad if I say yes?"

"Yes." But even *I* didn't believe me. "You have to kind of work the lather all over. Like you do with your own hair, but without massively tangling the length of it."

"I'm on it." By the time my hair and scalp were thoroughly clean, his fingers felt so good that I let him keep going just for the fun of it. "I think we're ready to rinse, right?"

"Not just yet. Keep scrubbing."

"Are you sure?"

"My hair was *really* dirty."

Justus scooped up a cup full of water and dumped it right over my face.

I sputtered at him in shock and wiped my eyes with my right hand. Then I flicked water at him. "Jerk."

"Sorry. I couldn't resist. Let me rinse your hair for real. I'll be good, I promise." But I was no longer sure I wanted him to be good.

After the shampoo, I let him rub conditioner into my hair, but then I made him leave the room to let it sit while I washed the rest of myself on my own. One handed.

While he was gone, I heard the microwave buzz, and the scent of lasagna wafted in from under the door.

Then he came back to rinse out the conditioner, and he

even closed his eyes while he helped me out of the tub. I dried off, careful of my left arm, then stepped into the clothes he brought me while he set up the first aid center at the table in the other room.

We shared the microwave lasagna right out of the box, eating with plastic forks, washing down bites of cheese and pasta with sips from lukewarm cans of soda. Then his gaze settled on my still mostly-open wound.

His phone buzzed with a text while he was peeling the seal from the bottle of alcohol. I glanced at it, and the blood drained from my face. "Why is Vic texting you?" I demanded. "What did you do?"

He gave me a guilty look. "I didn't mention that? Marc's sending them up from Phoenix to meet us." He glanced at the text. "And they're evidently about an hour away."

"No!" I grabbed the phone from him, but I didn't know the code to unlock it. "They'll take us back to the ranch, Justus!"

"Um…that's kind of the plan."

"No!" I stood and backed away from him, clutching my still oozing arm to my chest. "That is *not* the plan. We're going to get you that other vote."

"Well, we're going to have to do that from the Lazy S. If Blackwell gets you into his territory, he can try you for trespassing there, under his own terms. Marc says he won't hurt you, but he seems to think the old man's not above using you as a pawn to get to me. Or to force some other decision to go his way with the council. We *have* to take you home, so you can be tried there. Under Marc and Faythe's terms."

"But what about Taylor's vote?"

"We have a long drive back to think about that. And we'll still be together." He sighed. "Please sit down and let me clean that cut out before it scabs over."

"There's no real danger of that. I've broken it open about four times."

"Then let's bandage it up." He laid a clean, folded rag from the bathroom on the table. "Set your arm here. Come on, Kaci, I'm trying to help you."

"I liked the shampooing help better than the kind where you decide to take us back to Texas without consulting me."

"You were kind of out of reach at the time, and I had to call Marc. I didn't know if Jared was taking you on behalf of the Southwest Pride, or for his own nefarious purposes, and without knowing that, I couldn't tell whether he'd taken you north or south. If I hadn't called him, I wouldn't have found you, and you'd be back at the old man's compound right now, getting ready for a hearing in his puppet court."

"No, I'd probably still be in that little patch of woods."

"Bleeding," he insisted. "Waiting for Jared to get free of the paramedics and come after you. Or for Blackwell to send more of his men for you."

"Fine." He was right. But I didn't have to like it. I sank into the chair he'd pulled out for me and laid my arm on the rag.

"This will sting," he said as he lifted the bottle of alcohol.

"It's not my first cut, Justus," I snapped.

He sat in the other chair and leveled a gaze at me. "Would you rather do this yourself?"

"No. I'm sorry. I just…"

"You just what?" He poured alcohol into the lid of the bottle, then dribbled it from the lid onto my arm.

My wound bubbled, as if the alcohol were as angry as I was, and the burn was pretty fierce. And cathartic. "I don't want this to be over, and once Vic and Chris get here, it will be. They'll break this spell, or whatever this is."

Justus set the bottle down and took my right hand in both

of his. "Kaci. This won't be over until *you* want it to be over."

"That's cute." I sounded so bitter I even surprised myself. "If we don't get you that vote, they're going to convict you. If we run, they'll come after me. This will be over no matter what we want, one way or another, and I've known that the whole time. It's just…as long as it was you and me on a road trip we kept inventing reasons to prolong, 'together' at least looked possible. Hell, 'forever' looked possible. But now, Vic and Chris are on their way, and we're going to lose this…" I squeezed his hand. "…this private moment in an hour."

"I'm sorry." He picked up a long strip of sterile bandage and began to wrap it around my wrist. "I had to call Marc. I wasn't going to risk losing you just because…"

Because he was too afraid or proud to ask for help. He wasn't going to say it out loud. But that was the truth. He'd given up his chance to run, so he could go after me.

Justus secured the end of the bandage in place with a metal butterfly clip. "It'll probably need stitches soon, but…"

I stood and climbed into his lap, straddling him on the cheap, armless hotel dining chair.

"What are you doing?" His hands settled onto my hips. His heart began to race, and the sound gave me an exhilarating, powerful feeling.

"Whatever I want."

"Are you sure?" His gaze bored into me, searching for doubt.

"Don't read too much into this," I whispered as I leaned toward him and my wet hair fell over us both. "I just want… Um… I want to at least pretend this is forever."

"This doesn't have to be pretend." He slid one hand behind my neck and kissed me. "I'm not asking for the ring back." Another kiss. "I wouldn't take it if you *tried* to give it back."

His lips moved down my throat, and I let my head fall back. His hands tightened on my hips, then slid up my sides, over my shirt, and suddenly that wasn't enough. I wanted to feel his hands on my skin.

But I couldn't ask for that. I couldn't even *tell* him that. So maybe…

I leaned down for another kiss and as I tugged his lower lip into my mouth, I slid my hands beneath his shirt, over each ridge of his abs, pulling the material up as I went. "You're so…" I murmured against the corner of his mouth.

"So what?" He seemed hungry for my answer. As if he needed to hear the words.

"So…hard."

Justus threw his head back, laughing, and my face burned.

"What?" I demanded, humiliated, as I tried to stand up.

"No, don't go." He held me in place on his lap, his grip firm, but not unbreakable. "It's just, that's not usually what girls are touching when they say that."

"Usually?"

He frowned. "No. Never mind. There is no 'usually.' There is only now. Only you."

"But there *was* a usually?" I let his shirt fall back into place. Of course there was. Justus was gorgeous, and rich, and funny. He could have any girl he wanted, and he probably had. "How usual was this usually? I mean, other than Ivy."

"Kaci, don't…" He stopped and took a deep breath. "Let's make a deal. I'm not going to ask you that, and you won't ask me."

I shrugged. "You can ask me."

"But I wouldn't. I heard you bring guys back to the ranch

at least once a week, but I'm not going to ask you for a number."

"I'm going to give you one anyway." I crossed my arms over my chest, careful of the bandage. "Zero."

"What?" His head tilted in a look of skepticism that would have been adorable, if it weren't so obviously insulting. "How can it be zero?"

"Because it's zero. I've never…had sex."

"Whoa. Wait." He picked me up and set me on my feet, then stood and backed away.

"Where are you going? Virginity isn't contagious, Justus."

"I know, I just… *How* can you be a virgin?"

I shrugged. "None of the shifter guys were interested, so…" I frowned, my gaze narrowed on him. "You mean, out of all those conversations we had on our 'wedding night,' I never told you I was a virgin?"

"No." He scowled. "And do *not* put 'wedding night' in air quotes. That really happened. We really got married."

"Then why are you standing across the room now, like you're afraid of me?"

"Because… I'm not…" He scrubbed his face with both hands, then started over. "You never answered the question. Which is still, 'how can you be a virgin?' You're beyond gorgeous. None of the guys at school…?" He shook his head again, and I got the impression he was waiting for me to take it all back. To tell him I'd been joking. "None of the guys in the barn? You can't tell me none of them were interested. Until a few months ago, I was a human guy, and I would have…" He waved one hand in a vague gesture at my body. "In a heartbeat."

"So then, why are you standing all the way over there? If

we're really married, you're allowed to…" I threw his hand gesture back at him.

"Are you asking me to?" He propped his hands on his narrow hips. "Have we switched sides on this?"

"I don't know." I ran my hands through my hair, just to have something to do with them. "Do you not want to, now?"

"Do *you* want to?"

"I *always* wanted to. Wanting you wasn't the problem."

"Oh my God, Kaci," he groaned, as if I'd just said the most erotic thing in the world. He started to reach for me, and my pulse whooshed in my ears. Then he stepped away again and gripped the back of one of the dining chairs so hard that the wood creaked.

"Okay, you can't do that anymore, Justus. This back and forth is…not good for my ego. Do you want me or not?"

Another groan. "More than anything in the *world*."

"Then what's the problem?"

"Nothing." He scrubbed his face again. "Virginity is a lot of pressure for a guy."

"And it's not for a girl?"

"That's not the same. And don't tell me that's sexist. A guy's going to have a good time either way. But a girl is… harder to please. And the first time is…"

I waited for more, but nothing more came. "So, you wish I'd already been with a few guys, so this would be easier for you?"

"*Hell no*," he growled. "I just…I don't want to mess this up."

I laughed, and I have to admit, I was a little happy to see *him* actually flush. "Are you telling me you're not any good?" I teased. "Because that's fine, if that's what you're saying. I won't know the difference. I just didn't expect you to admit that—"

195

Justus scowled. "That is *not* what I'm saying. I've never had any complaints."

"Out of all those girls…" I teased. "How many was that again?"

"Nice try. I'm sorry. This isn't a deal breaker, obviously. I just wasn't expecting it."

"Well, if being your wife's first is too much pressure for you, I'm sure I can find someone out there willing to do the job. We *are* at an eighty-nine-dollar-a-night-motel, after all." I stepped toward the door, reaching for the knob. "There's bound to be—"

"No," he growled again as he slid between me and the door, his gray eyes flashing. "Mine." He picked me up by the waist and swung me around, and I squealed as he tossed me onto the bed.

"Well, that was a quick change of heart." I scooted backward toward the pillows, ignoring the ache in my bandaged arm.

"Says the girl who wouldn't even let me see her in the bathtub." He climbed onto the bed and crawled toward me like a predator stalking prey, his gaze pinning me, his mouth turned up into a heated grin.

"You've seen me naked," I said as he crawled over me, sliding his knee between my legs on the way. "You weren't missing anything."

"I've never seen you naked in the tub." He kissed his way up my neck, and my pulse raced. "Dripping wet."

I trailed my hands slowly over his back. "So, should I get back in the shower?"

"Yes," he said, and I pushed him off, laughing as I sat up on the bed. But he tugged me back down. "Later. First I want to see you naked here."

"Just like that?" I said, as he slid one hand beneath my

shirt, his fingers skimming my stomach. Every nerve ending in my body felt like a live wire. I'd been touched before, but it had never felt like this. "Just 'take it all off, Kaci'?"

"Oh, you want more romance?" he whispered into my ear. Then he bit my earlobe, just a tiny nibble of pressure.

"Hell yes," I practically purred as his tongue trailed down my neck. "I want *all* the romance. I think I deserve it, considering that I can't remember our wedding night."

He sat up, abandoning my neck, and I groaned over the loss. "I'm never going to live that down, am I?"

"Never," I teased. "But maybe you can make up for it with the best night of my life."

"Wow. You really know how to turn on the pressure."

"Again, I have nothing to compare it to. The bar's pretty low."

"I still haven't figured that out. How does someone as smart, and funny, and hot as you are make it out of high school without…?"

I shrugged, and the comforter bunched beneath my shoulder. "No one was special enough. Until now."

Justus went absolutely still, like only a shifter can. He didn't even seem to be breathing. Yet his gaze held mine, and suddenly all the humor was gone. There was nothing left in his eyes but a deep, aching hunger, and some sense of… possession I could suddenly scent on his skin. In his pheromones.

And it was delicious.

Did I smell that good to him?

"I want to give you all of that," he whispered, still staring straight into my eyes. "All the romance. But I'm suddenly very aware that we're in an eighty-nine-dollar-a-night-motel room, and I've just fed you microwave lasagna from the freezer section of the pharmacy. I can't even identify the material this comforter is made out of. But it doesn't smell especially…new."

"I don't care." I tugged him down for a kiss, and when I opened my mouth for him, he groaned. Then he pulled away again.

"*I* care. We just got married. We should be sipping champagne on a beach in some country where you're old enough to drink. There should be fresh flowers in the room—with a bloom behind your ear—and…"

I propped myself up on my elbows and kissed him again. "I don't need any of that." Another kiss, and I slid my hand into the hair at the back of his skull to hold him close as I whispered into his ear. "Please don't make me ask you again to touch me."

He groaned. "I don't think you've actually asked me to yet."

I lay down again and gave him the sexiest smile I could muster. "Touch me, Justus. Please. But first…take your shirt off."

He laughed as he pulled his tee over his head, then tossed it onto the floor. I ran one hand over his chest, marveling at the flat planes and hard ridges. "Human guys don't look like this. They don't feel like this either. Not normal guys, anyway."

"It's the shifter metabolism, and all the hunting. Lots of exercise and large amounts of protein make for a very low BMI."

"BMI?"

"Body mass—" He shook his head. "Never mind. That's not romantic. What I'm saying is that shifter metabolism looks good on everyone. But *especially* on you." He leaned down to kiss me, and his hand slid beneath my shirt again.

I sucked in a breath, startled not by his touch, but by how badly I wanted it.

"Are you sure?" Justus propped himself up and looked down at me, frowning. "We don't have to do this just because we're married. That really just means we have the rest of our lives."

"I'm sure." I pulled him down for another kiss. "Show me what I've been missing, Justus." *In case we never get another chance…*

"Yeah. Okay. Come here." He stood and helped me off the bed with one hand, then held my gaze while his hands skimmed slowly up my sides beneath my shirt, dragging it up as he went. And as good as that felt, the sexiest part—the part that made me forget to *breathe*, was the eye contact. The way he watched me while he touched me, holding me there in that moment with him, creating an indelible connection between the delicious sensation and the man behind it.

When he got up to my bra strap, I lifted my arms, and he slowly pulled my shirt off, careful not to snag the bandage on my left arm. My shirt hit the floor and he stepped back to look at me. His nostrils flared and his pupils dilated. His pulse began to race.

Heart pounding in sync with his, I reached back to unsnap my bra, but he stepped closer, his chest brushing my breasts through the material, and stilled my hands. "Let me. That's part of it."

I nearly melted into a puddle on the carpet.

He gently tilted my head and nibbled his way down my neck to my collarbone, then over my shoulder, dragging my bra strap out of the way, and each new touch—each new place his mouth found to explore—set off a fresh wave of sensations inside me. I wanted to tell him to hurry up.

Yet I never wanted it to be over.

His fingers trailed around my back, and my bra got tighter for a second, then gaped loose. Justus slid my bra down my arms and let it fall. "You are *so* beautiful."

"Thanks, but…you say that as if you've never seen me naked before."

"I haven't. Not like this. This is different. This is *real*," he said, and somehow, I knew exactly what he meant. He stepped forward until his body was pressed the length of mine, and this time when he kissed me, my nipples got suddenly, embarrassingly hard. He groaned into my mouth, his chest pressed against mine, and my breasts felt both heavy and… achy. As if they needed—

Justus ran his left hand up my side, then stopped. His thumb brushed the lower curve of my right breast, but went no further.

"Please," I gasped against his mouth. "Touch me."

He moaned, then lifted my breast, and it was the simplest, yet most erotic sensation I'd ever felt. That same hand had touched my arm a thousand times in the past two days, and it was nice, but it hadn't changed my life.

That hand had touched my face, and my lips, and my waist, and I'd wanted more, but not enough to beg for it.

But this—

He bent and licked a line from my collarbone straight down my breast, so slowly that by the time he got to my nipple, I'd nearly lost my mind with impatience. With anticipation. His tongue circled the tip of my breast, drawing my nipple into a harder point than I'd thought possible. I groaned and pressed myself into him. Aching for his mouth.

Then his lips closed over my nipple, a warm, wet pressure.

"Oh," I breathed, as his tongue flicked over me. He

sucked lightly, and I arched toward him with no conscious thought, my body demanding more all on its own.

Justus squeezed my breast as he sucked and licked, and I buried my hands in his hair, holding him in place while I rode a wave of sensations unlike anything I'd ever felt.

I ran my hands over his chest as he came back up for a kiss. "How's it going so far?" he whispered, the stubble on his chin scratching my cheek as he kneaded my breast gently.

"What, you want a score card?"

He chuckled, and his whole body rubbed against mine. "Maybe just a ranking, on a scale of one to ten."

"Eleven. Please don't stop."

Justus groaned, then lifted me by my hips and laid me on the bed, with my legs hanging over. He lay next to me on his side and licked my other, neglected nipple while he skimmed one hand slowly down my stomach.

My breaths came in soft, fast pants.

"You can say stop whenever you want," he whispered into my ear.

"Keep going. Don't stop. Green light," I moaned, and he laughed. Then his fingers slid beneath my waistband and I sucked in a breath. My hips arched toward him, of their own accord, and I might have died of embarrassment if I weren't actually desperate for his hand to go just a little…bit…lower.

Instead, it moved back up, his fingers lightly skimming my skin—then he unbuttoned my jeans, one handed.

"That was impressive," I whispered.

"Just wait…" His mouth closed over my nipple, and I groaned again.

"Feeling more confident about this high-pressure situation?" I asked.

He laughed. "You're giving great feedback."

"You're giving great…everything."

Justus crawled off the bed, and I groaned, aching with the loss of him. Until I felt his hands at my waist. He tugged my jeans over my hips, dragging my panties with them, and my heart thumped so hard I was afraid for a moment that I might actually be having a heart attack.

Wouldn't that figure? VIRGIN DIES DURING FORE-PLAY. They'd probably carve that on my tombstone.

But then my jeans hit the floor, and his hands glided up my legs, pushing them slowly apart. He dropped a kiss on my left thigh, beginning a trail of warm nibbles leading all the way up—

Someone knocked on the door.

"Justus? Kaci?" Vic called out.

"Oh my God go away!" I shouted. Then I slapped both hands over my mouth, equal parts humiliated and really fucking pissed off.

Justus's growl told me he was just as frustrated. Reluctantly, he stood. "You're going to have to let them in." He grabbed my shirt from the floor and handed it to me.

"They can wait." I reached for him, and he took one more indulgent look down the length of my body. Then he pulled me up by one hand.

"They *won't* wait. And you're going to have to be the one to let them in." He slid my hand over the firm, warm lump in his pants. "I need a minute."

"Oh shit." I smiled as I reached for my underwear. "How long will that take?"

He headed for the bathroom. "It'll be gone the minute Vic steps through the door."

SIXTEEN

JUSTUS

I FLUSHED THE TOILET BEFORE I CAME OUT OF THE bathroom, but Vic did not look fooled. Based on the determination in his jaw line, I gathered that Marc had told him to stay between me and Kaci. Physically, if necessary. Marc might have no plans to separate us, but he wasn't—evidently —going to let us eliminate the legal possibility of an annulment by consummating the marriage.

But Vic was too much of a gentleman to ask what we'd been up to. Not that he'd need to, after Kaci cursed him through the door.

I nodded at the cast encasing his left arm and hand, except for his fingers and thumb. "Sorry about that. I assume you didn't go to the ER for the cast?"

"Of course not. One of Blackwell's grandsons is a medical intern. He took care of it."

"Can you shift like that?" I'd never really thought about

what happened to a shifter with a broken bone. And suddenly I felt even guiltier.

"Not for a month or so." He turned to Kaci, effectively dismissing the entire subject. "Okay, let's take a look at you." With his good hand, he tilted Kaci's chin up and carefully pushed hair back from her forehead to examine the wound on her temple. A growl of warning built in my throat the moment he touched her, but I swallowed it and settled for clenching my fists instead.

Marc wasn't kidding. Something had changed.

Kaci was *mine*. Not to own, but to…love. To protect. I knew damn well that Vic meant her no harm, but deep down, some part of me no longer trusted him, despite the fact that he was bigger and stronger than I was and had far more experience.

Deep down, I *knew* that no one else in the world could give Kaci what she needed better than I could, be that physical protection or…pleasure. And I didn't want anyone else to try.

I didn't even want anyone else near her.

But before that thought had even fully played out in my head, I recognized the danger inherent in it.

While Vic assessed Kaci's injuries and I stood stiffly to the side, Chris started the coffee pot set up next to the second sink, just outside of the bathroom.

Because motels suck.

"This one's scabbed over nicely, and you look pretty alert." Vic let Kaci's hair go, and it tumbled over her forehead.

"I'm fine," she snapped. "Seriously, did you guys check in yet? Because there are plenty of rooms available. You can totally go get your own. Like, now."

Vic snorted with a glance at me. "We're not staying."

I tried not to sound gleeful. "That's too bad. Do you want something to eat before you go? We could order a pizza…"

Another snort, this one from Chris, as he clicked the coffee carafe into place beneath the drip. "None of us are staying. We're hitting the road as soon as Kaci's taken care of. Thus, the coffee. If this even qualifies," he added with a skeptical glance at the packet the grounds had come from.

"Okay. Well, I'm hungry, so why don't you guys go get some food and give us, like, half an hour?" Kaci glanced at me with raised brows, and I couldn't resist a grin. "Or forty-five minutes? To finish getting ready to go. We'll meet you in the parking lot in, like, an hour. Tops."

"Sit." Vic looked almost amused as he pulled out a chair at the table for her, evidently well aware that he'd interrupted us just in time. "Let's look at your arm."

"I already cleaned it," I said as I started gathering up our things from around the room.

Kaci sank into the chair, her jaw clenched. "I'm fine," she said again.

I stuffed her dirty clothes into one of the empty plastic bags from the pharmacy, then squatted next to her chair, one hand on her knee. "Please let him look. And try to relax." I stood, then leaned in to kiss her cheek and whispered into her ear. "We were stalled, not stopped. It will happen. Some place much nicer than this. When we have plenty of time to get it right."

She looked doubtful. But she laid her arm on the table in front of Vic.

He gave me an almost respectful nod, then carefully unwound her bandage using only his good hand. "Yup, that's a bad one." He aimed the light from his phone at it. "The muscle looks like it's already starting to heal, though."

"You can see that?" I leaned in for a closer look, and Kaci rolled her eyes at us both.

"If you know what you're looking for. Have you shifted since this happened?" he asked her.

"Twice."

"That was wise."

"Yeah, and she'd probably be much better off now if she hadn't climbed a tree right after one of those shifts and ripped it open again."

Kaci kicked me under the table. "Tattletale."

"Okay, well, it needs stitches on the surface," Vic said.

I nodded. "That's one of the reasons we're going back to the ranch."

"No need to wait." Chris set a green canvas zip-up pouch on the table, then he started removing cellophane from four disposable coffee cups.

"What's that?" I asked as Vic opened the pouch and began pulling out sealed packets of sterile wipes, gloves, and a couple of instruments that looked like scissors without blades.

"It's a field medicine suture kit."

"You're going to stitch her up now?" I demanded. "Are you qualified?"

"He is," Kaci said. Though she didn't look pleased.

"Qualified, yes. Able?" Vic stood and held his broken arm up for emphasis. "Not at the moment. Chris?"

Chris took the chair next to Kaci's and sterilized his hands with one of the alcohol wipes. Then he pulled on a pair of sterile gloves that were latex-free, according to the package.

I scowled as he opened a packet containing a thin, curved piece of metal that seemed designed to cause pain.

"It's a suture needle," Kaci explained, and I made a mental note *never* to cut myself around these guys.

"Unfortunately, I don't have anything for the pain. I probably shouldn't do this, but…" Chris glanced up at Vic, who nodded and set an unopened fifth of whiskey on the table in front of Kaci. "If it was good enough for civil war soldiers…"

"Amputation and gangrene were good enough for civil war soldiers!" I snapped. "She needs a local. An injection."

Vic exhaled slowly. "This is more like a field medic's tent than a doctor's office, Justus. If you'd kept a better watch on her—"

"This isn't his fault," Kaci insisted. "It's mine."

"No, he's right." I peeled plastic from the cap of the whiskey bottle. "I shouldn't have let you go out there alone."

"Fuck you both!" Kaci snapped. "I got taken because I wasn't paying attention. That could have happened to either one of you. And I got myself out of it, thank you very much."

"And right into this." Vic lifted her arm into her own line of sight. "But that's nothing that hasn't happened to all of us." He pushed up his short sleeve to show off a jagged scar winding around his left bicep.

Chris lifted his shirt to reveal a thin white line zagging across a stomach that gave me an inferiority complex about abs I'd been pretty proud of half an hour ago.

I unscrewed the lid of the bottle and pushed it toward Kaci.

She shook her head. "No way."

Chris shrugged. "That's your call. But don't say we didn't offer." He laid her arm across the rag I'd used earlier, then began to dribble alcohol over the wound.

The alcohol bubbled and Kaci hissed. "Why does that hurt worse now than it did before?"

"Because now you're focused on the pain. Before, you were busy being pissed at me."

Vic snorted. "Why don't you piss her off again?"

"While that does seem inevitable," Kaci snapped. "I'd love for this to be a little less entertaining for the three of you." She grabbed the whiskey bottle with her free hand and scowled at it while Chris threaded his sterile needle. "This is what you and the guys do?"

Vic nodded. "A time-honored tradition. Take several gulps, and we'll wait a few minutes for it to kick in. Not too long, though, because we tend to process alcohol pretty fast."

"She has *no* tolerance," I told him. "So we need to be careful."

"Do I want to know how you know that?"

"Probably not."

"Just…throw it back?" Kaci asked, drawing Vic's attention before he could decide to press the issue.

"Wait. You'll want a chaser." I turned to look for the sodas I'd bought at the pharmacy, and Vic slapped an unopened can into my grip. "Thanks." I popped the top and set the can in front of her.

"Slow, right?" She lifted the bottle toward her mouth.

"No, this time the point is to get a little drunk. You want the alcohol to hit all at once, make you happy for a few minutes, then just sort of fade away."

"So, take a couple of big drinks in a row." Vic pulled the carafe from the coffee maker and started awkwardly filling paper cups, one-handed. "Then just sit back and wait."

Kaci nodded. Then she gulped from the whiskey bottle, and made a terrible, adorable face. Then she gulped some more. "That is *awful*," she gasped as she set the bottle down.

Vic laughed. "Good."

I handed her the soda, and she drank half of it at once.

Vic set a cup of coffee in front of Chris, then one in front of me. Both black. Then he sank onto the edge of the bed and aimed an unreadable stare at me over the top of his own cup.

"While we're waiting, why don't you tell us what the hell possessed you to steal Chris's car and take off for Vegas."

"Technically, *I* stole your car," Kaci told him Chris. "And considering my recent history, I think you should be kind of grateful that it's still in one piece."

I screwed the lid back on the whiskey bottle. "I feel like I should make sure you guys aren't going to hold anything she says while she's drunk against her."

"She's not drunk yet," Chris pointed out.

"I know. I'm just covering all the bases."

"Or trying to deflect whatever she's about to say about you?" he challenged.

"Nope. This whole thing is my fault. Not hers. But she'll probably say something different in a few minutes."

"I can *hear* you," Kaci said.

"I overheard Vic talking about the enforcer grapevine. I knew I wasn't going to get a fair trial, so I was going to try to make enough cash in Las Vegas to get out of the country." Vic rolled his eyes, and I bristled. "It's not as crazy as it sounds. I know what I'm doing. I was up to two hundred thousand before I lost it."

"Wow." Chris whistled. "I'm not sure if that makes you a really good poker player or a really bad one."

"Sometimes there's not a lot of difference between the two," I admitted. "How you feeling, Kaci?"

"Fine. Normal." She shrugged, and the motion looked just a bit unsteady. "You should go," she said.

"What?"

"I mean, we should have an hour or so alone together. But then you should go. They won't chase you. Faythe said so. So you and I should... And then you should just get on a plane."

"What's she talking about?" Vic asked.

I shrugged. "I think she's drunk."

"But why does she want you to get on a plane?"

"I can *still* hear you. And I'm not drunk. I mean maybe a little, but seriously, I think this stuff is just some kind of truth serum." She picked up the whiskey bottle and contemplated it seriously for a moment. Then she set it down again without drinking. "Justus needs to get on a plane and get out of the country, so they can't execute him. "If you assholes will get out of here for a few minutes and let us consummate this sham of a marriage, he can go, and you can drag me home, and everyone will be happy. I mean, except me. And the council. But everyone will still be alive and intact."

"This isn't a sham, Kaci." I took her good hand.

"I know. But it needs to be. You'll be alive and gone, and you'll find someone else. And Faythe's right. Eventually one of those asshole enforcers will learn to live with the idea of marrying a freak, and I'll—"

"No," I growled, squeezing her hand. "I'll kill anyone who even tries—"

"Maybe we should do the stitches now," Chris suggested as he carefully guided Kaci's arm back onto the towel. "While she's clearly feeling…despondent."

Vic sipped his coffee. "Was she like this the last time she drank?"

"No. Last time she was happy, then she vomited, then suddenly she was asleep."

"You know what would be great?" Kaci asked, and I turned to find her staring at the wicked-looking suture needle. "If I could forget this, after it's over. Like a memory exchange. I wish I could remember marrying you, and forget about this entirely."

"You can't remember your wedding?" Chris picked up the needle, and I watched, half fascinated, half horrified, as he began stitching her arm back together.

Kaci hissed in pain and turned to me. "Whiskey is *not* a painkiller."

"No," Vic admitted. "But it calms you down and helps you care less."

I took her free hand again. "Just look at me. Think about us. Tell me something. Just keep talking and it'll be over in a minute." I glanced at her arm again. "Chris looks like he's pretty good at this."

"He's not as good as Vic. Vic's been the top enforcer since Faythe and Marc took over the territory, when I was a kid." She flinched again. "But *someone* put our best suturer out of commission."

Chris frowned, but seemed too focused on his task to take serious offense.

"So, what happened?" Vic asked. "Why did Jared take you?"

"He said I was being apprehended on charges of trespassing."

"Which you're guilty of," Chris mumbled as he tugged the needle through Kaci's flesh again, and she flinched. "But why? What good does it do Blackwell to actually charge you? I can't think of a tabby ever being charged with trespassing."

"I believe Faythe was charged with trespassing once," Vic supplied.

"Okay, but that was different. That was trespassing with a side of murder. But it's not like Blackwell thinks Kaci was staging a coup against him or anything. And why would they take her, but not Justus?"

"Because they didn't have to take him." Vic frowned over his coffee cup. "Jared saw them together. He knew Justus would follow Kaci."

"He used me as bait." Kaci scowled. "That bastard! How insulting."

"But what do they want with me?" I asked. "To hold me in custody to make sure I show up for my trial? Faythe said they wouldn't chase me if I left the country, because they don't care whether I'm dead or gone. That they just want me out of the way."

"So then why lure him into the territory, if they would be just as happy to see him flee the country?" Kaci asked.

Vic shrugged, "There has to be more to this. Something we're not seeing."

"I feel like that all the time," I told him.

"Okay, I think we're done here." Chris tugged gently on the tiny knot he'd tied in the thread coming out of Kaci's arm. "Let me just…" He took a little pair of scissors and clipped the thread as close to the knot as possible. Then he tossed me a tube of antibiotic cream. "Wash your hands and apply that, then re-bandage her. We'll pack up the car."

"Where are you supposed to drop the rental?" Vic asked as he stood with his coffee.

"Denver," I told him. "That's where I was going to catch my flight."

"Well, I'm afraid you're on the hook for whatever penalty comes from dropping it off somewhere else." Vic caught my eye in the bathroom mirror while I washed my hands. "Good thing you're rich."

"Not yet, he's not." Kaci giggled as I dried my hands, then sat next to her at the table. "Though he would have been, if you'd been a few minutes later."

Vic's brow rose. "I assume that made sense to you?"

"I don't actually have access to my money yet. Hold still," I admonished as I spread cream on Kaci's fresh stitches with a clean cotton swab.

"But he will be if we have sex." She giggled again. "And seriously, we were *so* close."

Chris looked surprised. "You haven't…?" Evidently Marc hadn't *quite* filled them in.

"Not the point," Vic growled. "I'm actually not sure what the point is. Why would sleeping with your own wife make you rich?"

"Because then we'll really be married." Kaci took another drink from her soda can. "*Consummated*. Then he can inherit."

"You're a trust fund brat," Chris said, and I nodded.

Vic tossed Kaci's bag to Chris, then threw my duffle over his shoulder with his good hand. "Someone fill me in."

"There was this guy in my high school who had a trust fund," Chris said. "He had something like three million dollars coming to him. But not until he turned twenty—or got married. I swear, that stupid fucker proposed to half the girls in the school, trying to get his hands on his money early…"

They both turned to me, as the realization sank in. Vic growled. His eyes began to…churn with color. Which is when I realized they were shifting. As were his teeth. "You married her to get your money?"

"No!" I stood and backed away as they came at me. I would defend myself if I had to, but I'd rather they understand the truth. "Well, yes, but it wasn't like that. I didn't just do it for me. I did it for us. We were *both* going to go. Together."

"Forever on an island," Kaci muttered, staring at the table, her gaze unfocused. She looked sleepy. Which meant her buzz was wearing off.

"You worthless bastard." Vic advanced on me, his broken arm still strapped to his chest, evidently ready to beat me to a pulp with the other one. "She's barely eighteen years old, and she's had it rougher than you can imagine. For some rich, pretty-boy predator like you to—"

"Stop." Kaci stood, wobbling on her feet. "It's not like it sounds. This isn't his fault."

"It's okay." I reached for her, but Chris stepped between us and steadied her by the shoulders.

"Don't touch her," he snapped.

"Take her to the car," Vic ordered. "Justus and I are going to have a chat.

"Leave him alone." Tears stood in Kaci's eyes. She shoved Chris with her injured arm, then hissed at the pain. Blood leaked through her bandage.

"Let her go," I growled, struggling against a protective instinct that felt extreme, yet somehow also entirely warranted. "If you try to take her out of this room without me, I will break every bone in your body."

"Okay, everybody calm down." Vic held one hand up, palm out, moving slowly and carefully. His gaze narrowed on me, and I realized he recognized the same hormonal mayhem in me that Marc had heard in my voice over the phone. "We're going to get in the car and head straight back to Texas. Justus will sit up front with Chris, and I'll sit in the back with Kaci."

"No…" she mumbled.

"Put her in the car." Vic's voice was low and calm.

Chris led Kaci toward the hotel door, and she turned to me, eyes full of tears. She looked confused and afraid, and seeing her like that—

I burst into motion. My arm slid around her waist and I spun her carefully away from Chris as I kicked him in the chest. He went flying. Kaci clung to me with her good arm.

Vic stared at us both in astonishment.

"I said *no*," she growled at him. "I'm staying with Justus."

"I believe the lady has spoken," I said through clenched

teeth, struggling to control my racing pulse, as well as the urge to pull his arms off and beat him with them. She wanted me. She was *mine*. And I would shred anyone who came between us. If they couldn't see that, they could damn well learn the hard way.

"Fine." Vic glared at me. "But whatever you've done to her—however you convinced her that this was real—you should be *ashamed*. Marc will skin you alive when he finds out."

"Just shut up," Kaci snapped at him. "You don't know what you're talking about." Her grip on me tightened, and she turned a defiant, if slightly unsteady gaze on Vic. "I love him. *That's* why I married him. Because while the rest of you fuckers were whispering about me behind my back, he actually *had* my back. He made me feel beautiful, and wanted, and normal. So I—"

Kaci gasped and clasped one hand over her mouth. "It was my idea. I suggested we get married. *I* proposed to *you*! In front of that fountain at the hotel!"

My pulse began to slow and I smiled as I squeezed her tighter. "You remembered."

"Why didn't you just tell me?" She looked horrified. "I was so *mean* to you the next morning, and the whole thing was my idea!"

I shrugged. "I didn't think you'd believe me, if you couldn't remember it."

"Okay. That's beautiful, and all, but we have to get on the road." Vic's phone buzzed and he pulled it from his pocket to read the incoming text. "Oh, damn."

"What?" Chris leaned over his shoulder to look at the phone. He frowned. "Paul Blackwell just died."

"We need to get home." Vic headed for the door. "Right now."

SEVENTEEN

KACI

"So, what's going to happen?" I asked, watching as Faythe bounced baby Ethan with every step she took. "What does this mean for Justus's hearing?"

"We're not sure yet." Faythe paced back toward me, still bouncing. "We know that Blackwell's son-in-law, Robert Taylor will officially take over the Pride after the funeral. Which is scheduled for tomorrow."

"Wait, Robert Taylor?" Justus said. "Any relation to Ed Taylor?"

"His brother." I stood and held my arms out. "And Jared's dad. Faythe, why don't you let me take him?"

"Thanks." She laid baby Ethan gently in my arms, then snatched a pacifier from the edge of her desk. "Don't forget to support his head." Then she frowned. "How's your arm?"

"Fine. It was just a gash, and I shifted twice this morning. Your mom's going to remove the stitches this afternoon."

"Okay." With a sigh, she sank into her rolling chair and

propped her elbows on the table, then she turned to Justus. "So, Paul Blackwell's name was drawn at random for your tribunal. His son-in-law's name was not. Robert Taylor is insisting that he'll inherit a position on the tribunal when he takes over the pride."

"Is that a problem?" Justus asked. "Do we not want that?"

Faythe shrugged. "Blackwell ruled the Southwest Territory with a notoriously closed fist. He never let anyone speak for him. Because of that, other than vague rumors that Robert is a little less conservative, I know nothing about where he stands on the unresolved issues on the council's plate. Which currently include your hearing and your brother's formal petition to have the Mississippi Valley Pride officially acknowledged. And frankly, having a brand new Alpha on the council has thrown a potential wrench into both of those proceedings."

"Because you don't know how he'll vote?" Justus guessed.

"And because we have a potential new alliance in play."

"The Taylor brothers," I whispered, as I rocked the groggy baby in my arms. He was surprisingly heavy.

"Yes. Since the war, we've largely fallen into two camps, divided along the stray-split: where each of us stand on acknowledging strays as citizens and accepting Titus onto the council. Ed Taylor has never taken a firm position either way. He and Jerald Pierce were always potential swing votes. But now that his brother is also on the council, there's a better-than-excellent chance that they'll vote together, to establish a new power dynamic. And no one knows how that vote will go."

"So, there are currently two Wades on the council—Rick and Isaac—and they're allied with you and Marc, and Vic's dad, Bert Di Carlo. That's four votes in the pro-stray camp." I was narrating aloud both for Justus's benefit, and because the singsong pitch of my voice seemed to be lulling the baby toward sleep. "Nick Davidson, Wes Gardner, and Milo Mitchel usually vote together, and Blackwell would have been in their camp before—four anti-stray Alphas. Leaving Jerold Pierce and Ed Taylor as unallied and undecided. Except that now the two Taylors could be going either way."

"Or their own way," Faythe confirmed.

"How would that work?" Justus asked. "An alliance of two doesn't seem to have much swing in a pool of ten votes."

Faythe nodded. "Which means they're probably planning to stand with one side or the other."

"And until we know whether they'll swing toward the pro- or the anti-stray camp," Marc said from the doorway. "We won't know whether or not it's safe to let Robert Taylor replace Blackwell on your tribunal."

"Well, Ed was planning to vote with Blackwell, against Justus," I said. "Doesn't it stand to reason that Robert will too, if they're allied? If so, that doesn't change anything." And we *really* needed to change something.

Faythe frowned. "Are you sure that's how he was planning to vote?"

"That's definitely the impression I got," I whispered, because the baby had fallen asleep.

"Here. Let me put him to bed." Marc reached for his son, and I handed the baby off to him carefully. He tilted his head to the side, clearly listening to something, then glanced toward the front of the house. "They're here. I'll let them in."

"Thanks." Faythe turned back to us as her husband left with the baby. "Okay, then we need to fight Robert Taylor's appointment to the tribunal. And the question now becomes whether or not we ask for a total redraw. If we do, we could lose Di Carlo's friendly vote."

"But we could gain another friendly one, couldn't we?" Justus asked.

I shrugged. "It could go either way."

Footsteps clomped up the porch steps, and from the hall came the whisper of the front door being opened. "Come on in," Marc said softly from the hallway. "They're in the office. And both boys are asleep, so shhh…"

"It'd be starting from scratch," Faythe said. "With all the risks and benefits of the original tribunal draw, minus the chance of drawing Blackwell. May God have mercy on his withered old soul."

"So, what's the procedure?" I sank onto the couch next to Justus and took his hand. "Who decides whether or not to ask for a redraw?"

"It's a full-council vote. Simple majority. I think we have the votes for that—"

"No," a new voice said, and we turned as one. Titus Alexander stood in the office doorway, with Robyn looking over his shoulder from the hallway. "No redraw."

"Titus!" Faythe stood and pulled him into a hug. "It's good to see you again! Though I am sorry for the circumstances."

He shrugged and gave her back a pat. "From what I've learned so far, everything's an emergency when you have a whole Pride to run."

"True." She let him go and moved on to greet Robyn while Titus turned to his brother and me.

Justus stood and tugged me up, and my heart seemed to be beating its way out of my chest. I'd only met the stray Alpha once, about a year before, and I hadn't given him much thought. He was hot, in an older-guy kind of way, but he was all business and I'd still been very dedicated to going out every weekend with any human guy who caught my eye—my way of waving my middle finger at every tomcat asshole who'd called me a man-eater behind my back. And, in retrospect, my way of reassuring myself that *someone* wanted me.

But now Titus was my…brother in law. Whether or not he knew it.

He pulled Justus into a hug, and I could hear the emotion in his voice when he scolded his brother. "I said 'don't do anything stupid.'" He let Justus go and looked into gray eyes so much like his own it must have been like looking into a younger mirror. "What the hell were you thinking?"

I couldn't tell whether Justus was being scolded for trying to flee the country or for marrying me, and my groom didn't seem sure either. "Later," he grumbled.

Titus nodded and turned to me. "You must be Kaci."

"We've actually met before," I said, and it took actual effort to project volume. It wasn't Titus's status as Alpha that was making me nervous. It was the fact that he was the only family Justus had left, and I desperately wanted him to like me. Or at least not hate his brother for marrying me.

Or me for marrying his brother.

"Of course. I remember." He shook my right hand, then held onto it for a second. "You were still in high school."

"Titus!" Robyn snapped at him. "Don't be an asshole!"

Justus groaned. "Leave her alone."

"It wasn't an insult." He clapped his brother on the arm. "Just making sure I have the facts right here. Though I do reserve the right to be insulted that my own brother—my only living relative—didn't invite me to his wedding." Titus lifted my left hand and studied the rings on my finger. "Quite the occasion that must have been."

"I'm afraid none of us were invited," Faythe gave me a sympathetic look, but made no effort to bail me out. Her message was clear. If I was old enough to get married, I was old enough to deal with my in-laws—er, my one in-law—on my own.

Fair enough.

"It was kind of a last-minute…event," I told him, my chin held high. "I'm sorry we didn't tell anyone. Like, *really* sorry." Almost as sorry as I was that I couldn't remember the event myself. Though I had hope that it, like my proposal, would eventually come back to me. "Maybe we could have a reception or something. Here, at the ranch? We could do the cake-cutting thing and throw a bouquet, and I could probably be convinced to put on a dress. Faythe didn't want much fuss for her wedding, so Karen kind of felt cheated out of a big party. She'd probably help us plan something." I smiled, kind of excited by the idea, but Titus only stared at me.

"That sounds great." Justus slid his arm around me and kissed my neck. I fought the urge to cling to him. I hadn't been this on-edge when Jared's car had flipped with me inside it.

And still his brother stared.

"Titus, we think we have a good chance at getting a more favorable tribunal, now that Blackwell is out of the picture." Faythe crossed her arms over her blouse and sat on the edge of her desk. "Isaac Wade would be a best-case scenario."

"That's Jace's brother-in-law," I whispered to Justus.

"And I think Jerold Pierce would be a reasonable judge."

Titus turned to Faythe. "I'm sorry, but could my brother and I possibly have the use of your office for a few minutes?"

Faythe blinked, obviously surprised. Then she stood. "Of course. Ladies, could I interest you in a cup of coffee? Or Robyn, maybe a glass of wine?"

"Sure. Thanks." On her way out of the office, Robyn went up on her toes to whisper something to Titus. I couldn't make it out, but she sounded angry. Or maybe embarrassed.

"Don't worry," Justus whispered to me as he kissed my cheek. "He's mad at me, not you."

But I didn't believe that for one second. I'd proposed to Justus. Within hours of running off to Las Vegas with him. Titus probably thought I was using his brother for his money. Which was a hilarious irony, considering that Marc and the South-Central enforcers thought Justus was using *me* to get to his money.

It would be great to have just one person who could understand our relationship for what it was.

It would be even better if that person were *me*.

I grabbed Faythe's arm the moment the office door closed behind us. "He hates me," I whispered.

"I'm sure he doesn't—"

"Faythe, he *hates* me."

"Okay, calm down." She turned to Robyn. "I'm sorry to abandon you, but…" Faythe tilted her head in my direction.

"No worries," Robyn said. "I'll just snoop around here on my own."

"I'm sure if you wander into the kitchen, my mother will try to feed you. Or offer you a drink."

"Sounds good. Thanks." Robyn headed into the kitchen, and Faythe followed me into my room. Where I'd slept for the past two nights without Justus. Vic, from what I'd heard, had started sleeping in front of the guest house door to keep him from sneaking out to 'see' me.

And for the record, there is nothing in the world more humiliating than knowing that the entire South-Central compound knows you're trying unsuccessfully to get laid.

Faythe hadn't tried to talk me out of sleeping with my husband, but she'd refused to step in on our behalf with Marc and Vic until after the hearing, because she thought we should take everything slow until then.

Logically, I couldn't argue. But logic didn't mean much when I was around Justus, and when I'd tried to point out similar incidents in her own past, she'd only frowned and told me to learn from her mistakes.

But what I'd learned was that if the tribunal was redrawn and that draw didn't go our way, Justus would still have to flee the country. And he'd need access to his money for that. I wanted him to have that access. I wanted him to live, even if I couldn't go with him.

But if the draw *did* go our way… If we got to stay in the states, a legitimately married couple…

I sank onto the end of my bed, and Faythe took my desk chair. "I've ruined this, haven't I? I should have called Titus when we got back to the ranch? Or I should have made Justus call him? I don't even know who told him about the wedding."

"I did," Faythe said.

"How'd he take it? Was he mad?"

"He was…surprised."

"Why does that sound like a euphemism for really fucking mad."

"Language," Faythe said.

"Sorry."

"Kaci, you stole two cars, ran off to Vegas, and married an underage gambler. Without bothering to tell either of your families. You knew there would be consequences for that."

"Yes. But I didn't think those consequences would include his family hating me."

"Titus will get over it. But you're going to have to give him time."

"There isn't much time for me to give him. Justus's trial is in less than three days. Unless you think forcing a redraw will delay it…?"

Faythe could only shrug. "I'm not even sure we're forcing a redraw yet. Titus seems set against it."

I frowned, picking at my ragged fingernails. "Why would he want to keep Robert Taylor on the tribunal?"

Faythe turned a serious glance toward the door, as if she could see through it. "I'm assuming he knows something we don't."

EIGHTEEN

JUSTUS

"WHAT THE HELL WERE YOU THINKING?" TITUS DEMANDED again the moment the door closed behind Kaci, and I could tell from the volume of his voice alone that he knew the room was virtually soundproof.

He'd commandeered Faythe's office to yell at me.

"Do you mean the cash advance on my card, or trying to flee the country?" I sank onto the couch, trying to look calm and in control—and nothing like the kid he obviously still thought I was. "Or marrying Kaci?"

"I mean all three of them. Somehow you've managed to commit a trifecta of stupidity, and you dragged a traumatized little girl into it."

"She's not traumatized. She's…scarred. Healed. She's strong, and she's smart. And she's not a child."

"She's eighteen years old!"

It wouldn't do any good to point out that it was perfectly legal to get married at eighteen, or that eighteen was old enough to vote. He would only point out all the things eighteen wasn't old enough for. So I went with a different kind of truth. "She's older at eighteen than I was."

"She's probably older at eighteen than you are now!" Titus snapped. "*Please* tell me you haven't slept with her."

Anger flared inside me like fuel dumped on a bonfire. I'd never really fought with Titus, yet suddenly, he felt more like an enemy than the lifelong ally I'd always thought of him as.

My brother knew what it was like to fall in love at an inconvenient time. He should be celebrating with me. Not grilling me.

"What Kaci and I have done is none of your business," I growled.

"Do *not* take that tone with me," he growled back, and I fought an infuriating instinct to cower away from him. This Alpha crap was bullshit. *I* was in the right. Kaci and I were both of age, and we'd made a legal and binding decision. One I would stick with until the day I died.

"She's my wife, Titus."

"Don't—"

"You should be happy for me. You should be cracking open a bottle of fucking champaign and welcoming her to the family, not yelling at me. Not interrogating me."

His mouth snapped shut, and he seemed to be consciously trying to edit whatever he wanted to say as he sank onto the couch across the rug from me. "She's a child, Justus. So are you. Tell me this isn't binding. Marc said he didn't think you'd…consummated. I've spoken to my lawyer, and we can get this annulled if you two haven't—"

"None. Of your. Business." I managed to keep from growling that time, but only barely. "The things I will listen to from you right now include, 'Congratulations, Justus, I'm so happy for you!' and 'She's wonderful. Mom and Dad would've loved her. I hope you two are very happy.'"

His gaze darkened. "Mom and—"

"You *have* to say that, Titus," I growled at him. "Someone has to say that, and you're the only one left. They would love her. You *know* they would love her."

"Of course they would love her. She's fucking adorable, and Marc says she's smart, and quick on her feet—hell, she wrecked a car to get away from a kidnapper—but none of that is really relevant. Do you have any idea what you're doing to me? To all the people in my territory who depend on me? I'm fighting to get our territory recognized. To provide basic civil rights to a population that's been disenfranchised for centuries. To protect them. To protect *you*. Marc and Faythe took you in as a favor to me. To help you. And you run off and sleep with their fucking daughter. You marry her to get your damned inheritance."

"You *know* that's not true." I launched myself off the couch and paced toward Faythe's desk, then turned to face him and sat on the edge of it.

"It's not about what I know. It's about what the council will think. It's about the facts, and the picture they paint. In college you were with a different girl every week, until Ivy. Whom you're on trial for *infecting*. Who died because she cheated on her boyfriend with you."

"Do *not* throw that in my face. You know Drew—"

"I know what Drew did. I know that wasn't your fault. I'm on your side. But *they're* not. Half of the council—maybe more —is looking for any excuse to execute you. To make an example of you. You have to give them a *reason* to be on your side, but you skipped straight from infecting a girl you were cheating with to manipulating a traumatized eighteen-year-old tabby so you can access your trust fund, on your way to fleeing the country!

What are they supposed to think? How are they supposed to rule in your favor now? How are they supposed to rule in *my* favor?"

"This isn't about you, Titus."

"*Bullshit*." He stood, gesturing with both hands, just like our dad used to do when he was mad. "This is about *all* of us. Whether you like it or not, out here, you represent all strays. You don't get the luxury of making mistakes any natural-born tom would get away with because when natural-born cats mess up, people assume they've made an isolated mistake, but when we mess up, they assume we're demonstrating an innate inferiority. That we're justifying their prejudices."

"That's bullshit!" I snapped.

"Yes." Titus's nod was short and sharp. "But it's also reality. What your mistakes are telling the people who have the power to keep guys like you and me from becoming citizens is that if they let us into their world, we might steal their cars and gamble under age—either of which could draw the attention of the human authorities—and drag their precious daughters into a fucking crime spree! Tabbies are everything out here. You may not understand that, but—"

"I understand. I've been living the shifter immersion program for four months, Titus. But Kaci's not like the other tabbies. They don't think of her like that. They…" Anger flared inside me at just the memory of what I'd heard from Brian Taylor, and from Kaci herself. "They call her the man-eater."

My brother blinked, his head cocked to the side. "What?"

"That's what they call her behind her back. Though she hears them. She's grown up like that. Feeling like a freak and a monster. Like no matter what she does, no one will ever want her, despite how rare and precious women are in their world, and how desperate they are for female shifters."

"Why?" Titus's forehead furrowed; obviously Marc hadn't told him that part.

"Because when they found her, she'd been living on her own in the woods, stuck in cat form for so long that she'd nearly forgotten she was ever human. She was terrified and starving. She found a human corpse, and she ate from it to survive. But these assholes out here don't understand shit like that. They've never been stuck in one form. They've never thought they were losing their minds, when their bodies start doing things they don't understand. Demanding things they don't want. They've never *not* known how to handle hunger, or rage, or bloodlust. But Kaci has. She's just like us. Titus, she may have married me for the money—so we could both get the hell out of here—but I married her because I understand her. And because I knew after just one night with her that no one else would *ever* understand me like she does." I sucked in a deep breath, then spit out the truth. "I fucking love her, man."

"You...? She... She's a stray?" He combed through his hair with one hand, and I enjoyed his confusion way more than I should have. Historically, there had been very few things that I understood but my older brother did not. "I thought Robyn was the only one."

"She's not a stray. She's what they call a genetic recessive. Her parents both had the werecat gene, and one of their daughters inherited two recessives—which activates the gene —and the other didn't. Kaci was born to human parents who had no idea shifters existed. Then she hit puberty, and one day: *bam*! She shifted into a big cat. Out of the blue. She wasn't scratched. She didn't grow up in a house full of shifters. She was a human, then she was a cat, with no preparation, warning, or infection."

"Holy shit," Titus whispered as he sank onto the couch again. "I didn't even know that was possible."

"I didn't either. Evidently no one did. They theorize that she wasn't the first incidence of that. She *couldn't* have been. But Marc can tell you all about that. What I know is that after she shifted, she was terrified and freaked out, and she accidentally killed her mother and her sister, when they found her in the back yard." I frowned. "Well, actually what they found was Kaci's clothes, and a big black cat growling at them. They tried to defend themselves. She tried to defend herself, and shit went sideways. She's been through things neither of us can imagine, Titus. So, you're going to be fucking *nice* to her."

My brother stood and pulled me into a hug. "I'm sorry Justus. I didn't know. And Mom and Dad *would* like her."

"Yeah. They would." And for a second, I thought I'd actually gotten through to him. I thought maybe I could bring Kaci back in, and we could start over and be a happy fucking family for a few minutes.

But then I realized there was something off in his expression. In the sad but determined way he was looking at me. Like he looked at me the day he told me our parents had died.

"But Justus, that doesn't change anything. Sit down. Please."

"No. Just say whatever you're going to say, so we can get on with this argument." Because that was clearly all this discussion would ever be.

Titus held my gaze as he sank onto one of the couches again. "I'm releasing your funds."

"What?" I sat on the sofa across from him. That wasn't what I'd been expecting.

"I'm releasing your funds. I have that authority, as the executor. I've already bought you a ticket."

"A ticket." And suddenly I understood. "You want me to run? No. I'm not going, Titus. Not without Kaci."

"You don't need to run. The tribunal is going to rule in your favor, *in absentia*, the moment they have confirmation that you're out of the country."

"How do you know what they're going to do?" And, more important, "Why would I need to leave, if they're going to acquit?"

"Because that's part of the deal I made. In a few years, after Kaci—" He had the decency to look uncomfortable with whatever he was about to say. "—has married and given birth to at least one child that isn't yours, you can come back. Live a normal life. Still a member of the South-Central Pride, if you want. Or you can come to the Mississippi Valley. You'll always be welcome at home."

"But not until Kaci marries someone else." *This can't be happening. This makes no sense.* "Not until she has someone else's *kid*." Rage made my vision go dark around the edges. "She won't do that. You can't make her do that. How the *hell* could you make a deal like that? We're not toys for you to play with Titus!"

"Of course not." To his credit, he looked distinctly uncomfortable with the deal he'd struck. "I made no promises on her behalf, and no one's going to make her do anything. But you won't be welcome back until and unless they're sure Kaci won't be handing the keys to the kingdom to a stranger, for lack of a better analogy. That's the only way this will work, Justus. The only way I could guarantee that they're not going to execute you."

"I don't need your help! Kaci was working on the vote. We only needed one more. And if I don't get that, she's coming with me."

"Grow up, Justus," Titus's voice had gone hard, his gaze

narrowed and impatient. "That's not how the world works. If she goes with you, they'll hunt you both down to get her back. She's not old enough to defect. And there's nothing you can do to get that extra vote, now that Blackwell is dead. The Taylors will vote together."

"You don't know that."

"In fact, I do."

"Because you made your deal with them." I sounded as stunned as I felt with that realization. "Without even *talking* to me. *That's* why you don't want to redraw names for my trial! You *want* Robert Taylor on the tribunal."

He shrugged. "They called me and made an offer. They're using you to get to me—to get me to cooperate—and they *will* vote to execute you if I don't give them what they want. I'm trying to save your life, Justus."

"I didn't ask you to do that! Kaci's *already* married. To me. And I'm not leaving her."

"You have to. That's part of the—."

"I'm not taking your deal." My jaw ached, as if my teeth no longer fit in my mouth. I stood, and the urge to rip into something—to *destroy* something—was so strong it was all I could think about. My fingers cramped. They curled up, as if they were grasping for something.

I knew what was happening. The rage storming through me was familiar enough by then that I understood exactly what my inner cat wanted. As far as feline-me was concerned, I would be with Kaci, or I would *rip the world to shreds to get to her*. There were no other options.

Kaci, or the utter destruction of everything and everyone who came between us.

"Justus…" Titus stood. "Your hands."

I looked down and discovered that I had claws. I ran my tongue over my teeth, and one of my incisors drew blood.

"Walk it back," he ordered, his voice low and calm. "Reverse the shift. You can*not* lose control in here."

"I'm not losing control." Kaci had said the partial shift was normal. Useful, even. I didn't have to worry unless my skin started to itch or my bones started to ache, which would indicate that my entire body was about to shift. "What do they want, Titus?" I demanded. "What is this deal you made? What is so important that you're willing to tell a girl who loves me that she has to be with someone else. Someone who thinks she's a monster. Who will only ever use her for the children he can—"

My bones started to ache at the thought of someone else touching her. Someone who might not recognize the vulnerability in her eyes when she took her clothes off. Someone who might not recognize the responsibility and the fucking honor that went along with—

I closed my eyes and clenched my jaw shut to keep my teeth in check. To keep the bones of my face from reforming —though it was actually the willpower behind the act that made that possible. And when I was sure I had it under control, I opened my eyes. I pinned my brother with my gaze.

"What on earth could be worth that, Titus? What do they want from you?"

"My vote."

"What vote? You don't have a vote."

"But I will. Blackwell was the last holdout on officially hearing my petition. On setting a date. Now that he's gone, the Taylors are willing to push it through. Immediately. And they've agreed vote in my favor and in yours—to accept the Mississippi Valley Pride and to find you innocent—if I vote to help them oust Rick Wade as council chair."

"What? Why?"

Titus shrugged. "All the usual reasons, I suspect. Power,

mostly. They're working on an alliance, and they know that as a swing vote, I'd be against them on most issues. So they want the chair position as a concession. To maintain the balance of power. We have the majority on most issues, but they'd have the tiebreaker on anything close."

"That's bullshit. That's not how a democracy works."

"This isn't a democracy, Justus! It never was. Deals are made before the votes are ever cast. No one comes to the table until all that is worked out beforehand. That's just the way it goes."

"This isn't for me. It's for *you*," I growled. "This is for your fucking Pride."

His gaze looked sad, but firm. "That's not true. I gave up the Pride to protect you."

"And now that you have it back, you're trying to make me give up Kaci to protect your Pride."

"No. The Taylors came to me. They told me they'd vote to convict—to *execute*—unless I vote for Ed as council chair."

"That's why they took Kaci. They were trying to lure me into the territory so they'd have me in custody when Ed Taylor called you."

"Sounds about right. They're calling an emergency meeting, and when they have my vote, they'll move to drop the murder charge against you. Then, when you're out of the country, they'll drop the infection charge. Tit for tat. Once piece at a time, until everyone has what they want."

"Everyone except Rick Wade. And Kaci and me."

"Yes. Rick is collateral damage. But he'll accept that like Vic evidently accepted the broken arm you gave him—it's an occupational hazard."

"And Kaci? How will she take this?"

Titus sighed. "Okay, you're looking at this all wrong. What you'll be doing—it's for Kaci too. You two just met."

"We met four months ago."

"Four *whole* months?" He rolled his eyes. "Well then obviously it's true love."

"Don't be an asshole. How long did you know Robyn before you were willing to go to war over her? *War*, Titus. You were willing to risk other people's lives."

"That wasn't just for Robyn. That was for sovereignty over our own territory. To protect my men. To keep the council from invading."

"To keep them from taking Robyn back," I spat at him.

"It's not the same, Justus. You two are kids! It's young love. It's *first* love. You can't know that's real until you've lived a little more. Gained a little experience. She's hardly out of high school. You're probably her first boyfriend."

"She's eighteen, not eighteenth *century*. I'm not her first boyfriend. And you're full of shit. This is just as real as you and Robyn, and you—" My mouth snapped shut, and my newly feline teeth didn't fit well into my human mouth.

He knew. He *knew* everything he was saying was utter crap, and but he was saying it anyway because he was…scared.

That's what I was seeing in his eyes. Fear. For me.

I wasn't going to talk him out of what he'd decided. Not with it coming from a place of fear. But that didn't mean I had to do what he wanted me to.

"Does Brian know?"

Titus frowned. "Who's Brian?"

"Brian Taylor. Faythe's enforcer, and Ed's son. Does he know his dad and uncle are trying to sell out Faythe and Marc's closest ally?" I sank onto the couch again as the connection finally hit me. "This isn't just about power. This is also revenge. Titus, they're unseating Rick Wade, because his daughter picked Jace over Ed Taylor's son! Abby Wade and Brian Taylor were supposed to get married. Someday Brian would have inherited Rick Wade's territory. That would have put two Taylors on the council."

"Three." Titus groaned. "Robert Taylor's been waiting for Paul Blackwell to step down for decades. Jace told me that any other Alpha would have retired more than twenty years ago, but Blackwell's been putting it off so long that he has great grandchildren."

"Then this is actually a play they've been trying to make for at least four years."

Titus frowned. "How'd you come up with four?"

"That's how long Abby and Brian were engaged." I leaned back on the couch, one hand over my forehead as another connection fell into place. "Oh shit."

I wish *I didn't know what I know about Kaci, because* someone's *gotta make a mom out of her*.

The memory of Brian Taylor's words sent chills marching across my skin. "They want to pair her with Brian. He said something the other day, and I didn't really process it, but that *has* to be what they're planning." I leaned back on the couch, staring up at the ceiling as I followed the logical breadcrumb trail to its end. "When Abby ran off with Jace, Rick Wade lost his heir, and soon he'll have lost his leadership of the council. Eventually the council will have to place a fertile tabby in his territory, and Kaci's the only one without a home of her own. If they can pair Brian with her before that happens, he'll get control of Wade's territory *and* his seat on the council. Right?"

Titus frowned. "From what I understand of the council's origins and procedures, that *does* seem to be a possibility. Every Alpha gets a seat on the council, and traditionally, an

Alpha must be married to a tabby and must father her children. Faythe and Marc's partnership being the obvious exception."

I nodded. That was my understanding too. "So when Rick Wade retires, if the council gives his territory to Brian and Kaci…" I let my brother draw the obvious conclusion for himself.

"The Taylors will have taken *everything* from the man they blame for letting Abby break her engagement to Brian."

"And they'll have used us to do it," I told him. "They're playing us like chess pieces."

Titus exhaled, and he seemed to still be processing. Then he looked me in the eye. "When did you get so smart?"

That seemed to be a serious question.

"It runs in the family." I huffed. "Though I wasn't so sure, for a minute there."

"Are you calling me stupid?"

I shrugged. "You were saying some pretty stupid shit. If they're willing to wait *that* long, to put *that* many pieces into play, and to threaten to execute me to get you to go along… you have no way of knowing they'll stick to their word, Titus. You could do what they want, and they could *still* hunt me down and bring new charges."

"But once they have what they want, why would they bother?"

"Because they know what my own brother doesn't seem to have figured out yet. Executing me is the *only* way they'll be able to keep me from Kaci."

NINETEEN

KACI

"So, this whole thing was Ed Taylor's attempt to take the council chair position from Rick Wade?" I could hardly wrap my mind around the web of back channel manipulations. The kidnapping. The deal the Taylors had tried to make with Titus. "Just because Abby wouldn't marry Brian?"

"I'm sure that isn't Ed's only grudge," Faythe said from her perch on the front edge of her desk. "I knew he was upset about the loss of the potential for grandchildren, but I have to admit I never expected him to make a power grab. That doesn't sound much like Ed."

Marc shrugged from the couch across the rug from Justus and me. "I suspect his resentment has been brewing for a while, and his son's broken engagement was the final straw. And we all know how miserable Robert Taylor has been under Blackwell's thumb for *decades*. The Taylors probably believe they're simply claiming what should have been theirs all along."

"I'm so sorry they dragged you into this." Justus's hand tightened around mine, and the leather upholstery creaked as he leaned closer to me on the couch. "And I'm even sorrier that I gave them that opportunity."

"Oh, please. I did that to myself. But the Taylors are responsible for their own actions."

"Why didn't you tell me about this?" Robyn twisted out of Titus's embrace to glare at him. "We drove all this way, and you didn't say a thing!"

"I'm sorry. I wanted to talk to Justus first." Titus glanced from one of us to the next while he spoke. "I owe the rest of you an apology as well. I had no right to agree to anything without consulting everyone affected by my decision. Rick Wade has been nothing but kind and fair to me and to my men, and the last thing I want to do is cast myself as his adversary. But all I could think about when Ed Taylor called was saving Justus's life."

"I suspect Rick would understand that," Faythe said. "Not that we need to tell him. Because he would also be *very, very angry*. So let's just count this as an impulsive lesson learned. We are all better off counting on one another than taking drastic measures alone." She aimed a pointed look around the room, from Justus and me on one couch to Titus, Robyn, and Marc on the one across from us. "And we *have* to be able to count on one another."

"Of course." Titus looked both embarrassed by and ashamed of what he'd done. Which was *almost* enough to make me forgive him for trying to separate me from his brother.

Almost.

Marc snorted, aiming an amused look at Faythe. "This coming from the valedictorian of the 'I can do it all on my own' school of leadership."

"The *former* valedictorian," she corrected with a smile. "I've learned a lot on the job."

"Are we sure Brian was in on this?" I asked.

Marc nodded. "We're pretty sure he at least knew about it. And if he did, that's grounds for dismissal—as our enforcer, his loyalty should lie with the South-Central Pride, not his birth-Pride."

"So, you're going to fire Brian?" I felt guilty for how happy that thought made me, after what he'd said about me to Justus. But only a *little* guilty.

"Not yet." Marc stood and headed for the liquor cart on the end of the room opposite the desk. "If we fire him, his dad will know we're on to him."

"So then, what's our move? What are we waiting for?"

Titus joined Marc at the cart and poured himself an inch of whiskey. "Ed Taylor's planning to call an emergency meeting to vote on my petition."

"That call went out an hour ago," Marc confirmed. Then he took a big sip from his glass.

Titus nodded. "This morning he informed me that as soon as I'm an official member, they're going to call for a new vote on the council chair position, and that if I don't support Ed Taylor over Rick Wade, he and his brother will vote to execute Justus. But that if I support them, they'll make all his charges go away…" He leveled an apologetic glance at Kaci. "As long as Justus stays out of the country until Kaci remarries and has a child."

"Bastards…" I hissed beneath my breath.

"Language," Faythe snapped. "It's not new information that the council wants women to have children and strays to get lost."

"But I thought things were changing! I thought you and

Marc were trying to drag the other Alphas into the twenty-first century!"

"They have, and we are," Faythe insisted. "But change takes time."

Marc drained his glass. "And sometimes a little spilled blood."

Faythe scowled. "This is *not* one of those times. The object here is to avoid bloodshed."

"And to keep Justus in the country. Alive," I added. "So, what's going to happen? We can't let them vote to execute Justus, just to get back at Titus for rejecting their 'deal.'"

"They won't have the chance," Faythe assured us. "We're going to press for a redraw for his tribunal. But first…" She smiled. "If Ed and Robert Taylor want to help us get the Mississippi Valley Pride recognized, I say we let them."

"I can't believe they were willing to assemble so quickly!"

"Assemble." Laughing, I wound my fingers through Justus's in the shade of the apple tree. Beneath us, the bench swing swayed gently in the hot summer breeze. "Superheroes 'assemble.' Alphas just convene."

"Whatever." He rolled his eyes. But he was smiling.

On the side of the tree opposite the swing stood three headstones, marking the graves of Faythe's father, Greg, and her brothers, Ethan and Ryan. They'd all died during my first year in the territory, and Ethan was the only one I really remembered very well, five years later.

I still missed him. He would have liked Justus.

"Anyway, it's not like they had any choice." I shrugged.

"Faythe said Robert Taylor was officially recognized as Alpha of the Southwest Pride this morning, and the Taylors are eager to put their plan into motion before your trial starts tomorrow." I shrugged. "Naturally, Faythe volunteered to host the vote."

Justus's smile faded. "How mad do you think the Taylors will be when they figure out Titus isn't going through with his promise? I mean, I know they'll be pissed, but how badly could this bite him on the ass later on?"

I shrugged. "Shifter politics are like low-key war. Politely worded insults and backdoor deals. Someone's always pissed off. If the Taylors weren't out to get Titus, someone else would be. And they took a risk, making him an offer. They *have* to know it might not pay off."

"Who's that?" Justus sat straighter as a car turned into the driveway and rolled beneath the arched gate.

I squinted to see through the windshield. "Jerold Pierce. That's the last of them." I twisted on the bench swing to face Justus, looking for any sign of fear. Any indication that he wished we'd gone with our original plan and were sipping drinks on a beach somewhere, rather than getting ready to face not just a tribunal, but the entire council, ten Alphas strong. Eleven, counting both Faythe and Marc. "You ready for this?"

"Nope. Let's go." Justus stood and tugged me up by one hand.

When we got to the house, we found Faythe's office crowded with Alphas, most sipping from short glasses of amber liquid, though it was hardly four p.m. The atmosphere was tense, and the clusters they'd gathered in clearly illustrated their alliances, both fledgling and long-standing.

Faythe sat behind her desk, with Marc standing at her side. Gathered around them were Rick Wade—the current council chair—Isaac Wade, his son, and Vic's father, Bert Di Carlo.

On the opposite end of the room, in what I privately thought of as the anti-stray corner, Milo Mitchell, Nick Davidson, and Wes Gardner stood just feet from the liquor cart. Ed Taylor and his brother Robert, representing the Southwest territory for the first time, had staked their claim on the space near the far wall, where they were deep in whispered conversation with Titus Alexander.

Surely that wouldn't be happening unless they still believed he was in their corner.

Justus and I slipped into the room as quietly as we could and took seats on one of the couches, where we tried to eavesdrop on all three groups at once. But a couple of minutes later, when Karen Sanders escorted Jerold Pierce into the office, Faythe stood behind her desk. "Gentlemen, it's pretty crowded in here. Why don't we hold this meeting in the dining room? I believe my mother has brewed coffee in the kitchen. You're all welcome to grab a cup on the way."

I couldn't resist a small smile. In any other territory, the Alpha's wife would have served coffee, and possibly pastries. But despite the fact that Karen actually liked showing off her baking skills and loading trays full of beautifully presented mugs, Faythe thought it sent the wrong message for her to serve the Alphas. Men capable of running entire territories, she reasoned, were just as capable of getting their own drinks.

A few of the older Alphas grumbled, but most of them were already holding glasses, so they moved as one tense procession straight to the dining room, where Rick Wade took the seat at the head of the table, with Bert Di Carlo on his right and Faythe on his left.

Ed Taylor took the seat at the opposite end, and I could

tell from his smug grin that he had no idea that Wade or his allies knew all about the coup he was planning.

Marc sat on Faythe's left, with Titus on his other side. But when Justus and I took up positions behind them, against the dining room wall, Robert Taylor turned to us with a stern expression. "Our first order of business doesn't concern the two of you."

I glanced at Faythe, and she nodded toward the hallway. Which was when I realized that her choice of venue had been very deliberate. The office was virtually soundproof with the door closed, but the dining room was open to the central hallway on one side with an arched doorway, and to the kitchen with a smaller doorway on the other side. Justus and I would be able to hear everything that was said from nearly any room in the house.

In the kitchen, we poured cups of coffee and sat at the island, where I realized that if I moved my bar stool *slightly* to the left, I could see most of the dining room table through the arched doorway.

Rick Wade stood at the head of the table. "First of all, let me thank you all for agreeing to meet on such short notice. And thanks, of course, to Faythe and Marc, for hosting our meeting. I'm sure I speak for all of us when I say how very sorry we are for the Southwest Territory's loss. Paul Blackwell was an institution, and in some parts, practically a legend. He held the record for the longest serving Alpha, and though we didn't always agree on the issues, I believe with all my heart that he always voted his conscience."

Robert Taylor—I could only see him in profile—nodded in recognition. "Thank you for saying so, Rick. I will pass on your condolences to my wife and the rest of our family."

"Thank you." Wade cleared his throat. "That said, I see no need for debate on the issue at hand today. We've been discussing the subject for months, and I suspect we all know where we stand on the issue of whether or not to formally recognize the Mississippi Valley Pride with Titus Alexander as its Alpha." He frowned. "Unless Robert would like to take some time to solicit opinions, question Titus, or consider the proposal, since he's new on the council?"

"No, thank you, Rick," Robert Taylor said. "I believe I'm all caught up."

"Great. Then I propose that we call a vote immediately."

"I second," Faythe said.

"Very well. We'll go around the table, starting from my right. Vote yea or nay. The issue is this…" Wade pulled a folded sheet of paper from his pocket, then he unfolded it and began to read aloud. "The Mississippi Valley Pride seeks formal recognition as a member of the coalition of American Prides. Recognition would include the following stipulations: The Mississippi Valley Pride will be admitted as a full member of the coalition with all the same benefits and obligations of the other Prides, bringing our membership from ten territories to eleven, to be considered effective at the moment of a majority vote in the affirmative. The territory recognized as belonging to the Mississippi Valley Pride will be the entirety of that currently considered the Mississippi free zone. The new Pride will be recognized with Titus Alexander acknowledged as its Alpha and as the eleventh member in full of the Territorial Council, with all the duties and privileges belonging to the other ten members. The new Pride will be responsible for the same dues owed to the council that the current members pay, and will be subject to the same increases and decreases voted on in the future. Mr. Alexander and his territory will be held to the very same standards and laws that we all abide by, and the Mississippi Valley Pride members shall be guaranteed all the same rights, considerations, and advantages that we currently enjoy. Without exception." Wade pocketed his statement and glanced around the table. "Any questions or objections?"

Several heads shook.

Wade nodded. "Then let's go around the table, beginning on my left. A simple majority will be considered an affirmative vote. A tie of five-to-five will be considered a negative vote." Which meant that Titus needed six yea votes.

"Marc and I vote yea," Faythe said. No one looked surprised.

The vote skipped Titus, and to his left, Jerold Pierce said, "I vote nay. It's nothing personal. I just don't think we need another Pride."

Titus nodded in acknowledgement, his lips pressed firmly together.

Next came Nick Davidson. "Nay."

"Yea," Isaac Wade said, tying the vote. As Rick Wade's son and Jace's brother-in-law, the youngest Alpha on the council had so far reliably voted with Faythe and her allies.

Then all eyes were on Ed Taylor, at the end of the table.

Taylor leaned back in his chair, enjoying the moment with his arms crossed over his chest. "For the moment, I'd like to abstain."

A shocked silence settled over the dining room. Mitchell, Wes Gardner, and Nick Davidson wore identical scowls, which I could only see in profile. They'd been sure Taylor would vote with them.

Justus shifted on the bar stool next to mine, frowning. I shared his nerves. *We'd* been sure Taylor would vote with Marc and Faythe. What the hell was he doing, abstaining?

"Well, I guess technically that is your right," Rick Wade said. "Rob? How will you be casting your first official vote as a council member?"

Robert Taylor sat a little straighter, obviously aware that all eyes were on him. "I vote in favor of recognizing the Mississippi Valley Pride, with the stipulations read aloud."

To his left, Wes Gardner frowned. If his mental tally agreed with mine, he understood that the vote was now three-to-two, in favor of the Mississippi Valley Pride. "Nay," Gardner said, without being asked.

With the vote tied, Milo Mitchell voted nay.

On his left, Bert Di Carlo gave a booming "Yea," tying the vote again at four.

"Yea," Rick Wade announced. "The count is five to four, in favor of the yeas. Ed, if you vote nay, the measure will fail. If you abstain, the measure will pass, with a simple majority of five out of nine votes. If you vote yes, it will pass with six out of ten votes. What do you say?"

Justus sat straighter on his bar stool, and I could feel tension rolling off him. In the dining room, all eyes were on Ed Taylor. Titus's hands were clenched on the table, as if he were silently praying. Marc's foot tapped softly, and Faythe put one hand on his knee. This vote—recognition of the first stray Pride—meant almost as much to him as it meant to Titus and Justus. As it meant to me.

Ed Taylor cleared his throat, and suddenly I understood why he'd abstained. So that his would be the deciding vote.

"As I sit here, I'm very well aware that as a group—as representatives of the entire American coalition—we find ourselves at both a political and a philosophical crossroads. The decision we make today will set our trajectory on both fronts for the foreseeable future. This decision sets a prece-dent we must all consider in countless future debates and votes."

Justus took my hand and squeezed it, passing a little of his tension on to me. But it took everything I had not to roll my eyes at Ed Taylor—I had no patience for his political grandstanding.

Though his obviously rehearsed speech *did* seem to bode well for a vote in Titus's favor; surely, he wouldn't be trying so hard to sound like the council leader if he weren't confident that his deal with Titus would put him in that very position.

"I believe it's time that we, as a group, acknowledge that our stray brothers—and at least one sister!—are entitled to all the same rights and privileges that those of us born into the shifter world enjoy. So it is with great optimism for the future that I vote yea!"

Mitchell, Davidson, and Gardner stared in shock as Ed Taylor stood and rounded the corner of the table with his hand extended for Titus to shake. Titus stood and accepted it, along with a hearty clap on the back from Taylor. "Welcome to the council, Titus. And I want to extend an enthusiastic welcome as well to the men and women of the Mississippi Valley Pride!"

Justus's hand squeezed mine so tightly that my joints groaned in protest. My sigh of relief was nearly audible.

The vote was over. It was *real*. Titus's Pride had been officially recognized—a victory Faythe, Marc, Jace, and Titus had spent well over a year working toward. That moment should have felt victorious. Euphoric. But I have to admit that my joy was tempered by the arrogant nerve of Ed Taylor practically taking credit for the whole thing—*while* he was trying to blackmail Titus and oust the current council chairman from his position.

"Yes." Rick Wade stood. "I do believe congratulations are in order. And I'm going to call a fifteen minute break before we get to new business."

Individual comments got lost in the quiet chaos of the

next few minutes, as Titus's friends and allies gathered around to congratulate him, while those who'd voted against him sat in silent shock. And since the chairman had called a recess, I grabbed Justus's hand and pulled him into the dining room, where we joined the crowd around his brother.

"Kaci." I turned at the sound of my name to see Jerold Pierce looking down at me. "I hear congratulations are in order," he said, with a glance at my grip on Justus's hand. Where my rings were easily visible. "So…congratulations."

"Thanks." I wasn't sure what else to say.

"And congratulations to you as well," Pierce said to Justus. "The news caught us all by surprise, but I wish you the best."

"Thank you," Justus said just as his brother emerged from the small crowd.

"Titus." Pierce extended his hand. "No hard feelings, I hope. My objection was to an unknown dynamic with an eleventh member on the council, not to your presence specifically." He lowered his voice to little more than a breath of sound. "If it had been an option, I might have voted someone else out and taken you on as the tenth."

Titus's smile was tight, but not unfriendly. "Of course I have no hard feelings, Jerold. And I look forward to working with you. I believe our interests are bound to align on several fronts."

"I hope you're right." Then Jerold Pierce excused himself to refill his glass.

"Well, that was awkward," Justus breathed.

"Keep watching," his brother whispered with just a hint of another smile.

"What's the plan?" I demanded in as low a voice as I could muster, but Titus only patted my hand, then headed into the kitchen to join Faythe and Marc around the coffee pot.

"Is he always that…tight-lipped?" I asked Justus as we headed into the hall.

"No, usually you know exactly what he's thinking. Whether you want to or not. Though it's possible that's my perception because the bulk of my interaction with my brother has been with him in the role of my legal guardian."

"I have a similar perception of Faythe," I murmured. "Though I suspect in her case, it's accurate."

The Alphas began heading toward the dining room again, and this time no one shooed us out when we slipped into the room. Evidently Ed Taylor didn't mind if we watched his attempt at a coup.

"Okay," Rick Wade said from the head of the table, when his colleagues were all seated. "The only new business on the agenda for today is regarding the tribunal for Justus Alexander's upcoming trial. The names drawn include Alberto Di Carlo, Ed Taylor, and Paul Blackwell. But since we've lost Paul, we have a decision to make." Rick folded his hands on the table. "As I understand it, we have two proposals on the table. Robert, you believe that since you inherited Paul's leadership of the Southwest Pride and his seat on the council, you should also inherit his position on the tribunal."

"Stands to reason," Robert Taylor said with a firm nod.

"But Faythe, you and Marc contend that Robert should not sit on the tribunal unless his name is actually drawn. If the council sides with you, the options for a redraw include drawing for an entirely new tribunal, or drawing to fill only the vacant seat. Which option are you intending to pursue—"

Ed Taylor stood. "Rick, if you don't mind, we actually have one other, more pressing bit of new business."

Rick Wade's surprised look was impressively realistic. "Well, I guess if it's pressing…"

"I'd like to call for a new vote on the council chairman position."

Wade's brows came together in a fierce scowl. He stood slowly. "That position is not up for vote." His surprised fury was highly convincing. Though the fury part was likely very real.

"With all due respect, Rick, we all just voted to give Titus the same rights, obligations, and privileges the rest of us have, and one of those rights is to vote on the leader of this council. Which he has not had a chance to do. You voted to accept him. You must also accept any potential changes that vote brings."

Wade hesitated. "Is that how you all feel?"

Several heads bobbed, from both sides of the table. Faythe aimed an unsure glance at Ed Taylor. Then she turned back to Wade. "For argument's sake, I'd like to point out that historically, we've never called for a new vote on the chair position simply because the council gains a new member. However, today we've actually gained *two* members, which means that nearly a fifth of us didn't have a chance to help select our leader. A new vote *does* seem like the fair thing to do for both Titus and Robert." She shrugged. "A vote doesn't necessarily mean leadership will change, Rick. In fact, I'm betting it won't. But this time, if you're re-elected, you'll know for sure that you have the unwavering support of the majority."

"Well said." Ed Taylor nodded, as if he'd expected nothing less from the most progressive member of the council, but I could see surprise hiding in the crinkles around his eyes. He and Faythe disagreed as often as they agreed.

"Well then I won't object." Rick Wade stood straighter and glanced around the table. "But I think a simple raised-hand vote will suffice." His gaze narrowed on Ed Taylor. "I assume you're throwing your name in as my opponent?"

"Well, I think *someone* should," Taylor said. As if he hadn't been planning this all along.

I did the math in my head. Faythe's alliance was virtually guaranteed to vote for Rick Wade. Which would give him his own vote, as well as his son's and Bert Di Carlo's, as well as the vote Faythe and Marc shared. Which was four out of ten.

No, out of eleven.

Taylor could count on his own vote, as well as his brother Robert's. He'd likely also get votes from Mitchell, Davidson, and Gardner. Which gave him five out of eleven.

Jerold Pierce had cast his previous vote in favor of upholding the status quo, which meant he might vote for Wade for the same reason. But I couldn't be sure of that. If he *did* vote for Wade, the vote would be tied. Titus would, as expected, be the tie-breaker on his very first council vote.

But if Pierce voted for Ed Taylor, Taylor would win, even without Titus's vote. And then he'd do his *best* to convict Justus, out of revenge.

"Okay, let's have a show of hands," Rick Wade said, and my heart beat so fast that Justus heard it and turned to me with a question in his eyes.

I let go of his hand. Then I stepped forward. "Is the vote limited to two candidates?" I blurted out.

Every head in the room turned my way, and the sudden, mostly disapproving attention of ten—no, eleven—Alphas at once felt like an iron weight on my chest. Like breathing was suddenly impossible.

"No." Ed Taylor fixed his weighty scowl on me. "But the candidate pool *is* restricted to members of the council. Which *you* are not among."

Nervous laughter burst from my throat. "I wasn't thinking of running. That's ridiculous, of course. I was just...curious."

Faythe gave me a perplexed frown, and I quickly—pointedly—glanced at one of her fellow Alphas. She followed my gaze, and her eyes widened. But I wasn't sure she was following my train of thought until she stood, abruptly. As if something had just bitten her. "If the vote isn't limited to two candidates, I'd like to nominate a third."

Ed Taylor's scowl darkened. "What—"

"Jerold Pierce."

"What?" Pierce's surprise was almost comical.

Marc nodded, clearly catching on. "That makes sense. Jerold, you're one of our senior members, and the fact that you're a frequent swing vote means that you're pretty middle-of-the-road, politically."

"So, will you run?" Faythe asked, while Rick Wade frowned at her in obvious confusion.

Pierce shrugged. "Well, I guess that couldn't hurt."

Faythe's smile lit up her face. "Then it's settled. Rick, I think we're ready to call for the votes. And I think we should start with Pierce, as the latest addition to the candidate pool."

Ed Taylor's face turned scarlet. His mouth opened as if he'd object, but before he could figure out how, Wade cleared his throat. "All in favor of recognizing Jerold Pierce as council chair, please raise your hands.

Pierce's hand went up immediately, and I exhaled in relief. If he voted for himself, he couldn't vote for Ed Taylor. Which Taylor clearly realized.

For a second, poor Pierce's was the only hand up. He looked pretty embarrassed. Then Nick Davidson shifted in his chair, and his hand rose slowly into the air. Followed by Wes Gardner's.

"That's three for Jerold Pierce," Wade said. "All for Ed Taylor?"

Ed raised his hand, his face crimson with fury. Milo Mitchell and Robert Taylor followed suit, and Ed turned a pointed look at Titus. Who returned his stare calmly. With his hands still folded on the table.

"That's three for Ed Taylor," Rick Wade announced, relief clear in his voice. He'd obviously done the math. "All in favor of me continuing to serve as council chair?"

Faythe raised her hand for the South-Central Pride. Isaac Wade and Bert Di Carlo raised their hands. Then Rick Wade voted for himself, and he'd officially won. Titus's vote wasn't necessary. But he raised his hand anyway—staring right at Ed Taylor.

"Looks like it's official!" Wade sank into his chair with obvious relief. "It will be my honor to continue to serve."

TWENTY

JUSTUS

"YOU ARE *BRILLIANT*!" I WHISPERED AS I TUGGED KACI INTO her bedroom and closed the door at my back. "Also, you're beautiful. Have I ever mentioned that you're beautiful?" I pressed her against the wall with my body and nibbled on the back of her jaw, just beneath her ear. "And delicious," I murmured against her skin. "How did you know that would happen?"

She giggled. Then she purred, deep in her throat, as she ran her hands over the front of my shirt. "I didn't know for sure, but I figured most people would vote for themselves, if they were nominated. And Pierce's was the vote I couldn't be sure of, so I thought we should try to take him out of play entirely. But I truly had no idea Davidson or Gardner would vote for him too."

"You totally split the vote." I ran one hand into her hair. The only thing sexier than Kaci Dillion, it turned out, was Kaci Dillion working to save my life.

"Yeah, I guess I did." She looked pretty pleased with herself, and the confidence—well deserved—made her even hotter.

"Hey—" The door lurched forward, throwing Kaci into me, and Faythe made a startled noise from the other side.

Kaci pulled me away from the door and opened it. "Sorry," she said as our Alpha stepped inside.

Faythe glanced at me, then at Kaci's disheveled hair. Then she pushed the door closed. "The recess is about over. I just wanted to…" She frowned. "That was…"

"Brilliant?" I suggested.

"Yes. Exactly." Faythe smiled, and she looked…proud. "I had no idea you had such a politically savvy mind!"

"Me neither," Kaci admitted.

I shrugged. "I knew." They both turned to me, and Kaci actually rolled her eyes. "Seriously. I knew from that phone call you made to Taylor the other day. No, wait, from the one you made to Faythe, while we were on the way to the airport!"

"What?" Faythe turned on her. "Well, I guess in retrospect, you *were* playing me."

"Like a fiddle," I agreed, and Kaci elbowed me. "What? I meant it as a compliment."

"Manipulating one's Alpha isn't generally considered a positive trait, but…well done out there," Faythe finished. "No matter how the rest of this plays out, you've given Justus a much better shot than he had going into this whole thing."

"So, what's the plan?" I asked as I slid my arm around Kaci's waist.

Faythe shrugged. "Our only real option is to try to put together a tribunal that will at least give you a fair trial."

"What are the chances we'll be able to do that?" I asked.

"Well, we're going to try for a redraw of *just* Paul Blackwell's seat, so that we don't risk losing Di Carlo's vote in your favor."

"But that means we'll also keep Ed Taylor's vote against him," Kaci said.

Faythe nodded. "Unfortunately, it also means we risk drawing Robert's name."

I crossed my arms over my chest. "That hardly seems fair, considering what they tried to do."

"It *isn't* fair," Kaci insisted. "Especially considering that Faythe, Marc, and Titus have to recuse themselves, even though they didn't do anything wrong."

Excitement shot through me, and I grabbed Kaci's hand as I turned to Faythe. "I might have an idea about how to even the field…"

"FOR OUR LAST ORDER OF BUSINESS IN WHAT'S TURNED OUT to be a longer-than-expected evening, we need to fill the empty space left on the tribunal by Paul Blackwell's death." Rick Wade looked particularly satisfied by his position at the head of the table. And the truth was that I was kind of happy for him, despite my belief that—as council chair—he should have been able to anticipate the Taylors' mutiny. "Faythe has asked that we keep the rest of the tribunal intact, so if there are no objections to that…?"

All eyes turned to Ed Taylor, but he remained silent. Of course he wasn't going to object, because if they redrew the entire tribunal, he'd likely lose his spot on it.

"Actually…" Several surprised faces turned toward Faythe. "We've decided we'd like to redraw both Blackwell's seat and Ed Taylor's seat."

"What? On what grounds?" Taylor demanded, his hands fisted on the table.

"On the grounds that you have an unfair bias against me," I blurted out.

Marc gave me a subtle but firm shake of his head. I knew it wasn't wise to butt in, unacknowledged by the council, but my life was at risk!

"Yes," Faythe said, drawing their attention away from me. Then she turned to my brother. "Titus?"

Titus cleared his throat. "Two days ago, Ed Taylor called to offer me his vote in Justus's favor, in exchange for my vote to help him unseat Rick Wade as council chair. He said he'd formed an alliance with his brother and that if I didn't help them, they'd vote to execute *my* brother."

"This is ridiculous!" Taylor stood, his face flaming.

Faythe actually rolled her eyes. "Sit down, Ed. Titus told us about the 'deal' you proposed just hours after you called him. Titus, Marc, Rick and I all knew coming into this meeting that you'd call for a revote on the council chair."

"It's true," Rick Wade said. "Don't dig yourself any deeper by lying."

"It's not against the rules to form alliances," Taylor insisted.

"No, though if there's nothing in our bylaws prohibiting you from buying votes, there should be," Faythe said. "Either way, it's pretty obvious that since Titus didn't take your deal, you'll be out to get Justus. Which means you have no business on the tribunal. I make a motion to remove Ed Taylor from the tribunal. And to remove Robert from consideration."

"Seconded," Titus said.

"All in favor?" Rick asked. Nine hands rose around the table. Only the Taylors declined to vote. "Motion carried. We will now be replacing both Ed Taylor and Paul Blackwell on the tribunal, through the traditional random draw. Faythe, Marc, Titus, Ed, and Robert are all excluded. As is Bert, since he's already on the tribunal."

Faythe set a plastic cup in the middle of the dining room table. "Coins in."

Each of the Alphas who hadn't been excluded stood and dug a coin from his pocket. "Quarters?" I whispered to Kaci. But they looked a little big for quarters. And they were copper, rather than silver.

"Territory coins," she whispered back. "Each one is engraved with the shape of the territory. They only use them to make quick work of drawing names, but they're kind of a status symbol, passed from Alpha to Alpha as they retire. Or die, in Blackwell's case." She shrugged. "I guess Titus will have to get one made."

Six Alphas dropped their coins into the cup, and Faythe shook it. "Bert, why don't you draw?" Faythe held the cup out to him.

Di Carlo reached inside without looking, and plucked out a coin. He held it up between his forefinger and thumb, so everyone around the table could see. "Wes Gardner. Great Lakes territory."

I glanced at Kaci to confirm what I was pretty sure I knew, and she gave me a small shake of her head. Gardner was not a friendly vote.

My chest felt tight as Faythe shook the cup again. The next coin pulled would determine whether I lived or died. Again, that fact seemed so infuriatingly *arbitrary*.

Di Carlo plucked another coin from the cup without looking. He showed it to the table, but I was too far away to make out the shape on the coin. "Isaac Wade. Appalachian territory."

Kaci's breath burst from her lungs in a sob of relief.

Faythe gave her a smile. And slowly, my fate sank in. Isaac was Rick's son. Abby's brother. Jace's brother-in-law. Faythe's cousin and ally. He was a friendly vote.

Even if the tribunal found me guilty, I was going to live.

Ed Taylor stomped from the room without a word. Robert followed him.

Faythe and her allies were all smiles. Titus looked…jubilant. Relieved.

Despite the fact that not a single vote had been cast—that my trial hadn't even started—it was evidently widely assumed that my fate had already been determined. My testimony would merely be a formality. As would the vote.

"Thank you, gentlemen—and Faythe." Rick Wade beamed at the room in general. "The tribunal will convene in Montana tomorrow for Justus's trial. Any interested party is welcome to attend, but I want to remind you that spectators are not allowed to speak during the trial. I will see you all there! Dismissed."

Kaci threw her arms around me, and I squeezed her so tightly I wasn't sure she could actually breathe. "Thank you," I whispered into her hair. "Thank you so much."

"I didn't really do anything," she said, her face pressed against my chest.

"Bullshit. You did *everything*." I let her go so that I could kiss her, and when we came up for air, I found my brother watching us from a few feet away, a smile hovering beneath his typically stern expression.

"Kaci." Titus took her hand. "I'm so sorry for what I did. I have no excuse, other than that I was scared for Justus's life, and the only way I could see to save him was to make him give you up. I hope you can forgive me."

"I forgive you." She smiled as she held her hand up to show off her ring. "I did something stupid to save him too."

I laughed and slid my arm around her waist.

"Welcome to the family, Kaci," Titus said.

"So, we can...be married for real?" She looked up at me with hope shining in her eyes.

"Whoa, whoa, wait a minute." Marc crossed the room in three steps. "Maybe we could talk about an annulment, then a long engagement?"

"I wasn't asking you," she informed him. Then she turned back to me, grinning. "So? Are you going to make me propose twice?"

"That is tempting," I teased. "But no. We're *already* married for real."

"You know what I mean," she whispered. As if the room full of shifters with super-powered hearing couldn't hear her. "I want to be married *for real*."

"I know what you mean, and they do to," I stage-whispered back.

"Okay, I'm out." Marc plucked his glass from the table and drained it in one gulp. Then he kissed Faythe on his way out of the room. "You let me know how that turns out. I'm going to check on the boys."

"I'll come with you," she said, shooting a meaningful look at my brother. "Titus, you're on chaperone duty. I have to get us packed for tomorrow."

"We should pack too," Kaci said as her hand curled around mine. "If we're actually going to show up for your trial."

"We are." I was ready to get it over with. To accept whatever non-lethal punishment they handed out, so I could get on with my life. With my *marriage*.

But Titus seemed to read my thoughts in my expression. "I'll help you pack," he said. "And I better not find any of *your* laundry in *her* hamper."

TWENTY-ONE

Kaci

THE MONTANA WILDERNESS WAS GORGEOUS. I HADN'T really noticed that during my first visit. Of course, back then I'd been stuck in cat form and literally starving. Which meant that Justus's trial had at least two advantages over Faythe's trial. For me, anyway.

For Justus, not so much.

The wooden porch steps creaked beneath me as I sat and stared out at the woods. The cabin at my back was the same one I'd stayed in with Faythe and her family after they'd found me in the woods. It was the same one they'd been staying in when Greg was murdered. I wasn't with them on that trip, but it was hard not to imagine it as I stared out over the grounds where he'd been shot.

But this trip was about Justus.

About justice.

About moving past his trial so we could get on with the rest of our lives.

I hadn't expected to be nervous. The votes were on our side. No matter what happened, Justus would live, and eventually I'd be able to convince everyone that they had no right to keep us from truly *enjoying* our marriage.

Eventually they'd let us be alone in a room together. Assuming Justus's sentence didn't get in the way.

It was entirely possible, according to Michael, that they would sentence him to "jail time." Which basically meant locking him up in someone's basement. Or they could take his claws.

Logically, I knew that taking his claws would be worse, because it was more permanent and would affect his ability to protect himself. But jail time would keep us apart...

The front door of the cabin squealed open at my back, and the scent of coffee wafted over me as the rapid-fire cadence of little Greg's footsteps thumped toward me.

"Kaci!"

"Hey, munchkin!" Before he could trip down the steps, I grabbed him around the waist and hauled him into my lap. "What 'cha got?"

"Fris-bee!" He clutched the plastic disk to his chest and struggled to free himself from my grip.

Laughing, I set him on the grass, and he toddled off with his toy.

"He found it in the coat closet," Faythe said as she sank onto the step next to me and handed me one of the two mugs she held. "How are you holding up?"

"Waiting sucks." I took a sip from my mug. The coffee was sweeter than I usually took it, but you don't complain when your Alpha brings you coffee.

"I know. I *remember.*" For a few minutes, we watched Greg try to throw the Frisbee. Nine times out of ten, he hurled it straight at his own feet.

"Where's the baby?" I asked, cradling the mug in both hands. I wasn't cold, but the warmth was still comforting.

"Napping. In Marc's arms. If we put him down in a strange bed, he wakes up screaming. My mom calls it 'electric sheet syndrome.'"

"I know." None of us had gotten much sleep in the two days we'd been in the mountains.

"This is what marriage is like, Kaci." Faythe sipped from her mug. "Marriage is kids—if you want them—and messes, and sleep deprivation, and compromise, and seeing each other go to the bathroom. It's cleaning up vomit at three am. It's all-night fever watches, and coffee breath, and arguing over who was supposed to pay the electric bill."

I shrugged. "Yeah, but it's also making out on your desk when you think no one's looking."

Faythe's brows rose. "Marriage for shifters is also being comfortable enough in your relationship to be okay with the fact that there's very little privacy."

"I know you're trying to scare me away from Justus, but I want all of those things. Well, not all of them. But I'm willing to deal with the vomit and the open bathroom door if I get all the rest of it. With *him*."

She sighed. "I'm not trying to scare you away from Justus. I just want you to understand what you're getting into. The reality, not the whirlwind trip to Vegas and the *huge* ring. And I want you to understand that even if you stay married, there's no rush for kids. You can and should still go to school first. As should he. You should figure out who you are as individuals—and as a couple—before you start making brand new people. Eighteen is *really* young, Kaci."

"I know." I fought not to roll my eyes.

"You may think you know, but—"

"Faythe." I turned to fully face her on the step. "I hear

you. Kids can wait. College shouldn't. I'm agreeing with you, so you can stop trying to convince me."

She nodded. Then she took another long sip from her mug with her brows furrowed. "It's just that…I'm not sure how you could possibly be eighteen already. I swear you were thirteen yesterday. And if you're ready to be married, then you probably don't need a mother-figure anymore, so—"

"I still need you, Faythe. I just need you at a little bit of a distance."

She smiled. "Well, you still have me. At a little bit of a—"

The door squealed open again, and I spun, sloshing coffee over my hand, just as Justus stepped onto the porch. The moment he saw me, he threw both hands in the air in a triumphant gesture. "Not criminally responsible for my actions due to psychological trauma!"

I set my mug down and threw myself at him.

He laughed as he lifted me in a hug. "You do realize they basically just said I was too irresponsible to be held account-able for my own actions, right?"

"That is *not* what they meant." I dropped a kiss on his mouth, then let myself slide down his body until my feet touched the porch. "Does that mean there's no sentence?"

Justus frowned. "What on earth is he doing?"

I followed his gaze to the grass, where little Greg was still trying desperately to get his Frisbee airborne. "Justus! Your sentence!" I demanded.

He laughed again. "One year of service as an enforcer, without pay." As if he needed a salary. "It's so that I'm 'prop-erly trained' to triumph over my own impulses and urges."

Unease settled through me. "Where?" What if they were sending him to the Northwest Territory? Or the New England

Territory? Or anywhere too far for me to drive to every weekend?

Instead of answering, he turned to Faythe with an expectant look.

She smiled. "He's replacing Brian."

"At home?" I squealed. "You knew!"

Faythe shrugged. "It was Marc's idea."

"Thank you!" I dropped into a squat and threw my arms around her.

She laughed. "We figured the best way to keep you around a little longer was to keep Justus close."

"Thanks, Faythe." Justus tugged me up by one arm. "We'll see you tomorrow."

"What?" I frowned at them both.

"Yup. Here you go." Faythe leaned back and dug a set of keys from her pocket, then dropped them in his palm. "Fill the tank on your way back, please."

"Will do." Justus led me down the steps toward one of the rental cars lined up in the driveway.

"Where are we going?" I asked as he opened the passenger's side door.

"You'll see."

"I want to know now." But he was already rounding the front of the car.

Justus got into the driver's seat and started the engine, then he backed out of the driveway. "If I tell you, I'll ruin the surprise."

"I'm kind of okay with that, considering that my last surprise landed me upside down in a car in the desert."

"This isn't that kind of surprise." But for the entire twenty-minute drive, he refused to even give me a hint, until we pulled into a parking lot in the closest little town to the cabin complex.

"A hotel?"

"Not just *a* hotel. The *best* hotel SmallTown, Montana has to offer."

"It's a Courtyard Marriot," I said as he pulled into a space near the front.

"That *is* the best hotel SmallTown, Montana has to offer. But I hear there's an available upgrade that includes a mini-fridge and an extra coffee pod." He got out of the car and raced around to open my door before I could do it myself.

"Do I get to guess why we're here?" I asked as he held the door open for me.

"If you need more than one guess, we might have a problem."

I laughed, hoping he couldn't hear how very fast my heart was beating. How loud my pulse was—at least in my own ears. "I'm assuming we're here because everyone at the cabin has shifter hearing. And thinks we're too young to be married." Although we were clearly here with Faythe's blessing, at least.

"That's definitely part of it."

"How long are we staying? I didn't bring my luggage."

"Everything you need is here."

"Is that your way of telling me I won't be wearing anything tonight?"

Justus groaned. "If you could just not say things like that until we're actually *in* the room…" He held the hotel door open for me, then he led me to the left, toward the elevators, rather than right, toward the front desk.

"Shouldn't we check in?"

"We're already checked in."

"Good night, Mr. and Mrs. Alexander," the clerk called.

"How does he know who we are?" I frowned. "Though

maybe we should have a talk about how I'm still Kaci Dillon."

"I don't care what your name is." The elevator doors slid open, and Justus walked me backward into it as he kissed me. Inside, he pushed a button on the panel, then pressed me up against the mirrored wall and kissed me some more. "When I made the reservation, I wasn't sure whether or not my sentence would separate us. I figured this might be the only night we get together for a while."

My heart slammed against my chest when the doors slid open, and he led me out of the elevator onto the fifth floor. "Unfortunately, there's no honeymoon suite at the Courtyard Marriott, so we might have to make do…" He pulled a key card from his pocket and stopped in front of the third room on the right. "…with the whole floor."

"What? Wait. You rented the whole fifth floor?"

He shrugged as he tapped the key card against the door handle, and the light flashed green. "I wanted privacy." He turned the knob and pushed the door open just an inch. "Close your eyes."

"Why?"

He dropped a kiss on my forehead. "You don't have to question everything, Kaci. I'm not going to hurt you. Ever. So please just close your eyes."

I closed my eyes. A second later, I squealed as he lifted me off my feet, cradling me in his arms like a baby.

No, like a bride.

His back thumped against the door as he pushed it open, then he turned sideways to carry me inside. Through my closed eyelids, the light level changed. It looked dimmer, yet…flickery.

"Okay. Open them."

I opened my eyes. Then I gasped.

The room was full of roses and...ribbons. I looked up. The ceiling was *covered* in red balloons. And candles flickered from every flat surface.

"Wait, those are...?"

"Battery powered." Justus shrugged as he set me on the bed. "The hotel has a policy against open flame, so I had to use fake candles. But the romance is real."

"Hell, yeah it is," I said as he lowered himself to his knees and slid my shoes off my feet. "This is *all* the romance."

He slid one hand up each of my legs until he found the button at the waist of my jeans. "Kaci, this is only the beginning..."

My Soul To Steal

If I Die

Before I Wake

With All My Soul

MENAGERIE

Menagerie

Spectacle

Fury

THE STARS NEVER RISE (YA)

The Stars Never Rise

The Flame Never Dies

BRAVE NEW GIRL (YA)

Brave New Girl

Strange New World

100 HOURS (YA)

100 Hours

99 Lies

ACKNOWLEDGMENTS

Thanks, first and foremost, to my husband, who has put countless hours into my career in the form of artwork, web design, brainstorming, and moral support—as well as a six-foot long white board on my office wall. You are my anchor and I love you.

Thanks also to Rinda Elliott, my long-time critique partner, who's been with me from the beginning.

Thanks to Jennifer Lynn Barnes who said, "You should write a "wake up in Vegas married" story!

Thanks to Elizabeth Taylor for edits and moral support. And thanks most of all to all the Shifters fans who asked for more.

ABOUT THE AUTHOR

Photo credit: Kim Haynes Photography

Rachel Vincent is a former English teacher and an eager champion of the Oxford comma. She shares her home in Oklahoma with two cats, two teens, and her husband, who's been her # 1 fan from the start. Rachel is older than she looks and younger than she feels, and she remains convinced that writing about the things that scare her is the cheapest form of therapy—but social media is a close second.

For more information...
www.rachelvincent.com

Printed in Great Britain
by Amazon